THE 2_
GIRLFRIEND

MARK EKLID

CARMEL,
GOOD TO MEET YOU
AGAIN

To Pam and Keith,
on reaching a fine half-century.

Chapter
One

I was lonely. It was as simple as that. That's why I went on the dating site. That's how I met Gina.

Had I known then how much trouble it would drag me into, I can emphatically say I wouldn't have bothered. Better to be lonely and remain in one piece than being shot at, chased, beaten up and threatened with having parts removed that I'd rather stayed attached to the rest of me. There was definitely no mention of looking for any of that in the profile I created on clickforlove.com.

Gina. I kind of knew from the start she was too good to be true, but I allowed myself to be taken in by her and by the time I realised what was going on, it was too late. I was stupid. I was vulnerable. As I said, I was lonely.

Eleven months earlier, I split up with my wife, you see. After thirty-three years of marriage, Louise decided I was too boring for her. The youngest of our three kids was no longer financially dependent on us and so Louise decided the last remaining purpose for us staying together was no longer applicable. She decided she wanted to travel – without me, obviously – and have more fun.

I thought we were having fun. We had two holidays every year – Spain in late May and the Isle of Man in early September – had a joint membership at the gym and formed half of a very successful pub quiz team (alongside our old friends Dave and Jo) every Tuesday night at the Frisky Dog. We still laughed, though not always at the same time, as I now recall.

I was aware there wasn't quite the same sparkle in our relationship as there once was, but isn't that what happens with every couple once they reach their fifties? Marriages evolve. You settle into a different kind of rhythm. A slower rhythm. That doesn't necessarily make it boring. I didn't accept we'd become stale, like Louise said we had.

That was the word she used. Stale. That stuck in my mind.

I didn't think she was serious those times she complained she was fed up with the same routine and that she craved adventure and that she believed I was suffocating her.

Suffocating her. She actually said that.

I thought it was just her time of life and that she'd get over it. I suggested she go to the doctors and get some hormone treatment. That suggestion didn't go down well.

Anyway, she said she wanted a divorce and I couldn't talk her out of it. Maybe I should have tried harder. The legal part went through surprisingly quickly, I thought. Less than six months. She quit her job as an orthopaedic nurse at the Royal Hallamshire Hospital and I agreed to buy out her half of our little semi-detached in Woodhouse, using up just about all the money I could pull together. I didn't want to have to move. Not at my age. Louise had no such qualms. She was off. For all I knew after that, she might have used the money to buy a chalet in the Dolomites and have hooked up with a twenty-eight-year-old Italian ski instructor called Giuseppe. She didn't show any inclination to stay in touch.

I took the split really badly. It hit me harder than I thought it might.

Our kids (we have two girls and a boy, fully-grown adults now, of course) were very supportive without taking sides. I got the impression they fully understood where their mother was coming from, as regards the being suffocated by a stale marriage side of things, but they demonstrated plenty of sympathy for my perspective as well. They showed me a similar level of pity as they might have offered an abandoned old Labrador they'd found tied to a tree, I sometimes thought. At least they tried, though, and the phone calls home became more frequent for a time. The number of and length of those calls has tailed off again more recently.

The people I work with at the carpet store were less helpful. The one person I thought might really understand what I was going through was Julie, one of the assistant sales managers who had struggled through her own considerably messier divorce three years earlier. I didn't actively seek her support but what I didn't expect was that she began trying to avoid me, as if overcome by dread at the prospect of me trying to hit on her now we were both single again. For the record, I'd not even remotely considered making a play for her affections. I thought we were friends and that was it.

My male co-workers, especially the older, still-married ones, came across as being wildly jealous of my new-found freedom and painted pictures of a fantastic world of opportunities now at my fingertips. Most of these utopian visions of my carefree future seemed to revolve around going to the pub as often as I wanted and watching non-stop

Premier League football on TV, which I thought reflected as much on the pitiful state of their shallow home lives as it did on their complete lack of understanding of mine.

Apart from Tuesday quiz nights, I've never been a big pub-goer and even that regular night out is no more. Without Louise, I could see little point in maintaining the team with Dave and Jo (The Four-midables, we called ourselves). We could have drafted in a substitute to justify sticking with the team title but it wouldn't have been the same.

As for watching endless Premier League football, not only had I no desire whatsoever to watch endless Premier League football, I didn't have the satellite channel subscription to enable me to watch endless Premier League football either, so that was a non-starter. The only sport I did like to watch was the tennis, especially during Wimbledon fortnight. It became a ritual Louise and I used to enjoy together right the way back to our early days, when Dan Maskell was commentating, though the cracks were beginning to show in that shared pleasure by the time Andrew Castle took over from John Barrett. That's no reflection on Andrew Castle. Or John Barrett.

In more recent times, Louise became visibly frustrated at my attempts to pronounce the names of the Eastern European women's players and would regularly storm off to watch it alone in the bedroom, accusing me of tutting because the players grunt every time they strike the ball. I'm sure I didn't tut that often, but I admit it's true I wish they didn't make so much noise. This year's tournament was the first since Louise left and I did switch on the highlights show one evening. It must have been the early rounds because one of the players was British. I tried it with the sound on and the sound off, but I gave up at thirty-love with the Brit having just dropped serve in the second set. It brought back too many memories, and not only of previous failures by the home-grown players.

I suppose the most important way everybody missed the point in attempting to visualise my post-divorce life was that they couldn't appreciate the fact I didn't *want* to be single again. I know the marriage had been turning sour for a while and it could even be argued that we didn't have a great deal in common from the start, but we were a couple and I liked being part of a couple. We were Barry and Louise. We were socially acceptable. We sent Christmas cards with both our names on. How are you meant to overcome the awkwardness of no longer being part of a pair? How do our acquaintances move past the embarrassment of my failed relationship? No longer Barry and Louise. Just Boring Barry whose wife couldn't wait to escape the stale relationship that was suffocating her. No wonder the Christmas card count was noticeably lower last year. Nobody likes a loser and that was what I'd become.

I moved through the initial pain and sadness to fear and uncertainty via regret and anger until I arrived at loneliness. That was when I decided I didn't want to spend the rest of my life alone.

The one saving grace of coming to the realisation I might have to go through the horrible courtship business from scratch again was that the process appeared to have changed. For the better, in my view.

I'd not even contemplated beginning a new relationship since I started going out with Louise, thirty-six years ago. We first got together a bit by default. I was invited to a house party by my mate Colin, who had a bedsit in Broomhill, lured by the promise that he'd invited 'lots of fit girls.' As it was, only six of us turned up. Steve and Karen had been with each other since they were fifteen but soon made their excuses and left when they realised there was no additional room to where they could slip away and shag in privacy. Colin made a play for a tall girl with backcombed streaked blonde hair who was a receptionist at the same company where he worked. She wore a permanent sulky pout because she thought it made her look like Kim Wilde. When they took to snogging in the corner, that left Louise and me.

It would be a lie to say we hit it off straight away. I was never very good at the whole chatting up thing. I went through a phase of trying to cover my inadequacies by approaching girls with questions I thought might prove thought-provoking – like 'Do you think the Anglo-Irish agreement will hold?' or 'What's your take on the Westland scandal?' I hoped it might speed up the process of identifying a like-minded potential mate, but it didn't work. By the time of Colin's party, I'd abandoned the strategy but hadn't yet formulated its replacement, so I didn't know what to say.

Louise kept looking towards Kim Wilde, willing her to finish exploring Colin's tonsils so they could both escape that dreadful excuse for a party, and I just sat awkwardly on a battered wooden chair next to her, cradling a lukewarm can of Skol. In desperation, I tried to break the ice by making reference to the following day's Wimbledon men's singles final.

'Do you fancy Pat Cash to beat Ivan Lendl?' I asked.

Louise made a funny blowy noise with her mouth as if I'd said something blindingly obvious.

'I fancy Pat Cash – full stop,' she replied.

I found this discouraging because I looked nothing like the ruggedly dashing Australian star, but I didn't let myself be crushed this time. I decided to accept the possibility we'd found some common ground and expand the conversation.

'Navratilova was too good for Graf today, though, wasn't she?'

She nodded. A good sign. She then turned to look directly at me instead of Kim and Colin. Another good sign.

It was the first time I'd dared to look at her properly. She was definitely within the parameters of what I would consider nice looking, with large brown eyes and naturally wavy long dark hair. She dressed smartly, in a cream blouse and navy skirt, but I suppose some might have considered her style conservative. It was fine by me.

'Martina's great,' she said, 'but I reckon Steffi's ready to take all her titles off her soon.'

'You think?'

'Next year or two, for sure.'

That was it. We were away. She was nineteen, a year and a half younger than me, and worked at Sheffield Town Hall in the planning department, but she told me she found it terribly dull and intended quitting to train as a nurse. I found that both impressive and a little bit sexy. Most blokes I knew around that time had a thing about nurses, for whatever reason.

Our first date, if you can call it that, was on the tennis courts near Frecheville Pond, close to where we both grew up. She won. Her serve was more consistent and she soon worked out my backhand was weak. We started seeing each other regularly and, astonishingly, we fell in love. We were married the weekend after the French Open men's final two years later.

About half the cards for our wedding day made reference to a 'perfect love match' or some similar tennis-related play on words. We were happy. She was just right for me.

She was right about Steffi Graf as well.

Anyway, thirty-six years later I knew I couldn't wait for another invitation to a party at Colin's bedsit to provide the spark for a new relationship, so I decided to look into the world of computer dating.

What a minefield that is! You have to be so careful. Some of the sites appeared to cater for folk who purely want to hook up and have sex. I mean, whatever floats your boat and all that, but I couldn't imagine the appeal of arranging a liaison just so you could have a knee-trembler against a tree on waste ground next to an industrial estate. That's not for me. Not with my hip.

I had in mind making a connection which had the potential to be a little more long-lasting and meaningful than that and eventually decided to sign up with clickforlove.com.

Connect with mature singles, it said. *It's never too late to click for love.*

That sounded more suitable. It also said you didn't have to pay a subscription, which appealed to my natural caution. I downloaded the app on to my phone.

It took ages – I mean days rather than hours – to fashion a short biographical profile to the point where I thought it vaguely acceptable, and then it took the best part of another week to completely re-write it. Finding suitable photos to upload also proved problematic because I don't like having my picture taken and, in later years, Louise wasn't keen on trying to get me to pose for any. I rejected using the mug shot from my work ID badge because I thought it made me look like a man arrested on suspicion of interfering with farm animals. I did find one from a day trip to Whitby three years earlier that I was OK with and another our youngest daughter, Lucy, shared on the family WhatsApp group of me opening a present at Christmas. They, I decided, would have to do.

With all required information uploaded onto the site, I left it another day in case I came to the conclusion it was all a dreadful mistake, but faced with the prospect of the computer wiping my efforts so far off the system due to unacceptable dithering levels, forcing me to have to go through the whole painful process again, I steeled myself to get on with it.

I hovered, finger poised over the launch button on the phone touchscreen, for so long that I developed a nervous twitch in my right arm. Finally, I jabbed at the button. The wheel whirred. It accepted me.

Welcome to your new love life, it promised.

I felt sick.

Chapter
Two

'Bloody teenagers!'

I wondered what Charlie was on about at first. We had just finished laying a Saxony pile in a back bedroom in Nether Edge and were on our way to fit a polypropylene twist on the landings and stairs of a house in Wadsley Bridge. He was driving. I thought he'd spotted some kids doing something daft by the side of the road.

I couldn't see anything that might have prompted his reaction when I glanced up.

'You!' he said, realising I didn't know what he was on about. Charlie was one of the other carpet fitters. We'd been working together at the same company for a long time. He's a bit younger than me.

'My fourteen-year-old spends less time with his face in his phone than you've done today. What are you up to? Have you got a new bird on the go, or what?'

I liked Charlie. He was always the one who dealt with the home owners when we were out on a job and would put in the order for cuppas when they were offered (white with two sugars for him, white no sugars for me). I preferred to avoid such interaction if I could. He'd happily fill the idle minutes in the van with distracting chatter and expect very little from me in return. We made a good team.

But I wasn't prepared to discuss the latest potential new development in my love life with him, or anybody.

'No, no.' I felt my cheeks flush. 'It's nothing like that.'

I didn't expand and Charlie, in fairness, didn't push. I took the hint and put my phone away, only sneaking a look for the rest of the day when Charlie wasn't around.

Needless to say, I was checking the clickforlove.com app for progress. Needless to say, there was none.

I was aware the way this online dating game was meant to work was that you identify what you're looking for in a prospective partner, the site filters out profiles of members it reckons are suitable, you look through to see if anyone catches your eye and you send them a message. They can then choose whether or not to respond and eventually, hopefully, you find someone you might be able to develop a relationship with.

I did look. There were plenty of women on the site who fitted the bill for me (aged 45-55, prefers the quiet home life, no smokers, Sheffield area), but I didn't send messages to any of them. I wasn't ready to deal with the inevitable rejections.

Instead, I decided to see if anybody would click on my profile and make the initial contact themselves. That way, I would know they were interested.

The messages count on my profile page stayed stubbornly at zero for the whole of that first day. Then, on the second day, while Charlie had nipped into the downstairs loo of a place in Handsworth where we were fitting a new laminate, I saw I'd had my first approach.

My heart leapt. I hurried outside as if there was something I urgently needed from the van. I opened the message. She was from just north of Barnsley. I've nothing against people from Barnsley, but it was beyond the limits of how far I preferred to travel. Not only that, she was clearly pushing the preferred limits age-wise.

If she really was fifty-five, as she claimed in her biography, I could only assume she had lived a hard life.

I decided not to respond. It made me feel guilty. I comforted myself by inventing a scenario in which Sandra from Monk Bretton struck up an instant rapport with a recently widowed former miner from Mapplewell in a series of online messages and they went on to share great happiness together. That made me feel better. We were not meant to be.

So that was a disappointing start, but the next contact, two days later, was a completely different experience.

By chance, it landed on a day when we'd managed to finish work early.

I'd just got in from a walk to the shop to buy some milk. I'd not been checking the app as often since Charlie's rebuke in the van, but reckoned I was due an update while I waited for the kettle to boil.

A red circle with a white number one told me there was a new message. I opened it.

Hi – Gina (44)

I opened her profile. I saw her picture.

Christ!

She was beautiful. Really beautiful.

They do say such a quality can be in the eye of the beholder, but this was beyond debate.

The photo looked as if it could have been posed in a

professional studio. She was reclining against the end of a sofa, casually cradling the right side of her jaw in the slender fingers of her cupped right hand. Her honey-blonde hair fell in a gentle flow over her shoulders and the warm smile that played on her pink lips drew the faintest of lines around her mouth and under her hazel eyes.

I know what you're thinking. Alarm bells. I heard them too.

I don't do social media very often, but I occasionally have friend requests from women in different parts of the world. Women with extraordinary cleavages and lips inflated to the point of bursting. If you scroll even a little bit down their timelines, you see that their lives appear to be taken up entirely with pouting into a mirror for their mobile phones, dressed in various seductive outfits. I delete those requests straight away, concerned that if I was to press the wrong button and accept I would be besieged by pornographic material forever more, or at least until I was forced to burn and bury my laptop to conceal the shameful evidence.

Originally, I thought this must be a similar deal. The originator of 'Gina' – and no doubt countless other mock accounts designed to trap impressionable lonely hearts – was probably a balding, fat con man in a basement in Istanbul.

And yet…

As I skimmed through the other half-dozen or so photos attached to her profile I got a different impression altogether.

They were all only of her. No one else to share the frame. Some were her in sleeveless tops and shorts, as if taken in a warm climate; one in a smart dress, ready for a night out; another was of her wrapped up against the elements on a clearly wild and windy venture into the open countryside. These were not glamour shots. No daring bikinis. No plunging necklines. Just an ordinary woman – albeit a particularly alluring one – in ordinary settings.

And do you know the overwhelming feeling I picked up from those photos? Sadness.

I've never been the most perceptive of men, but even to me it was unmistakeable. Clearly, someone was on the other side of the camera, pressing the shutter, so she was not alone, but I could see she wasn't happy. The smile she gave the taker was reluctant. Forced. The joy had been drained from those hazel eyes. I had no way of knowing what her relationship was with the person who took those photos, but why did it only appear to be just the two of them? Did she have other friends or family? If the photos she had selected represented a slice of her life in recent years, then there didn't appear to be anyone else.

To me, she appeared isolated. Trapped. I shuddered as I recalled one of the words Louise had used as a barb to sum up how she felt in our marriage.

Suffocating. The woman in these photos was suffocating.

I needed to know more.

Her biography said she was based in Sheffield, though not originally from the area. It said she was a self-employed web designer. It said she enjoyed cooking Italian food, watching films based on true life and reading historical mystery novels. It was her last line that got me.

I'm hoping to find someone who can restore my faith and make me believe there are still some good men out there.

I knew it!

I hadn't read those photos wrong! She had been stuck in an unhappy partnership and though she had shown the courage to escape, it had taken a toll. The wounds were still healing.

Why is it that beautiful women often attract the wrong men? Louise's friend, Alison, was a good-looking woman. Not necessarily my type, personality-wise, but physically attractive all right. Louise was forever on the phone to her, offering comfort over the latest break-up with one of a series of complete pricks who had turned her life upside down.

Maybe Gina had been similarly afflicted. Maybe her signing up to clickforlove.com was a final attempt to find the kind of relationship she always wanted. She was looking for someone who understood what it was like to have your heart ripped out by the person you believed would be your forever mate.

I understood.

I'm not an impulsive man. I can't recall the last time I took a decision without first weighing up the pros and cons at great length. It used to drive Louise nuts, but that's me. I'm cautious. It's surely better than diving head-long into something and then having to deal with the consequences of a poor choice.

But when I read that last line in Gina's biography I knew straight away I wanted to reply.

I began to compose my response. It took a while.

Hi Gina.

Good start, I thought. Casual. Friendly.

I'm so glad you sent me a message.

No. Too grateful, bordering on desperate. Delete.

Thanks for getting in touch.

Better.

I enjoyed reading your profile and I think you look great in the red dress.

Too creepy? I hoped not. I figured she chose the photo of her in the red evening dress because she thought she looked good in it as well. She did look sensational.

I also love Italian food, though I have to confess I'm better at eating than cooking!

I internally debated whether or not to include the joke for at least half an hour. Then I took a similar amount of time considering the merits of the exclamation mark. In the end, I decided both should stay. A little humour and humility never hurt, surely. I also wanted to show I'd read what she'd written and suggest we might have at least this one thing in common. Both statements were strictly true. I am a useless cook and I do like Italian food. Admittedly, I never eat anything more adventurous than lasagne or pizza, but that counts, doesn't it?

I couldn't think of much else to say, but I felt I needed to respond to her final line. This was the really tricky part. I decided to go with what was in my heart.

It sounds like you, too, have had to come through challenging times recently. I know how difficult that can be. I know as well that by doing this you have proved what a strong person you are.

Never lose faith.

That was it. I pressed 'send' and felt good about what I'd done, which is rare for me.

It didn't last.

Chapter
Three

Within two hours of pressing the 'send' button, I was a quivering mass of regret.

If there had been a 'retract' button, I would have tapped repeatedly on it until my forefinger left a permanent dent on the phone screen.

What was I thinking?

I had admitted I'd practically slobbered over a picture of Gina, compounded her sense of loathing with a crap joke and then finished off my message with a condescending attempt at greetings card philosophy.

The one consolation was that I'd almost certainly never hear from her again. A woman like Gina would probably have messages from thousands of men cramming her inbox – all of them considerably better written than mine. They would probably all be from better-looking guys, too. Guys with tattoos and soft-top Mercedes.

She was way out of my league. How could I imagine for a fleeting second that a beautiful, younger, smarter woman would really take an interest in a cranky old washed-up carpet fitter? It was a ridiculous thought. She probably sent the 'hi' message by mistake. Or out of sympathy. Or as a wind-up. Either way, I was stupid to believe it meant anything.

I resolved to delete my profile from the website. This was a sign I should resign myself to living the rest of my days alone. I'd been lucky enough to trick one woman into loving me and I'd lost her because I was too boring. That's your lot. You had one chance and you blew it.

Yet I didn't delete myself straight away. If I had, I would never have seen Gina's reply.

It landed that evening.

After eating my tea (breaded chicken fillet with potato wedges and peas) I settled down to watch a film about a man falsely accused of murder who was fighting to clear his name, but it wasn't very good. It felt as if I'd seen it before. My attention drifted and I picked up my phone, just in case. There it was.

Hi Barry.

Your kind message made me cry. I don't want to bore you with the details, but I have been through some tough times these last couple of years and your words have brightened my day like a ray of sunshine bursting through the clouds. I was beginning to wonder if I would ever see that sunshine again. How I wish I could have had someone close by me with your fabulous positivity through those many long dark months!

I knew, as soon as I saw your picture on the site, that you had a good soul. It seems silly to write that, but I just knew. Do you believe such a thing is possible?

Anyway, I wanted to thank you. You could never know how much your message meant to me. I don't expect for a minute you'd want to stay in touch with an old misery like me! You're probably looking for a woman who is able to share happy times with you, not someone who would drag you down to her level!

That's OK. I just wanted to say, 'thanks' and 'good luck'. Whoever you end up choosing to meet for a date, I hope she soon appreciates she is a very fortunate lady!

Gina x

Stunned doesn't even come close. I could hardly believe Gina had acknowledged my message at all, let alone that it meant so much to her.

I must admit I welled up and I'm not often taken to showing emotion. Louise used to say the last time I cried was at our eldest daughter Maisie's wedding and that was only because I'd realised how much it was going to cost me. That's not true. She hadn't stayed around long enough to see the last time I cried. But it had been a long while since I'd had such a strong emotional reaction to someone else's distress.

What dreadful suffering must Gina have been through to reduce her to such a low ebb? Devoid of self-esteem. The fire within her long since doused.

Who'd do that? What did they do to her?

Of course I was going to reply. I wasn't overcome by some sort of knight in shining armour compulsion or anything daft like that, but if I had played some small part in lifting the spirits of this poor woman and if I could do anything to raise them again, naturally I wanted to do all I could.

Hi Gina,

Do I believe it's possible to make a connection just through a photo on a website? Yes, I do! I felt exactly the same way when I first saw your pictures. I don't know how to explain that, but it's true. I could just kind of tell you were unhappy.

Maybe that's because there's been far too little happiness in my life lately as well. It's a long story and I guess the last thing you want is for me to offload my troubles on you when you've probably had to go through so much worse, but I think maybe that helped me see. I get what you are going through. I hope that doesn't sound too corny, but I don't know how to put it better than that.

But what I also saw in your photos was the person within, waiting to shine through when all the sadness is gone. I'd really like to get to know her.

I wouldn't suggest for one minute I have all – or any! – of the answers. I'm nothing special. I've probably got more flaws than most. What I can promise, though, is that I'll be a willing listener should you ever want to get in touch again. However much or however little you want to tell me, I'll be here. If, by doing that, I can help the real you to step back into the light, that will be enough for me.

Kind regards,
Barry

I wasn't sure about the 'kind regards' ending. A bit cold, maybe. Gina had signed off with a kiss. I certainly didn't think it would be appropriate for me to do the same, though. 'Cheers' would have been too off-hand. 'Yours' would have been too presumptuous. 'Kind regards' was the best I could come up with, so it stayed and I sent the message.

I felt good about it. It was honest. It wasn't pushy. Or pretentious. I thought the tone was about right. It put the ball in her court. If Gina wanted to extend the conversation, I'd hope she could do so without feeling pressured into opening up. If she didn't, then that was fine.

Except that I really, really, really hoped she would.
She did.

Over the next two days, we exchanged many more messages.

We chatted about our jobs, about what we liked and disliked on TV, about music, about going to the cinema and how we both wished they'd ban popcorn and slurpy drinks, about places we'd been (she said she'd never visited the Isle of Man but had always wanted to).

It really started to feel like we were beginning to get to know each other. We had so much in common. The conversation flowed more and more freely. It was as if the tension was melting out of our fingers with every line we typed to each other.

Then I told her about breaking up with Louise.

I held my breath for a while after that disclosure because I didn't want her to feel I expected her to respond in kind. Gina might not be ready to talk about it, especially as I was still, basically, a stranger.

Or maybe she was waiting for me to broach the subject first; to clear the way for her to say what she might have needed to offload for a while.

It was the latter.

Gina told me she'd lived her whole life in Bristol. She was an only child and her parents were both dead. She did a bit of modelling when she was younger (I might have guessed) and had used some of the money she made to enrol on a Multimedia Design course at University at the age of twenty-eight. After graduation, she earned a job with a company in her home city and it was there she met Jez.

At first, everything was perfect. Jez was a senior partner in the company, five years older than Gina and single. He told her he'd always been too dedicated to his career to commit to a long-term relationship, but that meeting her had made him re-evaluate. He promised her the world. He swore undying love.

Gina said she fell for him completely. He was handsome, rich, successful, charming. Sixteen months later, they got married and toured the Caribbean for five weeks. She was blissfully happy.

Looking back, she said, there were signs of what was to come within the first couple of years of their marriage. Gina was making a name for herself through her work and couldn't figure out why Jez responded to her successes by doing her down, often in front of colleagues. Then he began objecting to her seeing friends on her own. Gradually, their social life started to consist solely of trips together. He would book lavish holidays for them both without consulting her and, when they were away, they would be practically isolated. They would eat out, but never just sit in a bar and socialise. They hardly left the villa. They spent their days around the pool. He said he didn't want to visit public beaches because he didn't want other men looking at her.

Gina said she tolerated Jez's increasingly erratic behaviour because she loved him, even though the increasing seclusion of her existence was weighing her down. She tried to let him know how she felt but said communication between them became difficult. Then matters got decidedly worse.

A little under two years ago, she said, Jez announced they should start a family. Time was moving on. She was past forty and soon she would be too old. He demanded she abandon her career and prepare for motherhood.

Gina stood her ground this time. Her career was her lifeline. At times, it felt like her only contact with the outside world. She had worked too hard and achieved too much to give it all away.

As a compromise, Jez agreed to allow her to keep working until she was pregnant and four months before the due date, but he made it plain how unhappy he was with the arrangement. He started reading all sorts of crackpot theories about the best ways to prepare for conception and their eventual pregnancy and took it on himself to regulate even the smallest details of Gina's lifestyle to optimise their chances of achieving their dream. His dream.

She went along with it. Eight months later, she missed her period. She tested. A single blue line. A positive. He was overjoyed. She was wary.

Two weeks later, she miscarried.

Jez was furious. He blamed her. She cannot have followed his instructions to the letter. If she hadn't defied him by insisting on carrying on working it would have been different. She had killed their baby.

He wasn't going to let her do that to him again.

He used his influence as a senior partner in the company to take away her job. She was effectively sacked. She was to stay at home and do it right this time. His way.

Gina was a prisoner. Not allowed to leave home. Not allowed her independence in any way.

Their bedroom became a lab; the place they would perform joyless mechanical sex at optimum times according to Jez's calculations of when she was ovulating. She was given no choice in that. She was no longer his wife. She was the receptacle. She must conceive and grow his baby. He became increasingly obsessed.

She began to dread the arrival of her period but, with the inevitability of the mortgage payment direct debit, every month it came. And, with every month, Jez became angrier.

More and more hostile.

One night, he hit her. Not a slap. A full swing of a clenched fist which caught Gina just above the left ear and sent her spinning to the floor, scrambling her senses. As she lay there, the world swirling before her shocked wide eyes, wondering if the side of her head had split apart, he stood over her, yelling. That's what she had made him do. That's what she had driven him to. He even tried to make her feel guilty for the pain in his hand which he said was surely a broken bone.

He left her there, on the floor. He stormed out of the house.

When she had recovered sufficiently to stagger to her feet on shaking legs, Gina rifled through drawers for everything she might need – phone, passport, bank cards, as much cash as she could find – recovered her car keys from the place she knew he had hidden them away from her, piled everything into her largest handbag and walked out, not even stopping to pack extra clothes.

She drove away from Bristol for the last time.

I read Gina's story with the wide-eyed horror of someone watching a calamitous accident unfold before them, numbed by the powerlessness of being unable to do anything to prevent it.

I'm not a violent man and hadn't so much as thrown a punch since I found out it was Keith Whitmore who was responsible for spreading scurrilous lies about my mother at school. But if that Jez had been stood in front of me there and then, I reckon I could've quite happily beaten him to a bloody mush.

What a coward! How can any man believe they have the right to abuse any fellow human being like that, let alone someone they purported to love? It sickened me to the depths of my being.

He had put Gina through unimaginable torment with his obsessive coercion and had almost broken her, physically and emotionally. I wanted to wrap her in my arms and tell her everything was going to be all right from now on, but that was both impossible (as I didn't even know where she lived) and inappropriate (as we barely knew each other).

All I could do was reply – but what the hell are you meant to say which could come close to a suitable response to such a nightmarish tale?

Any words would be inadequate, so I kept it simple.

Gina. I'm so sorry for what you had to go through. I'm glad you escaped.

She typed back straight away.

So am I.

Then, within seconds, another message.

It feels better to have told someone. I'm sorry to have piled all that on you, but thanks for being so understanding.

Maybe it's time we met. I owe you a coffee.

Chapter
Four

Not really being an authority on cosy cafés, I was happy for Gina to select where we might meet. She suggested a place close to the cathedral in the city centre. That was fine by me. To be honest, if she'd proposed getting together in a rat-infested derelict Nazi-Satanist cult drug den I would have been up for that as well. We were going to see each other. In the flesh. That was all that mattered.

The following day was Sunday and, because neither of us worked on Sundays, it made sense to meet then. Around twelve-thirty? OK, I replied. I looked at my watch. It was already twenty to one in the morning. Already Sunday. We'd been exchanging messages all night. I hadn't even washed the pots from teatime.

The rendezvous was less than twelve hours away. That was probably a good thing. It meant less time to get too worked up about it.

I got there thirty-eight minutes early and sat at a table which gave me a good view of the door, so I wouldn't miss Gina arriving. I'd been up since just before seven and had spent most of the time between then and setting off deciding what to wear. In the end, I chose a shirt my youngest daughter bought for me two birthdays ago because it was probably the smartest one I owned. I thought it was a bit flashy, so I hadn't worn it before. It was basically checked but was predominantly orange and white. In my view, any item of clothing that included the colour orange had to be a bit flashy. I regretted having chosen to wear it. It made me look like a traffic cone.

The waitress asked me if I wanted to order something but I said not yet because I was meeting someone. As time ticked on and the café grew busier, I could sense her shooting me funny looks. I kept my eyes on the door.

I didn't realise it was Gina at first. She was even more petite than I expected, bearing in mind the only pictures I had seen to judge her stature by had no one else in them for scale purposes. She was only maybe five feet two or three and of a very slender build. Her eyes were hidden behind sunglasses and much of the rest of her face was obscured by the hood of a pink zipped-up sweatshirt.

I hesitated, unsure whether or not to stand and beckon her over because it might not be her. But then she noticed me and gave me a little wave. She took off the glasses and eased back the hood of her top, bringing her hair to life with the slightest flick of her head. She moved towards me and I felt my jaw drop. I must have looked like a startled clown fish.

The photos didn't do her justice. She was even more stunningly beautiful in real life. Kind of Jennifer Aniston meets Kylie Minogue – and that's a pretty intoxicating combination in my book.

'Hi Barry.' She extended her hand.

I took it. 'Nice to meet you, Gina.'

'Been here long? I hope I haven't kept you waiting?'

'Only a couple of minutes,' I lied. 'Is this table OK?'

I don't know what I could've done if she'd said not. People were queuing at the counter waiting for folks to leave. That must have been why I was getting filthy glances from the waitress.

'It's fine, only…' She stalled, unsure. 'Do you mind if I sit facing the door?'

'Yeah, yeah, of course,' I stammered, almost kicking the chair over in my rush to vacate the spot.

'It's just that I still don't go out much and I keep on thinking I'm going to see… You know.'

That explained the glasses and the hood. She still felt haunted by the abusive husband.

'Of course, yeah.'

She sat. I moved to the other side of the table and shuffled in with a loud screech of the chair leg.

'I like your shirt, by the way,' she said. 'Nice and colourful.'

'Thanks.' I cursed myself for not getting in the first compliment. A response in kind now would look like an afterthought, so I blushed and muttered: 'My daughter chose it. I thought it might be a bit flashy.'

'Not at all.'

The waitress pushed two menus at us. Gina chose a cappuccino. I asked for a tea. The waitress looked disgusted. Such a wait for that?

'Popular little place,' I said. 'Have you been here before?'

Relax! I might as well have come out with the old 'do you come here often' line. I needed to behave as if I was less anxious.

'Never.' She graciously ignored my dumb patter. She appeared nervous too. 'I saw it on Google. Good reviews. I haven't really got to know anywhere since I came here.'

'How long have you been in Sheffield, then?'

Gina's eyes kept flicking to the window and the view outside, almost compulsively.

'Just over five months. How about you?'

'I've lived here all my life,' I shrugged.

'I should leave the venue choices to you in future then.'

In future! I liked that.

'So when you left Bristol, what made you decide to come here?'

'Not sure, to be honest.' By the expression on her face it was almost as if she'd never even asked herself that. 'I just kept driving, trying to get my head around everything, and by the time I started thinking about where I would go, Sheffield was the nearest big city. I suppose I thought it was as good a place as any. I checked into a hotel for a week or two and shut myself away. I used the time to plan what I wanted to do next. I realised I had to stand on my own feet. I had a bit of money of my own – not a huge amount, but enough to get me started – and set myself up as a freelance web designer. I had plenty of contacts and people I'd worked for previously started putting work my way. It kind of took off from there. I bring in enough work to get by now and that side of things is going OK. I moved out of the hotel and found a flat in a place called Wincobank. Did I pronounce that right?'

'Like a native.'

That made her smile. It felt good to be the cause of it. The fact that she hadn't really pronounced it properly was neither here nor there.

The waitress brought our drinks, forcing a lull in the conversation. Gina was looking out of the window again.

'Do you think he will come looking for you?'

The question seemed to surprise her. Then she realised what she'd been doing.

'Am I being that obvious? I'm sorry. It's rude of me.'

I'd made her self-conscious. I didn't intend to do that.

'It's nothing to apologise for. I'm just concerned for your safety.'

She smiled again. 'That's sweet of you. Thanks. It's all in my head, I think. I've no reason to believe he'll come looking, or that he'll have the slightest idea where I am. I just can't get rid of the fear, you know? All I've had from him are texts, ranging from threatening to pleading. Pathetic really. I haven't responded to any of them. I hope, maybe, he's starting to get the message. Most of the time, when I'm working and dealing with clients, I'm fine, but I still find it difficult when I leave the flat. Perhaps after spending all that time shut away in Bristol I'm a bit agoraphobic. I need to shake myself out of it.'

'You will. It just takes time,' I said, as if I was an expert on agoraphobia.

'I'm sure you're right,' she nodded. 'I'm sorry for going on, but it's kind of helping me, talking about it. I'm comfortable saying these things to you. I trust you. I really feel as if we've connected.'

I felt that too. I'd go so far as to say I couldn't remember the last time I'd felt so closely connected with another person – Louise included. Isn't it weird to say something like that when your only knowledge of that person is an exchange of online messages and one face-to-face meeting so brief that I hadn't even had time for a first sip of my tea?

Yet it was real. I knew it and Gina knew it.

We chatted some more and drank our drinks. I settled up with the waitress (and gave her a tip as a peace offering), then we left.

I checked the time. I couldn't believe we'd been talking for almost an hour and a half. That had flown!

'Where are you parked?' I asked as we stepped outside into the warm August sunshine. 'I'll walk you there.'

'You don't need to.'

'I'd like to.'

That seemed to please her. She raised her hands to pull the hood over her head, but checked herself and left it down.

A good sign, I thought.

Gina wasn't parked far away. The multi-storey on Campo Lane. I wished it had been further.

'Well, thank you. That was really pleasant. I'm glad we met,' she said as we prepared to part ways.

'Me too.' I gathered my courage. 'I'd like to see you again.'

'I'd like that.' My heart rose. 'Should we exchange numbers? It'll be better than doing everything through the app.'

'Absolutely.' Another small confirmation. I gave her my number and she rang it.

'There. You've got mine as well now.'

We stood still for an awkward moment. I didn't want to be the one to make the first move.

'Anyway,' she said, turning. 'Actually…' She spun to face me again.

'There's a play on at The Crucible this week I quite fancy. Shall we go?'

I hadn't been to the theatre since one of the blokes at

work offered me a spare ticket to the World Snooker Championships in 1998. Ronnie O'Sullivan beat some Scottish fella whose name I forget. As for going to the theatre to watch a play... I'm not sure I'd ever done that.

'That'd be great,' I said. 'I love the theatre.'

'Which evenings are you free?'

I didn't need a diary to answer that one. All of them. Every week. However, I was sometimes held up at work and the last thing I wanted was to risk that happening on the one night I couldn't afford to be delayed. We do, though, have a day off in the week because we always work Saturdays.

'Tuesday would be good. I'm off Tuesday.'

'That works for me. I'll get the tickets and let you know what time it starts.'

'Wonderful!' I truly meant that. It was wonderful.

She reached out for my hand and squeezed it. With that, she turned to go and I stood watching her maybe a little longer than I should've.

I was euphoric. Was this really happening?

Chapter
Five

We exchanged dozens of text messages over the next couple of days. I was almost giddily excited at the prospect of where this new fling may be heading. Was it too early to classify it as a fling? Do people use that term these days? Anyhow, I was more upbeat than I'd felt in years.

Even my son, Ben, noticed the change when he made one of his irregular filial obligation telephone calls that Sunday night.

His calls often struggle to make it beyond the one-minute mark.

'Hey dad, how's it going?'

'Not bad, Ben, how are you?'

'Not bad.'

That usually just about covers it, but this time I surprised him by asking for specific details about the wellbeing of his girlfriend (a charmless, painfully thin lass called Destinee) and how he was getting on in his new job at the Benefits Office. The added scrutiny appeared to throw him completely.

'Is everything all right dad?' he asked. 'You seem kind

of… cheerful.'

Maybe he was going to have to get used to seeing more of the new me from now on.

I even looked up what the show was about – the one I was going to see with Gina on Tuesday. Apparently, it was a play exploring womanhood, body image and tradition. Despite that, I was still looking forward to going.

Then, at about quarter past six on the Tuesday evening, just after I had brushed my teeth for the fifth time that day and was getting ready to leave, my phone rang.

It was Gina.

'Barry, I'm so sorry.' She sounded fraught. 'I can't make it tonight.'

Perhaps crushing disappointment should have been my overriding emotion at that point but it wasn't. I went straight into bristling protective mode.

'What's happened, Gina? Is it him?'

I thought maybe that contemptible bully of a husband of hers had found her.

'No, nothing like that.'

That was a relief, at least.

'My Wi-Fi packed in. I haven't been able to get on with my work. I spent most of the afternoon on the phone to the broadband provider and they couldn't fix it. They said they'd have to get an engineer out and it might take them two weeks! I'm so far behind with a job I promised a client I'd get done by the end of tomorrow and I'm going to have to do it off a 4G signal through my phone. It's so slow! I might have to work at it all night and then I don't know what I'm going to do. Two weeks! I'll have to set up in a McDonalds or something.'

As I said before, I'm generally a cautious man. I've never

been known to launch impetuously into any form of meaningful decision-making, right down to the selection of what type of sandwich I want to buy when Charlie and I stop off for lunch. But all my natural circumspection vanished into thin air right there and then. I just came out and said it.

'You can come here.' Even as the words left my mouth I surprised myself. 'I have a very strong Wi-Fi signal at my house. You can set up in the spare bedroom and work from there.'

Gina seemed positively taken aback.

'Are you sure?' she asked. 'It's very kind of you but …'

'Absolutely, I'm sure,' I cut in. I absolutely was. 'I have to set off for work at seven-thirty, but you can arrive whenever you like. I'll leave a spare front door key in the hanging basket on the porch. I'll text you the address and the Wi-Fi details. You'll be able to do the job much faster and you can carrying on working from here for however long it takes them to get you back up and running.'

It appeared to me the perfect solution. I could see no flaw in it.

'I… I don't know what to say. You're so generous. If you're certain it's OK.' There was still an edge of anxiety in her tone but I wanted to believe it was beginning to melt from her.

'That's settled then. Do what you can tonight and come around here tomorrow to finish the job.'

She was quiet for a moment. I fancied there might be a tear in her eye.

'I'll do that. I'm so grateful for this, Barry. I'll make it up to you. I'll tell you what, I can cook for you every night I'm there. You said you liked Italian food, didn't you?'

'Love it.'

'Then I'll make you my favourite recipes. I'll provide all the ingredients. How does that sound?'

'Sounds great.'

Great? It sounded bloody marvellous! I began to picture a whole succession of rapturous evenings with Gina, sharing delicious food and a bottle of chilled Pinot – and all in the cosily intimate surroundings of my own home. It could not possibly be better.

'I can't tell you how relieved I am, Barry,' she said, sounding as if the weight of the world was off her shoulders.

'Not at all,' I graciously answered.

'Sorry about ruining tonight, though.'

I considered admitting I thought the play sounded a bit crap anyway, but I didn't want to risk spoiling the moment. I was missing out on a first proper date with Gina but I stood to gain so much more on the longer term. That was a win, as far as I could tell.

Cleaning the house only took me six hours. Domestic hygiene had not been one of my priorities since Louise moved out and now it was time to pay the price. After a raid of the Tesco Express cleaning products aisle, I set about scrubbing, scouring and polishing everything with the vigour of a manic charlady with OCD. The place was in a right state, but eventually it was spotless. I couldn't have Gina thinking I'd let it go to pot now that I was on my own, even though I had.

I crawled into bed at just after half past one and slept like a baby. Gina didn't show up before I left, but I hadn't expected her to. It was the beginning of a working day positively prickling with the anticipation of getting done and being able to return home. I may never have laid carpet faster. It took all my powers of restraint to limit myself to only three calls to Gina to check if she was able to find everything she needed.

Finally – finally – I was done and jumped in the car to drive home, risking three minor accidents at junctions and two fixed penalty fines for charging through amber lights. Her car was on the driveway, so I pulled up on the road outside the house. I casually strolled past her black VW Golf; resisting the urge to stroke it, reminding myself to keep breathing.

There was no sign of her when I opened the front door. Perhaps she was still working in the spare bedroom. I did, though, notice the small dining table had been pulled into a more central position in the living room and was set up with placemats, serviettes, candles – the lot. It looked lovely. The table had been abandoned against the wall with the top folded down for years. Louise and I used to eat our tea off trays in front of the telly, taking away any awkward compulsion to make polite conversation while we ate.

'Hello? Gina?' I called, tentatively.

She emerged from the kitchen with a radiant smile, wiping her hands on a towel.

'Oh, hi! I didn't hear you come in. How was your day?'

She was wearing the 'King of the Grill' novelty apron my eldest daughter, Maisie, bought for me a few years ago when I mentioned one day (it must have been in the summer) that I was considering buying a barbecue. I decided not to bother when I remembered why I didn't really like barbecues, but I kept the apron. It practically engulfed Gina like a Christmas cracker wrapping.

'It was fine, ta. Did you get everything done that you needed to do?'

'I did!' she announced, triumphantly. 'I honestly don't

know how I'd have managed if you hadn't allowed me to work from your lovely home. You're a life-saver, Barry.'

'I'm glad.' I was beaming inside. 'As I said, you're welcome to work from here for as long as you need to.'

'Thank you.'

We stood facing each other, almost the full width of the living room apart, for a few seconds, as if unsure what to say next.

I was reflecting on how good it felt to have someone to come back home to at the end of a working day. It had been too long. Even longer since that someone gave the impression they were actually happy I was home again. Maybe Gina was having similar thoughts of how nice it was to rekindle the memory of happier times.

'Anyway,' she broke the spell. 'I've just started preparing the meal, so you get changed and leave me to get on with it. You're not allowed into the kitchen or you'll spoil the surprise.'

I acknowledged the 'order' with a mock salute and marched upstairs for a wash and to get out of my work clothes. When I came back down, there was a glass of white wine waiting on the table beside my armchair. I sat sipping it while watching the end of Look North and the first half of The One Show, waiting to be called over to eat.

The food was a revelation! It was called Tagliatelle Carbonara. It's this flat spaghetti with ham, a bit of a sauce and powdered cheese on top. I don't know if you've ever tried it, but it's delicious. Gina said there was garlic in it as well and I began to feel sorry for Charlie in the van the next day but he never said anything.

Even if he had, it would have been worth it from my point of view.

Gina worked from my place for the next three days after that, Thursday to Saturday, and all the following week. She even came in on the Tuesday, which was my day off. I got on with the tasks you have to catch up on when you're off work and, apart from knocking on the spare bedroom door occasionally to offer a cup of tea, I left her to get on with what she had to do. It was impressive the number of hours she was putting into her business.

I treated us to a takeaway that night, for a change, but I much preferred when Gina did the cooking. She was a great cook. It wasn't Italian food every time. I bet even Italians have a break from pasta some days. Her shepherd's pie made me vow to never again buy the microwavable meal for one version I often picked up from the supermarket. It was such a joy to eat proper, home-made food again.

Best of all was the time we spent together after the meals. We had no need for the telly. We had too much to say to each other. Mostly, it was Gina who led the conversation. She was very smart and knew so much about a whole load of stuff. I found it fascinating to listen to her stories about places she'd been and people she'd known, but she also had a real way of drawing you into the conversation and making you feel like your experiences and opinions were just as interesting. It was so easy getting along with her. We were from different backgrounds but, in many ways, we shared so many similarities. Including our sense of humour. I hadn't laughed as much with another person for as long as I could remember.

Even when I was at work, all I thought about was Gina. I'd find myself smiling at the memory of something she'd told me the night before or at a silly joke we'd shared. Charlie must've thought I was turning into a simpleton.

Especially when he left me alone for a few minutes and I started ripping up the carpet in the wrong room at a bungalow in Fulwood. I just couldn't keep my mind on what I was meant to be doing. All I wanted was to get finished and get home to her. That second Sunday, when I was off and Gina stayed at her flat, was a nightmare. I didn't know what to do with myself. I had to practically physically restrain myself to keep from texting her or calling her all the time because I didn't want to appear to be coming on too strong.

You see, we were getting along incredibly well, but I was too timid to ask outright how she felt about me. I guess part of me was worried I might be reading the situation wrong and that she only thought of me as a friend. It was, after all, very early days in our relationship. Also, she was quite a bit younger than me and so much better looking. I was completely aware I was punching way above my weight and if it turned out my feelings for her were far stronger than hers for me, that would've made it awkward. I didn't want to risk spoiling what we had, but there was no doubt in my mind as to where my emotional state was heading.

I was falling in love with Gina.

I know what you're thinking.

The silly old bugger's rediscovered that his willy's got another purpose.

But it wasn't like that. Don't get me wrong, I fancied her like mad, but we were taking it one step at a time.

I was overtaken by the urge to kiss her one night, after a particularly lovely chicken in mushroom sauce with rice, but it didn't go as I'd hoped. Gina stiffened as I leaned towards her and turned her head away.

'What is it?' I asked. Not nastily. I was concerned I'd

overstepped the line.

'I'm sorry,' she said, turning back to me. 'I'm just not ready yet. It's not you. I'm still getting over everything that happened with my husband. Sex with him became this horrible power game where he used me as his slave. You're not like him, I know, and I want to trust you, but I can't yet. Not that way. Give me time, Barry. I promise I'll find a way to deal with it, but I can't…'

'That's OK.' I cursed my lack of sensitivity. I should've realised how deep the scars were. We had become so close in such a short time, but the frightened little mouse I first saw when we met at the café that Sunday afternoon was still not yet able to emerge from the shadows.

'I understand.'

I wasn't really trying it on. I only wanted to kiss her. I wouldn't have complained if it had led to more, but I wasn't being presumptuous.

Anyway, I didn't make the same mistake twice.

It was enough for me to have the chance to spend so much quality time with Gina.

I wished the engineer from the Wi-Fi company would never turn up to fix her broadband connection. I couldn't even bear to bring up the subject, in case she wrongly interpreted my asking as an indication I was getting fed up with having her around so much. That was most definitely not the case. My heart sank when she mentioned on the second Friday that the engineer had been in touch.

'But he couldn't offer me an appointment until a week on Monday. Can you believe that, Barry? I'm so sorry to keep imposing on you.'

'No, no – it's fine, honestly,' I replied, trying not to break into a little jig. I rejoiced in the company's inefficient customer service standards and clung to the hope that the hapless engineer would stand hands on hips after an hour of trying to get to the root of the router problem and confess he couldn't work out where the fault was.

A continuation of our current arrangement suited me just fine.

However, all that was to change.

Chapter
Six

I suggested we spend a day out. Tuesday was my usual midweek day off and Gina said she was well enough on top of her work commitments to be able to take some time off as well. The arrangements were made and I was delighted. It was to be the first time we'd been out together since the meeting in the café and I interpreted that as a positive sign. I hoped it meant being with me was making her more confident about going out in public.

What I had in mind was a drive in the Peak District, taking in Castleton, Eyam, Hathersage and Ladybower. That's about as idyllic a round trip as there is, in my view. Gina still didn't know a great deal about Sheffield itself but I wanted to show her what we have on the doorstep as well.

I told her the story of the plague village. I bought her a lovely Blue John necklace. I showed her the view of the reservoir from Bamford Edge before we dropped lucky and saw the plug holes in full noisy flow from up close. I even took her up the Devil's Arse.

It's a cave, by the way. Just in case you were wondering.

I could tell she loved it all. Louise and I used to take the kids out there, so I know the area very well, but visiting those familiar haunts with someone who was experiencing them for the first time was like seeing everywhere through fresh eyes again.

Time passed so quickly. We didn't realise how hungry we were until we were in the car heading home at just before five o'clock. Neither of us had eaten since breakfast, so we stopped off at a pub on the drive back for an early tea.

'It's been a fabulous day,' she declared while we waited for our food to arrive. She tipped her glass at me before taking a sip of wine.

'Glad you enjoyed it. It's a very special part of the world.' I couldn't have been happier. I didn't want the day to end.

'The company wasn't bad either.'

'Yeah,' she smiled. 'Not bad.'

She touched the necklace I'd bought her. It looked great on her. There was so much good energy between us. There was no way I could see any reason to believe I was misreading all the signs.

We chatted some more during our meals and decided to have coffees. I turned in my chair to try to attract the eye of one of the waiting staff and caught sight of the large-screen TV in the bar. The tennis was on. A match had just finished. Congratulations and commiserations were being exchanged at the net. I spun around, curious to find out who was involved.

'Is it Wimbledon?' Gina asked.

'US Open, I think.' I wasn't as up to date with the sport as I used to be, but the US is generally late August to early September. 'Wimbledon is earlier in the year.'

'Who's playing?'

I strained to see. The screen was big enough but my eyesight isn't all it once was.

'Looks like Coco Gauff has just won. Singles quarter-final, I think.'

'Is she good?'

'Excellent,' I turned back to face Gina. 'A real prospect, from what I've seen. Still only a teenager. They reckon she could be one of the stars of the game for years to come.'

She arched her eyebrows in feigned surprise. 'I never had you down as a tennis expert.'

'I used to watch it a lot. Not so much now.' It wasn't appropriate to go into the reasons why, but simply touching on the subject brought back a small wave of sadness. I hadn't expected that.

'Never been a fan myself,' said Gina. 'I did watch the Wimbledon final, though. It was when I was back in Bristol.'

She had become increasingly willing to drop mentions of her time in Bristol into our evening conversations over the last week and I was pleased about that. I thought it showed she was healing. Some aspects of her recent past remained too raw to talk about, but not all of her memories from those days were being blanked out for fear of the damage they could still inflict. Something about this recollection jarred with me, though. Wimbledon this year was the first two weeks of July. Didn't she say she'd been in Sheffield for five months? And how come she thought the tennis on the TV in the pub might be Wimbledon when she'd just told me she watched the final? Odd.

Maybe she was getting mixed up. She had been through a great deal of trauma.

'We can stay here and watch a bit more of the tennis, if you'd like.'

I didn't want that at all. So much of that day had been spent walking over ground I'd previously trod with Louise and I'd been fine with that, but watching tennis was somehow going too far. I didn't want to risk getting maudlin.

'How about we go to see a film instead?' I suggested.

'Sure,' she nodded. 'You choose.'

I was glad she said that, bearing in mind her selection of evening's entertainment at the theatre two weeks earlier. I looked up the options on my phone. There was a new film on featuring Denzel Washington shooting baddies and blowing things up, which was as far from a play exploring womanhood, body image and tradition as I imagine it's possible to find. I enjoy watching Denzel Washington taking out baddies and blowing things up. He does it particularly well.

'Do you like action films? There's one with Denzel Washington and he's always good.'

'Sounds great.'

It did to me, too. Our day out was not over yet.

We were a little early by the time we dropped into town and parked up, so we went to a bar. It was too trendy for my liking but it did have a coffee machine, which was useful because I was driving. I got the drinks (Gina decided to have another glass of wine) and we found a quiet table in the corner.

As we were talking, I noticed a guy at the bar by himself. He kept looking towards us. I'd begun to get used, during the course of the day, to Gina drawing the eye of other men and I must admit I kind of liked it, because she was with me. That's a male ego thing, I know, but I couldn't help it. This guy struck me as a bit furtive, though. He kept glancing over, even though Gina had her back to him. It was beginning to get annoying.

When Gina got up to go to the loo, he watched her all the way. I considered heading over to warn him off but I don't really like confrontations, so I gave him a hard stare to let him know I was on to him. He finished his pint in one gulp and I thought he'd got the message, but he walked towards me instead. I immediately regretted being drawn into some sort of alpha male challenge thing. I was a bit taller than him and hauling big rolls of carpet around all day gave me a certain toughness of body but he was a bit younger and, for all I knew, might be a martial arts expert or something. He didn't look like one but I imagine you can't always tell.

I puffed myself up like a pigeon in the mating season, just in case. He planted the flats of both palms on the opposite side of the table and leaned in towards me. I'll always remember what he said.

'Have you had your twenty-three days yet?'

That punctured my posturing. It wasn't what I was expecting. I didn't have the remotest clue what he was on about. He was obviously a nutter. It was the sort of thing only a nutter in a pub would say. No wonder he was drinking alone.

'What?' It was the best response I could come up with at the time. What else are you meant to say to a question like that?

With a flick of his head, he gestured towards the ladies' toilets.

'How long have you been seeing her? Less than twenty-three days, I'm guessing.'

This was getting downright weird now. Impertinent at best. In my head, I wanted to point out that such an inquiry was none of his damned business and that he should seriously consider heading for the exit before I was compelled to do something he would regret, but it didn't come out that way.

'Yes.'

'Good,' he said. 'You've still got time.'

He reached into his trouser pocket and drew out a business card. He lay it on the table and pushed it towards me.

'I'm only in Sheffield for one more day and I'm heading home tomorrow night. My number's on the card. Call me. You're going to want to hear what I've got to tell you.'

With that, he turned and ambled away. It was all a bit surreal, like I'd inadvertently stumbled into an old Bogart movie. I was totally flummoxed. I watched him until he disappeared through the doors and into the growing dusk of the evening. Then I became aware that Gina was returning and snatched up the business card before she could see it.

'Everything all right?' she asked as she sat. 'You look alarmed.'

I shook myself into a smile. 'Do I? No. It's nothing.' I checked my watch. 'We should be going in a minute.'

There are certain things that even Denzel Washington cannot divert your attention from and this was one of them. All through the film, I kept seeing the guy staring intently at me through his silver-rimmed specs from the opposite side of the table in that bar and churning his words over and over in my mind.

What did he mean?

The twenty-three days thing was the biggest baffler. If there was a significance to such a specific length of time then it was completely lost on me, but he made it sound like some sort of deadline. I did a mental reckoning of how long it had been since I first made contact with Gina and that was the nineteenth day. Christ! What the hell was he implying was going to happen in a few days' time?

The business card was burning a hole in my trouser pocket. He wanted me to call him. I was going to want to hear what he had to say, he told me. The very fact that I couldn't even imagine what it was he felt I needed to know so urgently made it impossible to contemplate ignoring him. I needed to find out – yet part of me didn't want to know. It was a proper conundrum.

I tried to blank it out on the drive back to my house, where Gina had left her car, but I'm not sure how convincing a job I made of it. I think she could tell something was wrong. We hugged on my driveway and she stretched onto the tips of her toes to give me a peck on the cheek.

'Thank you again for a lovely day.'

It had been lovely. Beyond lovely. Almost perfect. It was the 'almost' bit that was preying on my mind and that clearly showed. Gina's sharp hazel eyes pierced my feeble attempt to disguise it.

'Are you OK, Barry?'

'Just a bit tired,' I offered lamely. 'I really loved being able to spend today with you. You're wonderful.'

She drew me into another squeeze.

I wanted to say it. I really did. It was the ideal moment, holding her tight under the clear late summer night sky, two figures illuminated only by the light of the half-moon and a million stars. The council still hadn't come out to fix the broken street lamp outside my place by then. I wanted to tell her I loved her but I couldn't. The last thing I wanted was to scare her off, but I wanted to say it and I would've meant it.

If it hadn't have been for that guy in the bar, I actually think I would've.

'You're so sweet,' Gina said, releasing me. 'See you tomorrow, then.'

With another crushingly gorgeous smile, she turned to her little black VW. I watched her drive away and waved as she headed towards the end of the street.

My heart was bursting, not only because of my feelings for Gina but because of the new uncertainty introduced by that strange guy in the bar.

Until I found out what he said he needed to tell me, I knew I wouldn't be able to get him out of my mind.

A poisonous snake had slithered into my little paradise.

Chapter
Seven

ANDREW HAGUE
Regional Sales Manager
Duchamos Shower Supplies Ltd

I stared at the business card on my kitchen counter for so long that my cup of tea went cold. I still couldn't decide what I should do. I'd spent just about the whole of a restless night staring at the ceiling, running it over and over in my head. I could not settle on what to do for the best.

I'd like to think anybody in the same position as me would have found it to be a dilemma, but for someone who sometimes takes ten minutes choosing which pair of socks to wear in the morning, it was a bloody nightmare.

Just about the only time I drifted into a fitful doze, I was abruptly jolted out of it by a bizarre dream in which Gina transformed into some sort of ferocious spider monster with enormous fangs at the end of our twenty-third day together. It was plain that I had to get to the bottom of this or it was going to consume me. I couldn't try to forget the encounter in the bar had ever happened and hope the whole business blew away.

But how should I go about it?

The clock on the kitchen wall said nearly twenty past seven. I had to leave for work in just over ten minutes. Gina usually arrived at the house around eight. This brings us to option one.

Phone into work to tell them I'm going to be late. Hang on for Gina's arrival and talk to her about the guy in the bar. See if she recognises the name from the business card.

The main problems with this approach, as I saw it, were:

Gina was probably completely innocent of whatever it was this nutter shower salesman might be accusing her of. It was most likely a case of mistaken identity anyway (the guy was wearing glasses, so his eyesight can't be that good). If I waded in with even the slightest suggestion of impropriety, Gina would be perfectly within her rights to mark me down as the jealous type, it would shatter the delicate trust she had started to show in me and, basically, I would have blown it.

Option two.

Phone the shower salesman and listen to what he had to say.

Problems:

Why would I want to listen to what he had to say, why should I believe anything he said and who the hell was he anyway?

Despite this, hearing him out still appeared to me the better alternative. I would know what it was he was so keen for me to know, rather than tying myself in knots guessing what it might be. I could hear him out, dismiss him as the nutter shower salesman he undoubtedly was and happily get on with my blossoming relationship with Gina, no damage done.

This, I was coming to accept, was the better way

forward.

It was time to go. I picked up the business card and my car keys to leave. I called the number from the car park behind the storage warehouse at work.

'Hello, Andy Hague speaking.'

By the sound of it, he was in his car and on the move.

'We saw each other in the Snail and Porcupine last night. You said I should call you.'

The tone I was going for was guarded suspicion. I didn't want him to think he had me where he wanted me.

'I'm glad you did,' he replied. 'We need to talk.'

His tone was businesslike, no sign of emotion. He was still the one setting the terms. Damn. He did have me where he wanted me.

'OK, when?'

'I'm on my way to visit a few clients in Doncaster and then I've got to call in at a showroom in Rotherham, but I can be back in Sheffield late afternoon. How about four at the same pub?'

I wasn't sure how busy a day lay ahead for Charlie and me but I was pretty sure I could get to this proposed liaison in time. Charlie and me often covered for each other if one of us had an appointment to keep.

'Fine,' I said.

'Great. That's settled.'

I was about to hang up first, to make a point, when he spoke again.

'What's your name?'

I hesitated but couldn't think of a good reason to withhold the information.

'Barry.'

'Right, Barry. See you at four.'

Then he hung up first. Damn.

***

I arrived fourteen minutes early. I ordered a cup of tea and sat at the same table as the previous night.

Hague arrived nine minutes late. No apology or excuse offered, which was noted. He did, though, ask if I wanted another drink. I declined, on principle. He came back from the bar with a pint of lager and sat opposite me.

I don't normally rush to judgement on people I don't know, but this bloke struck me as a right prick. If pushed, I might, in truth, have struggled to explain why. He just did.

He was pretty ordinary to look at really. Edging towards under-tall, definitely edging towards overweight. Mid-fifties, glasses, dried blood on his neck where he'd rushed his morning shave. Hair no longer as dark as it once was or as thick as he would have liked but still styled the same way he'd probably had it since he was thirty years younger. Suit too tight around the waist and jacket crumpled. As I said, a right prick.

I waited for him to speak first. He took a mouthful of lager.

'So,' he said, wiping froth from his upper lip with the back of his hand. 'What's she calling herself these days?'

That was another thing I disliked about him. What gave him the right to make insinuations about my Gina?

'What do you mean?' The hostility in my delivery was deliberate.

'Your girlfriend. What's her name?'

So why didn't he just phrase it that way first time?

'Gina.'

'Gina. All right.' He took another drink and nodded his head like it was meant to signify something. 'And how long have you known Gina?'

'Two weeks or so,' I replied, intentionally rounding down the length of time to show I wasn't concerned about the random twenty-three days figure he'd mentioned, even though the number had been bouncing around my brain all night.

'And in those two weeks or so, I bet she hasn't let you put your hands anywhere near that lovely little body of hers.'

That was it. I'd had enough. I shot to my feet. 'I knew this was a bloody waste of time.'

'OK, OK.' He held up a contrite hand. 'That was unnecessary. I apologise.'

I remained standing. He was going to have to do better than that to make me completely withdraw my threat to walk out.

'Look, I'm here to do you a favour,' he said. 'Sit down and I'll explain.'

I stayed defiantly upright.

'All right,' he accepted with a bow of his head. 'Let me guess what's gone on in this last two weeks or so with you and Gina and if I'm on the right lines, then you sit down and hear me out.'

What peculiar game was this? I had to know where he was going with it.

'You met online, though a dating app,' he began. 'You didn't pick her out. She approached you, which was enormously flattering because she's a very good-looking woman, right? She lays it on thick with "woe is me, you won't want anything to do with me because I'm so miserable, but I thought you looked kind, so I messaged you" and you're instantly feeling sorry for her. You can save her! You start chatting online and she spins you a sob story about running away from her bastard of an abusive husband and by this time you're completely sold. You're ready to go to war for her. You chat some more and appear to be getting along great, so you arrange to meet up. But – oh, no! – she's been struck by broadband meltdown just at the time she has an urgent job to finish and has to cancel. However will she cope? "I know," says you. "Come and work from my place". Am I getting warm?'

Stunned doesn't come close. You could've sent me tumbling backwards with the slightest breath of air. I felt as exposed as a fish floundering on the bankside. There's no way…

I sat down.

'How…?' I spluttered. 'Have you been spying on us?'

'Spying? No.' He chuckled at the idea as he raised his glass again. 'I fell for exactly the same ruse two months ago. She was operating in Manchester then and called herself Diana. Different name, different place, same woman. I recognised her as soon as she walked into this bar last night and, before you ask, no I wasn't expecting to see her. I just happened to be in Sheffield for work and just happened to call in here for a drink or two after seeing my last client.'

He stopped talking, probably to allow time for my addled mind to absorb what he had already told me. Naturally, I wanted to find a way to justify calling him a liar, but I couldn't think of one. It was impossible for him to have known so many intimate details that I hadn't shared with any other person, unless…. Unless he was telling the truth.

'Look, Barry,' he added, calmly. I couldn't look at him.

My gaze was fused on my empty tea cup, which now somehow seemed to neatly symbolise my hopes for the future.

'I'm not telling you this to get back at her for dumping me or anything like that. She's a con artist. She's using you to dupe people out of money by setting up a fake online investment company in your name. If you don't do something about it now, you could end up with the fraud squad knocking on your door looking to pin it all on you.'

That tore my attention away from the tea cup. I gawped at him, open mouthed and wide-eyed. 'What? That's got to be nonsense. It's impossible.'

By his expression, he had anticipated my scepticism.

'You don't believe me? I can show you. Take out your phone.'

I retrieved it from my coat inside pocket.

'Search for "company information service" on the Gov.UK website.'

I opened the search site and keyed in the words, as instructed.

'Now type your full name into the search box.'

There it was. One company registered to that name. Sheaf Crypto UK Ltd. One officer of that company listed.

HAYWOOD, Barry Hagan
Role: Director
Date of birth: March 1966
Appointed on: 30 August 2023
Correspondence address: 41 Shinfield Drive, Sheffield, England
Occupation: Entrepreneur

My name. My date of birth. My address.

That date of appointment. It was only a week or two ago. About the time Gina first started working from my house.

'Congratulations.' I lifted my disbelieving eyes from the phone screen to see I was being toasted. 'You're now a company director.'

I didn't know what to say. I certainly didn't feel it was cause for celebration. I'd been tricked, deceived, conned, hoodwinked – call it what you like. Gina had preyed on my good nature and had played me for a fool. My whole being tingled with a combination of acute embarrassment and indignant fury at her deception.

Hague reached forward to lay his hand on my arm.

'I know what you're going through, believe me, but this next bit is important.' He stared at me with intent. 'She's been working on you for less than twenty-three days. You still have time. Go straight from here to the police. Tell them what I've told you. Get her arrested before she disappears again.'

I was finding it impossible to process what he was saying with a rational mind. It was all too much. All of it. I could pick out only one detail. The one that had been bugging me since the day before.

'Why twenty-three days?'

Hague sat back and released my arm.

'That's how long she stays for, then she heads away to set up in a different place to pick out a new victim. Look.' He visibly slumped on his stool. For the first time, I saw him as a kindred soul.

'In the short time Diana – Gina – was with me, I started to believe I could find love again. I'd been alone for four years since I got divorced. My fault. I had an affair with an assistant manager of a bathroom installation company in Halifax. Anyway, I met Diana and I thought we were made for each other but then, twenty-three days in, she just vanished without trace. Not a sign. I reported her missing and everything but there was nothing. Gone. I was devastated. I'm not too proud to admit I wasn't sure if I could go on.'

He tipped the last dregs of lager from his glass into his mouth.

'Then I started getting letters, addressed to me but referring to a company I'd never heard of. I ignored them at first. Didn't even open them. But then I got curious and decided to Google the company name. That's when I came across the website. Wouldn't you know it, my address was listed on the website as the company's base. The penny started to drop. There was never an answer from the phone number I had for Diana but I looked her up on the dating app, Amor4Mature, to see if I could trace her that way. Which site did you meet her on, by the way?'

'Er, clickforlove.com.' In the midst of a deluge of new information, I'd almost forgotten.

'Oh!' He curled his lip to suggest I'd made an inferior choice. 'Anyhow, she'd deleted her profile off the site but I know a couple who run about half a dozen sites like it. It's a lucrative business, this lonely hearts thing. I asked if anybody had reported a similar situation to the one that had happened to me and it rang a bell. The description fitted. They were good enough to put me in touch with this guy who had been taken in by a similar story, a guy from Peterborough, so I called him. She'd used the same profile picture with a different name and pulled the same con. I asked him to reckon up how long it was between her first making contact with him and the day she disappeared. Do you know what he told me?'

'Twenty-three days?' I guessed.

'Exactly,' he said triumphantly. 'Twenty-three days. That's how long you've got. That's why you have to act fast.'

Chapter
Eight

Andy Hague slipped the key into his front door lock and sighed. It had been a long and difficult day.

The life of a Regional Sales Manager for one of the biggest shower supplies companies in the north of England was not all glamour. He'd been behind schedule since the second appointment in Doncaster, where he had to sort out the mess of yet another order the warehouse had managed to get wrong. Then there was that idiot of a manager at the DIY superstore in Mexborough. He was always a pain in the arse. Then there had been an accident at the road works on the A57 just outside Sheffield. Then there was Glossop at the tail-end of rush hour. And the M57. The drive from Belle Vue to Rusholme alone had taken over an hour.

He was home far later than he hoped. All he wanted from the rest of his evening was to pour a large whisky and order in a takeaway. More urgently, though, he was busting for a pee.

Hague took care of his top priority and stared deeply at his reflection in the bathroom mirror as he allowed water from the cold tap to run freely through his fingers. He did not like what he saw.

'You're getting too old for this game,' he said to the miserably haggard face opposite him. 'Too old and too knackered.'

He was feeling sorry for himself. The source of his self-pity was not the journey home or even the DIY superstore manager at Mexborough. It stemmed from seeing her again.

It had, after all, only been just over two months.

He would rather have suffered the withering contempt of a million flat refusals from a million women in a million bars than have to go through what Diana put him through.

The agony of hope rekindled, only to be doused again just at the time its flickering new flame had begun to produce thin warmth and a pale light.

He thought he was getting over it. He thought he had channelled the pain of unexplained sudden rejection into anger after peeling back the layers of deception she had hidden behind that perfect superficial exterior. Diana never wanted him. She lured him close and sucker-punched him.

He thought he'd got that fixed in his head. He thought he's moved beyond the hurt with nothing worse than a never-again life lesson to carry into what remained of his unfulfilled late middle age. He even fancied he might be a wiser man for the experience.

But then, out of the blue, he'd seen her again and the protective barrier he thought he'd built began leaking like a badly installed shower enclosure.

At least he'd been able to tip off her latest victim. With luck, that dopey-looking bloke in Sheffield will have taken his good advice and gone straight to the police. She might even be under arrest by now. That would be something. Never mind the poor saps who had lost money. She had stolen something far more valuable from him. She should pay for that, too.

Hague pushed his glasses off the bridge of his nose with wet fingers and rubbed his weary eyes. Yes, it would be good to see her brought to justice. For now, though, he just wanted to switch off and try to carry on coping with life.

Starting with a large whisky while he ordered an Indian takeaway online.

The bottle was in its usual place, on the table in the corner of the living room. He picked it up. It was lighter than he expected. Less than a third full. He didn't recall hitting it hard the night before heading off to Sheffield. He made a mental note to consider cutting down his intake.

The glasses were in the kitchen. So were the takeaway menus. So was a very large, fierce-looking man.

Suffice to say he had not expected there to be a very large, fierce-looking man in his kitchen, but there he was all the same, leaning against the washing machine with his arms folded like he was waiting for someone who had promised they would be home earlier. He did not look happy. He was mid-thirties, at least six feet four and seemed almost as broad around the chest. The sheer bulk of him was exaggerated by the tightness of his plain white T-shirt and the snug confines of the tiny kitchen. At first sight, you might have thought he had close-cropped dark hair, but if you dared to look closer you would have seen there was not a single hair on his head. There was, however, plenty of tattoo ink in brooding depictions of demonic figures, screaming ravens, wild-eyed skulls and a dagger dripping blood down the length of his spine.

Hague was not eager to look closely at the ink on the man's head, or the ink that covered almost every centimetre of skin on his thick, muscly arms. Or anywhere else on his formidably large body, for that matter. He wasn't even that concerned, for now, how this very large, fierce-looking man came to be in his kitchen. His only immediate thought was to get out of the kitchen and as far away from the very large, fierce-looking man as possible.

Unfortunately, even if he had been able to form an effective escape plan and even if the shock had not turned his legs to jelly it was still unlikely he could have outrun the younger man. He made it only as far as half way across the living room before a meaty claw grabbed the collar of his shirt and brought his progress to a choking halt. He was jerked backwards and, off-balance, fell with a thud onto his back on the laminate flooring. The blow punched all the air out of him and sent his head spinning. As he regained his senses and drew in a deep breath, towering above him was the very large, fierce-looking man.

'Where's my fucking money?'

Hague blinked hard at the ferocious face looming above and tried to work out how this man apparently knew him when he didn't have a clue who this man was. He was absolutely certain he would have remembered such a recognisable visage if he had seen it before. He quickly tried to come up with an answer that might calm the situation. He could not.

'Money?' he stammered.

'*My* fucking money,' the man clarified. 'I want it back.'

The information was still not specific enough to help Hague make sense of it. He still couldn't place that face and he still didn't know about any money.

'What? I...'

The man stooped lower and, with his huge mitt,

grabbed hold of his cowering victim by the front of his shirt, lifting him off the ground.

'Do you know who I am?' he growled. Their faces were close enough for Hague to smell the whisky on the man's breath. He shook his head, frantically.

'I'm Thommo. I'm the hardest man in Skelmersdale. You don't want to cross me.'

That much Hague could easily comprehend.

'You stole my fifty grand. I checked my crypto wallet and it's gone. I want it back. With interest.'

Now the full fifty grand's worth of pennies dropped. This was one of the casualties of Diana's online financial services scam. She must have cleared out all the accounts and run off with the proceeds.

Since uncovering the extent of the fraud he had been duped into being part of, Hague had feared a knock on the door from a member of His Majesty's constabulary, demanding an explanation, but he hadn't considered he might be paid a visit by an irate customer.

How?

Of course! His address on the website. He hadn't been able to get the authorities to take it down yet.

The realisation did nothing to make him feel better about his current situation. He was still in a whole world of trouble. There had to be something he could say to make this man realise he was an innocent patsy in this con job as well.

'I haven't got your money.'

That wasn't it.

The hardest – and possibly the most heavily tattooed – man in Skelmersdale became really angry at that truthful but, in the circumstances, unwise admission. It wasn't what he wanted to hear. His eyes turned as wild as a wolf smelling fresh meat. His nostrils flared. His yellowing teeth gritted. He threw his prey back onto the hard floor and stretched to his full height again, lifting his right boot and clamping it down heavily on the left hand of the supine figure beneath him.

Hague yelped.

'Where's – my – fucking – money?' spelt out the man, gradually increasing the pressure of his foot on the hand. The first bone snapped with an audible crack. Hague cried out again.

'I know who's got it!' he offered, desperately.

'Who?' That wasn't enough to stop him exerting more weight on the hand.

Crack.

'It's a woman. She's a con artist. She used my name and address to set up a fake company. I didn't know at the time. Please believe me.'

The man tilted more of his vast weight on to his right side.

Crack. Crack.

Hague wanted to scream. The pain was immense.

'I know where she is now. I can give you an address, just please let me up. I'll get it for you.'

The man wanted a more immediate solution but could see this might be his best available option. He eased his boot off the hand.

'Give it to me.' He leaned to pull Hague to his feet with a handful of shirt. 'If you're lying to me, you're dead.'

Hague pressed his injured hand into his right armpit to try to ease the shooting agony.

'I need to get my phone.' He gestured towards his

jacket, folded over the back of an armchair. The man nodded his consent.

They had exchanged details in the pub, in case they needed to stay in touch. He had a name, phone number and email address. He only needed the name right now.

As quickly as he could, with only one hand available, he tapped 'Barry Haywood crypto' into the search engine. As he hoped, that brought up the link to the website for Sheaf Crypto UK Ltd. Soon he had the address.

'Here,' he said. 'See?'

The man peered at the small phone screen.

'Write it down.'

Hague hurried over to the pad and pen he often needed for scribbling down late instructions to do with work and copied down the details before tearing off the sheet to present it to his tormentor.

'Gina,' he read. 'That her?'

'That's her,' Hague confirmed. 'That's the guy she's currently with. That's his address.'

The man grabbed hold of his trembling prey by the collar again.

'You let them know I'm coming for them and you're dead. You go to the coppers and, you know what?'

'I get it, I get it,' Hague nodded. 'I'm dead.'

'So dead.'

He studied the paper again. 'Sheffield,' the man said, releasing his grip.

With that, he stomped towards the door.

Chapter
Nine

I walked to the car park I normally use when I go to town but I couldn't find the car. That was when I remembered I'd actually parked somewhere closer to the pub where I'd just met Andy Hague, the shower salesman. That was how much of a daze I was in after listening to what he had to tell me.

It started raining quite heavily on my way to the other car park. I have a vague recollection of people dashing across the streets as the traffic splashed by, while others took shelter in shop doorways in the hope that the storm would quickly pass. I just kind of trudged along, oblivious to it. By the time I reached the car I was soaked to the skin. I climbed into the driver's seat, water dripping off my nose and running off my sodden hair down the back of my neck, and sat there, allowing the blurring patterns made by the rain on the windscreen to swim before my eyes. I didn't want to move.

I couldn't believe it. Gina was a con artist? It was bad enough discovering she was not the person she had pretended to be, but to be told the sole reason she had spent the last couple of weeks with me was so she could set me up as the fall guy for her latest fraud made it infinitely worse. What an idiot I'd been, to be taken in so easily. They do say there's no fool like an old fool and that's exactly what I was. An old fool. To think I had believed a beautiful woman like Gina could have been even remotely interested in me without having an ulterior motive! How could I be so stupid?

Stupid. Stupid. Stupid.

I pressed against the centre of the steering wheel so that the horn blasted loudly and held the flats of my hands there for at least ten seconds while I yelled so deeply from the pit of my being that my throat was made raw. It's a good job no one cared enough to respond to the noise by coming to see if I was OK because I started crying. Convulsing sobs that held me powerless until they left me completely empty. I'd never experienced an outburst like that. It seems an odd word to use when nobody had died but I can only describe it as grief, though I didn't feel grief like that even when I lost my parents or when Louise said she was leaving me. There had been signs to prepare me for those moments. This had been so sudden.

As disabling as the crying was, it was also kind of cleansing. By the time I'd cleared my head and blown my nose, the storm inside had passed through. As had the storm outside. Andy Hague had been insistent that my first move should be to get the police involved but I didn't want to do that. Yet. I wanted to head home. Gina would be there. I needed to have it out with her.

The trouble was that as I drove, I became angry. Not violent angry. As I said earlier, I'm not a fighter and I absolutely would never raise a hand to a woman, but I was getting ready to confront Gina. By the time I arrived home,

I knew exactly what I wanted to say to her and I didn't care if the words came across pleasantly or not.

Her car was on the driveway. The sight of it normally gave me a little extra tingle, knowing it meant another lovely evening with Gina lay ahead. I know it sounds a bit strange, but I liked to run my hand along its sleek bodywork on my way to the front door – from the rear lights, across the roof and all the way along the front wing to the headlamps. Make of that what you want. Not this time, though. In fact, I had my house key in my hand and I used it to gouge a deep scratch in the black paint. It was petty and spiteful and I shouldn't have done it. But I didn't regret it at the time.

I could hear her in the kitchen as I walked in and closed the front door behind me. She stepped into the living room to greet me, drying a measuring jug with a tea towel.

'I thought it was you,' she said with the sort of smile that used to melt me. 'You're a bit later than you said you'd be. Did something crop up?'

I was finding it difficult to do the normal catch-up small talk. It was one of the things I'd grown to love, especially as there had been so little of it through the later years of my marriage, but now it just seemed like part of her act.

'Yeah. Something.'

She looked closer at me. 'You're wet through. Did you get caught in the storm? You go and get changed. I'm just starting to prepare the meal. Mushroom stroganoff OK for you? How was work?'

Her last words tailed away as she returned to what she had been doing in the kitchen.

'It was good,' I called, to make sure she heard me. 'I got a promotion.'

'Really?' Gina's head reappeared around the kitchen

door. 'That's great. What's the new job?'

I waited a second for added impact.

'Company director.'

Of course that confused her. I expected it to. I wanted to get her attention and set her mind whirring. I didn't expect it would spark an automatic confession but it was the first step in seeing how long it took her to come clean.

'For the carpet firm?'

Obviously, it was never going to be for the carpet firm. She knew that. She just said the first words that came into her head while she was processing what was going on. Stalling. She probably felt she had to say something.

'No,' I said. 'An online investment company. Sheaf Crypto UK Ltd it's called. It's a new start-up business but I'm guessing you've already heard of it. I must admit I hadn't. Not until a couple of hours ago, anyway.'

Cards on the table. It wasn't a direct accusation but it was as good as. I hoped she would at least have the decency to admit what she'd done and not attempt to wriggle out of it. I could tell by her body language she knew I'd rumbled her game.

'Look, Barry…'

'No, you look!' I burst in. My anger would not be contained any longer. 'How could you do this? You tricked your way into my life through a pack of lies, purely with the intention of exploiting my good nature. You picked me out because you knew I was vulnerable after the divorce and you'd be able to twist me round your little finger, didn't you? And, guess what, I fell for it. I felt sorry for you when you told me what you'd been through. I felt sorry for you when you said you had internet trouble. I invited you into my home, for god's sake! I trusted you because you made me believe you were a person who deserved a little kindness after going through a hard time and it was all just so you could get hold of all my details to run another of your sordid little con jobs. You're a liar and a thief, Gina. Gina! That's not even your real name, is it? Another lie!'

I still had my keys in my hand and I cast them across the room. They hit with a chink the tall black metal shelving unit Louise bought from IKEA years ago. I never liked it. I didn't throw them in Gina's direction but the suddenness of the action make her jump anyway.

'Give me one good reason why I shouldn't call the police and keep you here until they arrive? One reason.'

She didn't offer one. Perhaps she couldn't.

The fury abruptly drained from me as quickly as it had consumed me. I had to sit.

'How could you do this, Gina? How?'

A calming silence fell between us.

'I can understand why you feel let down,' said Gina at last. I snorted derisively. 'I get it. I took advantage of you, I know, but it was nothing personal. I'm very careful in what I do. You wouldn't have got into trouble because of it. For what it's worth, I do think you're sweet.'

For what it's worth? It was worth nothing.

Neither of us spoke again for a while. I couldn't even look at her. She was clearly starting to wonder how it had gone wrong this time.

'How did you find out, by the way?' she asked.

'You were seen last night in the pub. One of the guys you took for a ride before me. Bloke from Manchester called Andy Hague.'

I lifted my eyes to watch the dawning on her face as she recognised the name.

'Andy. Oh, yes!' It was all so cold. Like she was recalling someone she was once introduced to at a party a long time ago. 'Not a particularly nice man. Struck me as a bit of a prick, to be honest.'

I was going to admit I'd made the same assessment but I didn't want to take any step towards common ground. As a fellow victim, I was on his side.

'He was in love with you.' I wanted to strike straight at Gina's heart, if she had one. I wanted her to know this game she was playing was not without collateral damage.

'In love with me?' She laughed. 'That's ridiculous!'

'Why's it ridiculous?' It annoyed me that she was so dismissive. 'Don't tell me you aren't aware how physically attractive men find you because I bet you've spent half your adult life having to beat them off with a stick. You know how to make men do exactly what you want them to. It's what you've based this whole sorry fraud on in the first place. It's a guaranteed winner. A single man in late middle age, staring down the barrel of spending the rest of his life alone, is approached by a beautiful younger woman and he thinks all his birthdays have come at once. Normally, a woman like that wouldn't even look twice at him but not this one. She makes him believe she actually needs him. Naturally, he'd do anything to help her. In helping her, she heals him. She restores his self-worth. She makes him feel valued, wanted. She awakens emotions he feared would be dead to him for the rest of his life. Of course he falls in love with her. She makes him feel alive again.'

It dawned on me that I might have given a bit too much of myself away there. Too late. Gina saw straight through me.

'Oh, Barry, you don't mean…'

73

I said nothing. I could say nothing.

I might have expected a little sympathy at that stage, at least, but the realisation only appeared to make her cross.

'I never promised you anything.' There was accusation in her tone, like I'd failed to live up to my side of the deal. 'I might have played the part of little girl lost and I might even have flirted a bit, but I never gave you any reason to believe we would ever be anything more than just friends.'

'You didn't have to!' I couldn't hide the anguish. 'Look at you! You're gorgeous. Of course men are going to fall in love with you. It's in our nature. If you press the right buttons, we can't help it. History is littered with stories of men who've been brought to their knees by beautiful women.'

Maybe she'd have been within her rights to denounce me as pathetically weak and tread me into the dirt because I must have appeared pathetically weak, slumped in the chair with my head in my hands. I was naked and shrivelled. I was in no position to defend myself against anything else she could hurl at me. Instead, she softened.

'I'm sorry,' she said. 'I didn't mean to do that to you. It was purely for the money, as far as I was concerned, and I never considered the full potential implications. I am sorry.'

I neither accepted nor rejected her apology. There was no point. I'd said what I'd said and my words had got through. That was it.

'Look,' she added. 'We could be partners, if you'd like. The business I set up in your name has got off to a strong start and it'd be a pity to scrap it now. We could share the profits. It's easy money.'

So she really didn't get it, even after all that.

'No,' I said calmly. 'I don't want anything from you. All

I want is for you to get your stuff together from the back bedroom and to go. Just get out.'

She didn't move at first but then, without another word, she headed to the stairs. Five minutes later, she returned downstairs carrying three black bags over her shoulders, with two keyboards under her arms. She carried on walking to the door without so much as a glance my way and she was gone.

Chapter
Ten

That night was one of the longest of my life. I didn't even go through the motions of getting ready for bed because there would've been no point. There was no way I was going to get any sleep. For hours, I sat in my armchair – not on the sofa I used to like to share with Gina – and let all sorts of crap drift in front of my eyes on the telly. Game shows, reality cookery programme repeats, old episodes of The Vicar of Dibley. All sorts.

It did nothing to clear my head, so I decided I needed fresh air. I set out for a walk, even though it was still dark. I followed the lane all the way through the Shire Brook Valley Nature Reserve, up by the Rother through the Washlands and on to Waverley Park. I hadn't done so much walking since lockdown. Not surprisingly, there weren't many other people about. The occasional cyclist heading to or from work, a couple of dog-walkers. That was about it. No muggers, thankfully, though as I look back I didn't even consider the possibility I might run into any undesirables at the time. I guess I was past caring.

All I could think about was Gina and how she'd made a

proper mug of me. I was ashamed, to tell the truth, that she'd been able to truss me up and hang me out to dry so easily. I'd like to say the walking helped, but it didn't really. It did, however, make me realise that I hadn't eaten since lunchtime the day before, so I called in to the McDonald's near Handsworth Asda and had breakfast before heading home.

It was after seven when I got back. I must've been walking for three or four hours. I'd already made up my mind that I was in no fit state to go to work, so I phoned through and said I'd tested positive for Covid. I never called in sick usually. They could manage without me for a few days.

Besides, there was stuff I needed to do.

After a shower and a cup of tea, I sat down to figure out how to shut down the business I was unknowingly responsible for before it had the chance to blow up in my face. There was plenty of advice on the internet. Clearly, I wasn't the first innocent person to be duped by this fraud, which was both an eye-opener and kind of reassuring. There actually seemed to be a lot of it about. But the more I read, the more my natural indecision came out and the more I worried I might take the wrong course of action which would land me even deeper into bother. In fairness, it was the first time I'd ever had to extricate myself from a company directorship. I needed to be able to talk to someone who had already had to deal with this mess.

I called Andy Hague.

He'd given me his card and I passed on my details in the pub. He seemed quite keen to be kept in the loop, should Gina end up facing criminal charges, which was plainly his preferred outcome. I was prepared to lie to him about having gone to the police already, if he asked, but only because I wanted him to focus on my first priority.

It rang for quite a while. I was beginning to think he must be trying to sell showers somewhere when he answered.

'Hello?'

It was far from the buoyantly confident senior sales executive about town tone I got when I'd called him the day before. He sounded quite timid. Scared, almost.

'Andy, hello. It's Barry Haywood in Sheffield.'

It took him an awkward few seconds to respond, like he was on a time lag. I assumed he was in the middle of something.

'Oh Christ, Barry! You shouldn't have rung. I shouldn't be talking to you.'

Odd. 'Have I caught you at a bad time? I can ring back later if you'd like.'

Again, the silence. I thought I picked up the sound of heavy breathing down the line. What the hell *was* he up to?

'If you're at home, get out of there!' he yelled. 'Leave!'

I was totally confused then. I was about to ask him what he was talking about when there was a knock at the door. Three heavy thuds.

'Andy, I have to go. There's somebody at the door. I'll call back in a bit.'

All I heard as I lowered the phone from my ear to hang up were the words: 'Barry, I'm sorry…'

I pressed the red button to end the call. Strange man, I thought.

Three more heavy bangs. Someone's impatient.

I unlocked the door and opened it.

Good God Almighty, he was big. And scary. And I don't think I've ever seen anyone with so many tattoos.

That was my snapshot reaction to the sight I faced on my doorstep. A snapshot was all I had before the man pushed the flat of his huge hand into the centre of my chest and shoved me backwards. By the time I'd recovered my balance and my bearings, he was in my house, closing the door behind him.

'Give me my fucking money back!'

At that stage, I was too absorbed by the sheer scale of the bloke and the fact that he was in my home to really take in his demand. It wasn't so much that he was a good six or seven inches taller than me, he was about twice my size in just about every other proportion I could see. The months he must have spent in the tattoo parlour were clearly with the intention of adding to his ferocious demeanour and, if that was indeed the aim, it was time and money well spent. He was truly terrifying to behold. And he was in my home. And – what was that he said about money?

I read the situation almost straight away. One of Gina's dissatisfied customers.

'Look, mate,' I pleaded, trying to appeal to the reasonable side I desperately hoped was buried somewhere deep within that heavily-inked monstrous exterior. 'I think I know where you're coming from but, honestly, I had nothing to do with the scheme you got ripped off by. I got taken in as well. I'm sorry if you're out of pocket but I haven't got your money. My name was used without my knowledge. We were both conned.'

Remarkably, my words seemed to connect with him somehow.

'That's what the other one said.'

What?

'Sorry – other one?'

'In Manchester.'

Andy. That explained why he was so panicked on the phone. He must have passed on my details. I wanted to be cross with Andy for the betrayal but I knew if this massive slab of a man asked me under threat of violence to give up that kind of information I'd also have blurted it out without hesitation.

I just hoped the situation wouldn't escalate like that with me but any chance there was of conversing like two reasonable human beings immediately evaporated.

'I don't give a fuck about you and him. I want my fucking money!' he exploded and began a sudden, quite random search of my living room for his missing cash; tipping over chairs, throwing cushions, scattering a few framed pictures and ornaments off the table. I wasn't sure he thought he was going to find anything. Perhaps he was just following his instinct to wreck stuff. I let him get on with it.

He moved over to my sideboard and started ripping open doors. Inside one he found my modest booze stash. He grabbed the half-bottle of Glenmorangie my lad Ben had bought me for my last birthday. I'd only had a couple of shots from it. He slugged a good proportion of the rest straight down.

While he was momentarily calmed, I felt able to speak again.

'I haven't got any money in the house,' I said. 'Let's try to work this out. My name's Barry. What's your name?'

'People call me Thommo,' he proclaimed. 'And I'm the hardest man in Skelmersdale!'

I wasn't completely sure where Skelmersdale was, apart from somewhere the other side of the Pennines, and I certainly wasn't aware how hard you had to be to gain a reputation as its hardest resident, but I wasn't going to challenge his claim.

'Thommo. Let's see if we can find a solution here. How much have you lost?'

He slammed the whisky bottle down hard onto the top of the sideboard, sending a small droplet arching high out of the neck and landing with a small splash on the polished wooden surface.

'Fifty grand.'

'Fifty grand?' I spluttered. I'd expected him to say a couple of hundred.

'So you tell your girlfriend…'

'She's not my girlfriend,' I felt compelled to mumble.

'You tell your girlfriend I want my money back. In fact, make it sixty grand. For my inconvenience.'

He split the last word into four clear syllables, like he was trying out a new word he'd seen written down for the first time.

'She's gone,' I said. 'Probably in another city by now. I don't expect I'll ever see her again and, honestly, I don't want to ever see her again.'

'Then you'll have to find her!' he snarled.

His eyes darted around the room again, possibly targeting something else he could break. He spotted a pink envelope, propped behind the carriage clock on the sideboard, and picked it up.

'Miss Isla Mitchell,' he read and shook the envelope in my direction. 'Is that her?'

'It's my granddaughter,' I replied. I'd left it there to remind myself to post it so that she'd get the card in plenty of time for her third birthday the following week.

'Really?' he said, with a sneer and not at all in a "how lovely" kind of way. 'And this is where she lives, is it?'

Oh no! My blood ran cold.

'Thommo! Please!'

'I'll tell you what's going to happen.' He folded the card and shoved it into the back pocket of his jeans. 'You find your girlfriend and tell her to meet me here tonight, with my money. If she's not here, you're dead. If you get the coppers involved, then I get one of my associates to pay a visit to your little granddaughter. Do you understand?'

'But I can't…'

'Do you understand?'

What alternative did I have? I nodded.

'You've got twelve hours.' He pointed in my direction, then stormed off, leaving the front door wide open.

The shock of that final development rooted me to the spot. I looked at my watch. Twelve hours gave me until roughly half past eight that night. I couldn't imagine what I would be able do before then to resolve the situation in a good way. How could I find Gina when I had no idea where she was? But I had one shot. Thankfully, I'm not the most tech-savvy man in the world and I hadn't yet tried to work out how to delete Gina's number off my phone. Thank Christ!

I fumbled through my directory and pressed dial.

The person you are calling is not accepting calls at this time. This number may be out of service. The person you are calling…

I tried again. Same message. Perhaps she'd already binned the phone she'd used for this job, realising it might be a way to trace her if I'd gone to the police.

I tried again, just in case. Same message.

Now what? I sank down and sat on the floor. The stakes

were eye-wateringly high. It was bad enough that the lunatic sasquatch from Skelmersdale was threating grievous harm on me but I couldn't bear the thought that he knew how to get to my little Isla. I'd have rather died a thousand times than see her harmed in even the smallest way.

I had to work it out. I had to find Gina.

I grabbed my coat and my car keys.

Chapter
Eleven

I had to do something to try to find Gina. That was beyond doubt. Exactly how I was supposed to find her was the tricky bit.

I had one clue. I had a rough idea where she lived.

Back on the day when I met Gina for the first time, at the café near the cathedral, she said she'd rented a flat in the Wincobank area of the city. That stuck in my head because I told a little white lie when she asked me if she'd pronounced 'Wincobank' right. I said she had, even though she put too much emphasis on the 'o'. I only wanted to make her feel better.

But I'd never been to her flat. Almost all our time together had been spent at my house. I didn't have the slightest idea what her address might be. I didn't even know that part of the city very well. Perhaps people who live there don't buy many carpets. All I did know was that it was close to the Meadowhall shopping centre, which is a place I'd spent much of my married life trying to avoid visiting. I couldn't even be sure Gina was still in Sheffield. Maybe she'd already decided to move on to another city to pick out another poor sucker as the fall guy for her next con.

It wasn't much to go on but I couldn't just give in without trying. Doing nothing was not an option. Both my own safety and – more importantly – my granddaughter's safety were at stake. If the task had been to find a needle in a haystack, I'd have dived in and rummaged for as long as it took until I felt the sharp stab of metal on my fingertip.

So I set the satnav for Wincobank.

My strategy, such as it was, consisted of driving around looking for flats in the hope that one of them would have a black VW Golf parked outside. It wasn't a particularly refined strategy. It wasn't an especially successful one either.

The trouble with driving arbitrarily around an unfamiliar area, searching for a car and a person who might not be there anymore, is that it's hard to avoid the feeling you're pissing in the wind. I tried to approach the task methodically, street by street, but by the time you've been up one hill and down the next several times, past the same eclectic mix of Victorian terraces, post-War semi-detached houses, and more modern builds you see in so many other parts of the city, you get the impression you're going round in circles. Before long, you start wondering if that vape shop or this mini-market is a different vape shop or mini-market or the same one you drove past half an hour earlier. It's very disorientating; a mental assault made worse by the constantly rising tide of panic raging inside, a voice which screams at you that you're on a hopeless mission.

I had to pull over regularly, to try to restore my focus and to attempt to reach Gina by phone, in the increasingly forlorn hope she had decided to turn the bloody thing on again. No chance.

The person you are calling is not accepting calls at this time. This number may be...

The person you are calling is not accepting calls at this…
The person you are calling is…

There were blocks of flats. When I stumbled across them, I would stop and have a good look around, in case they provided parking areas hidden from view from the main road or even – and this was the desperate level of optimism I was clinging to by this time – by chance I caught Gina nipping out to empty the bins or something. Needless to say, that particular long shot fell woefully short of the target.

I knocked on some doors, trying not to appear too suspicious as I presented the picture of Gina I had on my phone and asked a succession of wary residents if they had seen her around. A couple of people feigned concern and wished me luck, most couldn't even be bothered to look properly at the picture before slamming their doors in my face and I finally had to abandon that approach when one old lady threatened to call the police if I didn't get off her property within two seconds. I'd already started to wonder if the sight of a strange man driving randomly up and down the streets, occasionally stopping off to snoop around the back of buildings, would be attracting unwanted attention and didn't want to take any unnecessary risks.

I thought I'd found the car three times, but the first was a Seat rather than a VW, the next had a scrawny late-teens kid just getting out of the driving seat and the last had a 'Powered By Fairy Dust' sticker in the rear window, which I'm pretty sure Gina's hadn't.

The light was already fading, even though it was not yet five o'clock. I'd been prowling the streets of Wincobank for ages and it had got me precisely nowhere. I had less than four hours left. While I couldn't say for sure I'd searched everywhere and tried everything, I was running out of time and knew I needed to try something else.

But what?

It's a sad reflection on how out of fresh ideas I was that the only one I could come up with was to try phoning Gina again. More in hope than expectation, obviously.

The person you are....

So much for that.

I sat in my car and scoured the dark corners of my brain for anything that might resemble a new plan. Clearly, it would've been pointless to carry on driving around until it got dark but I was reluctant to give up on what was, basically, the only lead I had. I tried to convince myself there was a case to be made for doing one last circuit before evening drew in and that maybe – just maybe – I might stumble on a back street I'd so far missed. Maybe that would be the one I was searching for. Maybe.

I was clutching at straws and I knew it. The situation was desperate and, all of a sudden, it all just kind of got too much. Pressure started building behind my eyes and in my ears. My pulse was thumping so loudly that I feared my heart wouldn't be able to stand the strain. My throat was constricting like it was being squeezed. I was sweating like a meat pie salesman at an Animal Liberation Front convention. I couldn't breathe. I couldn't think. I didn't know if I was having a heart attack or a brain explosion or both, but I was undergoing a crisis of some sort and I feared my number was up.

I flung open the car door and jumped out urgently, as if it was the car seat itself that was attempting to smother me. Leaning forward, my forehead pressed against the cool metal of the roof, I began to draw long drafts of chilly autumnal air into my lungs. I'd never experienced such ferocious panic before and I hope I never do again. I think the magnitude of what was at stake rose to the surface and attempted to swallow me whole. It was pretty frightening, let me tell you, but as the worst of the sensation receded it was as if a tidal wave had washed away the clutter that had been building over the previous hours. My head was clearing. I was able to recalibrate.

Time was against me and I knew I couldn't waste any of it. Less than four hours remained until I was due another visit from the hardest man in Skelmersdale and that left me such little leeway. The chances were I would not be able to do this on my own. I needed help. I could think of only one option, but it was a huge gamble. I climbed back into the car and started the engine.

***

It was only a couple of miles to the city's main police headquarters, an imposingly impressive new building on one of the main roads heading out of the centre of town towards the motorway. I'd passed it many times in the van with Charlie. My intention was to head straight there but, of course, the closer I got, the more I began to doubt whether this was the smart move.

There was a retail park opposite which I knew mainly because it had a drive-through Greggs. For whatever reason, Charlie was incapable of driving past it without feeling compelled to call in and buy something pastry-related. I didn't normally share his enthusiasm but because it had been ages since my very early breakfast and I needed a moment to gather my thoughts, I pulled in.

My only intention all day had been to try to locate Gina. Find her and persuade her to give the mad tattooed guy his money back. It was, as far as I could see, the only way to stop him kicking nine types of shit out of me and guarantee that he would leave my family alone.

When I expanded my potential options to include getting the police on my side, it was still with a view to finding Gina. Even if her phone was still turned off, I assumed they would have the technology to track down her car or pinpoint where she lived when she wasn't travelling around the country fleecing investors and duping vulnerable older men. However, the more I thought this through, the more I became aware of the flaws in my plan.

For a start, I didn't know Gina's registration plate number. On a considerably smaller scale, I'd already seen for myself how difficult it can be to find a car when all you have to go on is that you're searching for a black VW Golf. Not surprisingly, it turns out there are a lot of them about.

So that would be no help and neither, in all likelihood, would the only information I could give them about Gina. She'd told me her surname was McKenzie and that she was from Bristol but she didn't speak with any kind of regional accent, as far as I could tell, and I had every reason to believe the name she'd given me was a false one. She'd used a different one in Manchester to deceive Andy Hague and just about everything else she had told me had been a lie. All I could offer the police with certainty was the photo I'd downloaded off the dating site. Didn't they have some sort of face recognition computer programme or did I only see that in a TV drama once? Whatever the process, it was surely a bit more advanced than flipping through those huge books of mug shots like they had in the old films, but that's assuming she had a criminal record, of course. Perhaps she didn't. Even if she did, the process would be eating up time I didn't have. I checked my watch yet again. Ten past five.

All I could reasonably expect from the police, at this stage, would be to protect me and my family from the wrath of Thommo. I'd have to throw myself at their mercy and try to convince them I wasn't a fantasist or some sort of paranoid loon. They could lie in wait at my house until the appointed time, arrest Thommo and put him out of harm's way. I bet he was well known to their colleagues in the north-west and that would add weight to my appeal for protection. It would be my word against his, of course, and he'd only threatened to do something nasty. Hardly grounds for locking him up and throwing away the key. I would be no more than delaying the danger. I could hardly demand the police offer me and my family protective custody until the end of time. He knew where I lived and, worse still, he had my daughter's address too. I had no doubt he would come looking for revenge as soon as the heat died down. Just the thought of his threat to harm my granddaughter sent a shiver down my spine. I couldn't take that chance.

I was, not to put too fine a point on it, fucked.

Involving the police would only, as far as I could see, complicate matters further and increase the jeopardy of the situation. It was all on me. Either I find Gina and get her to pay him off or I take the consequences.

I'd lost my appetite for the half-eaten steak bake and tossed it, in its bag, onto the passenger seat. I was out of ideas and almost out of time. I tried to tell myself I could not give up. There had to be a way. Then I realised. Maybe I'd been approaching the search from entirely the wrong direction.

I'd assumed when Gina told me she had a flat that she'd offered me a clue – but what she'd actually served up was a red herring. And I'd swallowed it whole.

She hadn't set up home in Sheffield five months ago, like she'd told me that first time we met in the café. It was another lie. She was running a scam in Manchester only a few weeks earlier. Most likely, she'd moved on to Sheffield after getting all she needed from Andy Hague. She might have arrived when she was relatively certain she'd got me on the hook and that was only three weeks ago. Renting a flat at that short notice and for such a short period wouldn't make sense.

She must have been staying in a hotel.

Of course! I couldn't believe I hadn't figured that out sooner.

It felt like a lightbulb moment but it didn't necessarily mean I was closer to finding Gina. A hotel is the solution when you need accommodation at short notice, but it can be vacated just as quickly. The odds that Gina had already headed elsewhere might have increased.

I had to give it a go, though. Contemplation of how many hotels I might have to trail around made my head spin and I still had so little time. I needed to prioritise. Find a starting point with a higher chance of success.

The car was still the key. Locate the car and Gina should be close by.

Where would she stay? I tried to put myself in her shoes. If it was me, scouting for accommodation in a city I didn't really know, I'd look for somewhere in the centre. A safer option. Highly likely to be close to a larger variety of places to eat and drink, unlike some of the out-of-town hotels which can leave you stranded in the middle of what is basically an industrial estate. I'd also go for one of the low-budget chain hotels. Reliable, anonymous, cheaper if you're staying for several weeks. One problem there, as I knew from my own travels, is that so few of those city centre hotels have their own car park. But they do often have standing arrangements with the companies who run multi-stories to offer cut-price parking fees. That could be a consideration.

Gina had parked in a multi-storey when I met her at the café. The one on Campo Lane. I'd walked her there but hadn't stayed to watch her drive away. Perhaps she hadn't driven away. Perhaps she'd acted as if she was going to her car and had waited there a while until I was long gone, to keep up the deception of telling me she lived in a rented flat.

That seemed plausible enough to me. Besides, this new search had to start somewhere, so it might as well start there.

Chapter
Twelve

It looked promising as I drove past it in the car park, though I was well aware VW Golfs were not an uncommon make of car and black was a pretty popular colour. I'd risked causing a collision four times on my drive into the city centre when I spotted black hatchbacks and craned to see if it was Gina behind the wheel of them. I couldn't be certain in one case but don't think it actually was her. Neither was she the driver of the white SUV who gave me a blast of the horn for swerving into her lane as she tried to overtake. I wasn't that close to hitting her. Some drivers have serious anger management issues these days.

I took my ticket at the automatic barrier and noted the black VW Golf as I drove past it on the lower level, but I was unable to have a very close look because another new arrival was right behind me. The car park was busy. No spaces on the lower level but I managed to nip into what might have been the last space on the second. That must have been irritating for the guy following but, had he known, I'm sure he would've taken comfort in the knowledge that my need was more pressing.

After some manoeuvring (honestly, how do they expect

you to get safely in and out of bays that narrow?) I locked up and headed back down the ramp, trying not to build my hopes too high. It was definitely the right make and model. There were no unfamiliar identifying markers, like stickers, to rule it out. Neither could I see any reason to be certain it was the right car until – there it was.

On the rear nearside panel, between the brake light and the back door. A scratch about five inches long in the black paint, dug out with something sharp. My front door key. My heart leapt. It had been a disgraceful act done purely out of spite when I was at my angriest, shortly after being briefed by Andy Hague about Gina's scam. I wasn't proud of myself for it, but right at that moment I could have kissed that shameful little gouge of exposed metal. I'd found Gina's car. I was getting somewhere at last.

There was no parking permit issued by a hotel on the dashboard to identify where she was staying. I wasn't that lucky. There was still work to do and now I had less than three hours to do it. Lingering by the car on the off chance she decided to go for a drive was a complete non-starter, but to leave would be to risk not being there should she return to her car. I decided to write a note and pin it under her windscreen wiper, pleading the urgency of my situation, just in case. I had to hurry back to my car to find something to scribble on and a pen that still worked. Then I took a photo of her reg plate and left the car park to begin the next stage of my search.

She had to be fairly close by. A Google search brought up six candidates for hotels within a short walking distance, so I set off to investigate. I immediately discounted one because it seemed ludicrously expensive. The first two I checked out appeared to be private rental apartments with no reception I could see, so if she was in either of those, I was screwed. The next was more promising. Exactly the type of ubiquitous chain budget hotel I had in mind. Nothing doing, though. The young guy at reception listened to my attempts to convey the seriousness of the circumstances before staring blankly at the picture on my phone and shaking his head. He did have the good grace to consult a more senior colleague but neither could recall her staying there. Three down.

The fourth looked like a converted pub and was nice inside. No result, though. I had one more to check out before having to expand the radius of my search.

It wasn't the prettiest of buildings. Either it, too, had been repurposed as a hotel following a life as something mundane and functional, like a council office, or the architect was experiencing serious personal issues which stunted their usual creativity when they sat down at the drawing board to design it. I had a vague memory that it might have formerly been a police station, which would've explained its bleak outlook and, in a way, would have been an appropriate choice for Gina to stay at. In the spirit of clinging on to any hope I could, I took that as a good sign.

In contrast to its brutalist exterior, the designers had over-compensated on the inside, which was brightly lit and crisply colourful, making it look more like a Swedish furniture showroom. The young woman behind the reception desk stayed on-theme by bursting into a bright, broad smile as I approached. I didn't mind that at all. I was in need of all the friendly faces I could find.

'Hi,' I said, attempting to hide the growing anxiety from my expression, though possibly not convincingly. 'I'm hoping you might be able to do me a big favour.'

'Certainly sir. How can I help?'

She must have been in her early twenties; smartly dressed, heavily made-up and very pretty. She wore a name badge on her lapel but I resisted looking down to check what she was called in case she took my glance as lechery and it made her less inclined to be so amiable. I presented the picture of Gina on my phone.

'I'm looking for this woman and I believe she may have been staying at this hotel for the last three weeks or so. It's really important that I find her. Urgently.'

I tried to get over how pressing the need was but do it without appearing irrational. I reckoned if I allowed the bubbling desperation within me to show, she might fear I could do something erratic and start thinking how to instigate special procedures. In these days when companies seem to have statutory training for just about every other eventuality, I'm sure there must be a How to Deal With Unpredictable Nutters module for hotel receptionists.

I thought I saw a flicker of recognition instantly but she carried on staring at the picture for several seconds longer without saying anything. Possibly, she was running through a mental checklist before deciding what to do next.

'I'm sorry, sir, are you with the police?'

'No. I'm not police. I'm a friend.' I went back into the photos app on my phone and selected a selfie of Gina and me from our trip to the Peak District to show her, in the hope of removing from her thought process the possibility of my being a random stalker. 'We had a… disagreement and she's not answering my calls at the moment, but something's cropped up which she needs to know about straight away. That's why I've had to come looking for her. It's an emergency.'

The receptionist was uncertain. 'I don't know. We're not supposed to…'

'Look…' I decided to risk a glimpse of her name badge. '… Anjali, I get that you have rules to follow. I can show you some personal ID if that's any help. I'll happily say what I have to say here in reception, in plain sight, so you can see you're not putting anybody in danger. I know this must look a bit irregular but I wouldn't be asking unless this was genuinely my only option. It's literally a matter of life and death. Could you please just call her room to see if she's there and if she's not, or if she doesn't want to come down to see me, I promise I'll leave and not create a scene. I promise. Please.'

Short of dropping to my knees, which wouldn't have been the most dignified option, I don't know if I could've made my case more earnestly. I was certain I had found where Gina was staying. The receptionist would surely have given me the brush-off by now if I was in the wrong place. I was at Anjali's mercy.

She sighed and tapped on her computer keyboard. 'I don't know if she's back right now.'

'Thank you,' I breathed. 'Thank you.'

Anjali picked up the telephone and pressed in four numbers. The wait for a response from the other end only lasted a few seconds but it seemed an age.

'Hi, Miss Ryan, it's Anjali at reception.'

Ryan? Another false name? No matter. She was here and she had answered.

'I have a man here asking for you. He says he's a friend and he needs to talk to you urgently. His name's…'

She glanced up to prompt me to supply the missing detail.

'Barry. Barry Haywood.'

'Mr Barry Haywood,' she repeated. 'Yes, in reception now.'

Silence. It was agony. Gina was clearly contemplating whether to accept or refuse.

'Certainly,' said Anjali at last. 'I'll let him know.' She hung up.

I stared, wide-eyed. Beseeching. And?

'Miss Ryan says she'll be with you in a minute.'

My shoulders slumped, tension seeping from them.

'Thank you so much.'

I retreated from the reception desk, where a small queue of two couples with suitcases had formed behind me, waiting to check in. I wondered if they'd been listening and what they might have made of the exchange. No matter. It was more important that I thought about what I was going to tell Gina to convince her to help.

It took more than a minute for Gina to come down. More like six or seven. For an awful moment or two I wondered if she might have done a runner with a hastily packed case down the fire escape. Then there she was, walking down the last flight of stairs.

Seeing her again was strange. Aside from the obvious grateful relief of finding her, I wasn't certain how I felt about her anymore. The Gina I believed I was falling in love with turned out to be all for show. A sham with a scam. She'd played me for a fool. I meant nothing more to her than just another sad old man to unwittingly front her scheme. You can no longer love someone capable of treating the emotions of another human being with such contempt.

But, right then, I needed her. I had to set aside everything she had so callously put me through and implore her to do the right thing. I was the one in dire straits, but the situation was all of her making. Surely, she had to recognise that. She held the power in her hands to reach a resolution before anyone got hurt.

Never mind me. A nearly three-year-old child, for Christ's sake!

Gina grabbed my arm and ushered me towards an area at the far side of the open reception area, where there were four small round tables and wooden chairs. She said nothing until we were well out of earshot of anyone and then turned to fix me with a burning stare.

'What are you after, Barry? If you've come to threaten me, you should know I'm not easily frightened.'

'No!' Her aggressive response caught me off guard. It was a hardened side of her I didn't recognise. I'd only been allowed to see the soft-focus cute-but-fragile Gina before. 'I'm not here for anything like that. I'm genuinely in huge trouble and I need your help.'

She appeared unconvinced.

'Can we just sit down for a while?' I asked. 'Then I'll tell you all about it.'

Cautiously, Gina relented and lowered herself on to a chair. I sat opposite.

I told her all about the visit from Thommo. His menace. His demands. His threats.

She listened impassively. Not giving anything away. When I reached the end of my account, she wrinkled her nose and shrugged.

'I'm sorry, but this is your problem, not mine.'

Wow! Was she really that uncaring?

'Not your problem?' I was aware I was raising my voice and quietened it to almost a whisper. 'If it hadn't been for you tricking this man out of a very large sum of money, why the hell else would he have come knocking on my door, saying her was going to do me in and threatening my little granddaughter? How can you say it's not your problem? This is *all* on you, Gina. You've cheated, you've stolen, you've deceived and now your actions are having consequences. Face your responsibilities. Christ Almighty, woman, for once in your life you've got to do the right thing here.'

I was angry. There was no denying that. I also knew I might be risking her storming off and there would have been nothing I could've done to stop her, but I wasn't going to pussyfoot around and let her get away without hearing a few home truths. I was glad I'd said it. Now all I had to do was hold my breath to see how she reacted.

'What you are clearly failing to recognise, Barry,' she said, calmly, 'is that even if I did have such a large sum available and even if I did give this man his money back, it'll resolve nothing.'

That stunned me. I couldn't see the logic.

'He's got you on the hook. If I handed over fifty grand…'

'Sixty,' I corrected.

'If I handed over sixty, seventy, a hundred grand tonight, do you think for a moment that would be the end of it?'

I still didn't get her point. Surely, it would end everything.

'People like that never let go once they've got their teeth into you. They're animals. They're greedy. They keep coming back for more and when there's no more left to give, they'll do what they want to you or your family anyway. I'm not going to throw away everything I've worked to build up just to hand it over to some low-level thug.'

There was nothing I could think to say to that. It was crushingly detached thinking.

'As I see it, you've got two options,' she continued. 'You go to the police and get them to protect you and your family, or…' She hesitated.

'Or what?'

'You get to him before he can get you.'

'Seriously?' I thought I knew what she meant but it was so far removed from my world that I didn't want to be sure. 'You're saying I should….' My voice was lowered so the words could barely be heard. '…*kill* him?'

Gina sat back, nonchalantly. 'Why not?'

'Because,' I spluttered, 'I'm not capable of doing anything like that. I'm a carpet fitter, not an assassin. It's ridiculous to suggest that.'

'The police, then,' she said. 'Let them deal with him. I'll be long gone by then and all your problems will be out of the way.'

'Yeah, until he gets out of prison, or until he gets a few of his nutcase mates to call around and take revenge on his behalf. How long do you reckon the police will be able to protect us from that? What are we supposed to do? Uproot the whole family and move somewhere new with new identities? Is that even remotely realistic, never mind acceptable? We'd be hiding in the shadows, looking over our shoulders, for the rest of our lives.'

There was not so much of a flicker of sympathy from Gina at that. She remained leaning back in the chair and crossed her arms.

'I'm pleading with you, Gina. You've got to help me.' I

was at my wit's end. Begging was all I could think to do. 'I'm appealing to your conscience. I know we only had a few short weeks together and that it meant nothing to you really, but it meant a lot to me and I don't deserve for you to just throw me away like a used rag to be ripped apart. I promise I'll not report what you've done to the police – the fraud and all that – but I need you to at least try to bring this to as quick and as bloodless a conclusion as possible. Give this man his money. Up until a couple of months ago it was his anyway. I'm sure you won't miss it really. What have you got to lose? It's nowhere near as much as I stand to lose if you do nothing. It's not for me. It's for an innocent little girl. Come on, Gina. You've got to try.'

She let out a long, slow breath and bowed her head.

'I cannot fucking believe this,' she muttered. 'OK. I'll give it a go.'

Chapter
Thirteen

Perhaps it was just as well we drove separately from the hotel to my house. It saved a lot of awkwardness.

I was left in no doubt that Gina was distinctly reluctant to come to my aid in attempting to appease the heavily-inked lunatic from Skelmersdale. She replied to my suggestion we travelled together in my car with a curt 'No'. That was the only word I got out of her between her telling me she was going to get her things from the hotel room and her giving me the same monosyllabic reply to the offer of a cup of tea once we arrived back at my place. She wasn't happy. It was hardly my fault things had got complicated though, was it?

I totally understood why she was keen to get it over with as quickly and painlessly as possible. I was with her all the way on that. Especially the painlessly bit. I didn't even especially care that she wasn't overjoyed at the prospect of the job in hand. It was enough for me that she had kept her word. I fully expected her to change her mind, either once she got back to her hotel room or on the six-mile drive to Woodhouse.

It was a little after quarter to eight by the time we

arrived. Thommo was due by half past. I'd cut it fine, for sure, but I'd done what I needed to do. Against the odds, I found the needle in the haystack. Whatever happened next was largely out of my power, but the most pressing threat to my safety had been averted. That was an enormous relief, even though I realised the danger was certainly far from over.

I made myself a cup of tea and brought it back to the living room. Gina was sitting at one end of the sofa, simmering with the grudging compliance of a teenager told she had to miss her favourite band's concert to attend an aunt's seventieth birthday party.

'Shall I put some music on?' I suggested, hesitantly. I was tense enough as it was, without having to deal with Gina's frostiness. I thought music might help. We often played music in the background through our evenings in together over the previous weeks. Rapturous hours then. Tainted memories now.

'Suit yourself,' she mumbled.

I did. It didn't really help. Maybe, on reflection, I could've made a better choice than Joni Mitchell's Blue album in trying to lighten the mood.

After feeling like time was running on fast-forward through the day before then, the hands of the clock tipped agonisingly slowly towards eight-thirty. We sat separately, locked into our separate thoughts, neither of us saying a thing. As Joni sang about going home to California, Gina finally broke her icy silence.

'Leave me to do the talking.'

I nodded. Fine by me.

Eight-thirty came. And went. It was unbearable. My anxiety levels were through the roof. At ten to nine, I had to do something. Get up. Take the record off the turntable. Say something.

'I'm going to make another cup of tea. You want one yet?'

She didn't dismiss the proposal out of hand this time.

'Yes, I would like that,' she replied. 'Thank you.'

It was the closest we had come to a cordial conversation since I confronted Gina with Andy Hague's revelations just over twenty-four hours earlier. Before then, actually, because my tone wasn't exactly friendly through that exchange.

'Do you still think he'll come?' I asked. Obviously, I'd have been happy to have never seen or heard from Thommo ever again.

She sighed. 'I would imagine so. He's gone to some trouble to take it this far and I don't suppose he'll just give up on that now. People like him want to feel as if they're in control. Showing up late is to be expected. He'll be enjoying keeping us waiting but he'll be here.'

She was right. It was five past ten. My nerves were almost completely shredded by then. I practically leapt out of my chair when I heard the approach of heavy boots on the driveway and the front door burst open.

'Right then, you fuckers!' he announced. 'Payback time.'

He was dressed the same as when I saw him that morning. Spray-on white t-shirt and blue jeans which struggled to contain his muscular thighs. There was no need to ask how he'd spent the hours since then. Even from a distance of several feet, he stank of booze. God knows what else he'd been taking as well.

'Hey.' He noticed Gina, slowing rising to her full petite height from the sofa. It seemed to be an effort to make his eyes focus properly. 'They didn't tell me you was a proper babe.'

Thommo took a couple of lumbering steps towards her. I quickly shuffled sideways to put my body between them. He could've swatted my inadequate challenge aside easily but I succeeded in bringing him to an unsteady halt.

'Your boyfriend's protecting you. Isn't that nice?' he smirked, gazing directly down at me. I wasn't sure if his immense bearing or his breath was more likely to make me pass out first.

'I don't need protection,' Gina responded. I wondered where she got her nerve.

Thommo held me in his fixed manic stare. Petrified as I was, I wasn't about to budge. Slowly, a malevolent grin spread across his face.

'Just as well. Let me know when you'd like to try being with a real man.'

'I'll bear that in mind,' said Gina in a flat tone as I tried to keep my defiant stand together just a little longer. 'Now are we going to talk business, or not?'

He loomed over me a few seconds more, like a boulder wondering whether it can be bothered to roll over and crush the tiny creature beneath. 'Yeah,' he rumbled slowly. 'Let's get to it. You.' His leaned his head within two inches of my nose. 'Get me some whisky.'

I was about to move, happy for an excuse to escape the jaws of the beast, if only for now, but Gina spoke again before I could summon sufficient strength to my legs.

'You've had enough already. Get it over with. Tell me what you came for.'

That appeared to amuse, rather than antagonise, Thommo. He took a step back. I took the opportunity to melt away.

'I want my fifty grand back,' he spat. 'The fifty grand you stole from me. And I want another ten on top for my trouble.'

Gina laughed. He didn't like that. 'No chance,' she said. He really didn't like that. She wasn't finished with him.

'What are you into? Selling cheap wraps to hopeless addicts? Extorting small businesses? Robbing grannies on street corners? It's not legal, whatever it is, so don't give me that taken-what's-rightfully-mine shit. We're both crooks. You stole to get it and I stole it from you. That's the way it is. So you want me to hand over what's mine now? Why should I? No way. Stop pretending to be the victim here. It doesn't wash with me.'

I don't know if I was in awe of her courage or terrified by it. Talk about poking the bear! Thommo reddened as if he was an overheated pot about to blow. I doubt anybody talked to him like that, especially a woman half his size. I'm not sure he knew how to react but I didn't want to be in the way when he figured it out.

'You stole from *me* and nobody gets away with that,' he screamed, smouldering with indignation.

'Oh, get real! Who do you think you are? Everybody's fair game in our world and you know it. What makes you so different? Now go home to whatever north-west shithole you say you come from and steal a few more kids' dinner money. Just accept you've been outwitted by a smarter criminal this time.'

'I'll fucking give you real, bitch! I'll fucking smash that pretty face of yours so no fucker will know if they're looking at your head or your arse.'

The situation was spiralling rapidly out of hand. I was

stuck between dark worlds I could neither control nor comprehend and I was the one who stood to lose everything as they hurtled towards a collision.

'For crying out loud, will you both please stop posturing and sort this out?' The instruction had been to keep quiet but I couldn't help it. Remarkably, my little outburst shut both of them up.

'OK, look,' Gina switched from all-out assault to a conciliatory tone. 'We're never going to agree about the rights and wrongs of this. You think the fifty is yours and I say it's mine. One of us is going to have to take a hit, so I'll cut you a deal. We split the loss and I give you twenty-five.' She took the phone from the rear pocket of her jeans. 'Give me the details of an account and I'll transfer it right now. Take the money on offer and none of us need ever see or hear from each other again.'

An even split. Nobody gets it their own way but both parties save face. Had that been Gina's play all along? Maybe she was banking on my intervention in order to sell the compromise. I held my breath while I waited for Thommo's reaction.

I know I'm hardly one to talk when it comes to indecision but his thought processing wasn't the quickest. It might not be quite accurate to say he was thinking long and hard but it took a while all the same. Eventually, he tipped his head to one side and scowled.

'Nah.'

I wish I could've said I was surprised.

'No skinny bitch tells me what to do. That money's mine, so here's how it's going to go down. You're going to bring me my full fifty – in cash – here tomorrow at five o'clock and then you're going to give me ten grand every month until I say the debt is paid. That's because I told you to have it here today and you ain't got it. It's the last time I'm going to be this generous. One payment so much as a pound short or a minute late from here on and I burn down your boyfriend's granddaughter's house with cute little Isla inside. Even think about getting the law involved and you're dead. So dead. Now do we all understand each other?'

Neither Gina nor I said a word.

'Good.'

He edged slowly towards the back door, full of who's-the-big-man swagger. Enjoying his triumph. He held the ace card. The threat of unspeakable violence and the knowledge that no person with a shred of humanity would risk testing his willingness to see it through. Unless Gina was prepared to pay up – possibly even *if* Gina was prepared to pay up – I could see no way this was going to end well.

Thommo left. I trudged miserably back to my armchair and slumped into it, head in hands.

'Don't say I didn't warn you,' said Gina, unhelpfully. 'I told you once his type gets a taste for blood they won't let up until they've drained the last drop.'

About the last words I needed to hear right then were 'told you so', to be honest.

'We gave it a go,' she added. 'It was a long shot, but I tried because that was how you wanted to play it. Now we do it my way.'

At first, I was too wrapped up in thoughts of impending doom to register what she was suggesting. She said *my way?* What does she mean *my way?* Oh, wait!

'You're going to have him killed?'

'Not exactly,' she said. 'We're going to do it.'

'No, no, no, no!' I was in it deep enough already. That

was a whole new level. 'Pay him off. I'll sell everything I've got if needs be. There's got to be a better option.'

'You said it yourself. You and your family will never be safe as long as you know he can get at you. It's the only way we resolve this for good.'

'There must be another way.'

'I'm all ears. Tell me one.'

I couldn't. Throughout that nightmare day I'd been clinging to the hope that giving Thommo his money back might satisfy his brutish craving for vengeance. I'd pinned everything on that. I'd been unable to envisage another way of keeping both myself and my family safe. I'd been naïve. Gina was right. The solution was never going to be so simple. I'd attached rational values to circumstances where rationality didn't count for much and where one of the major players didn't play by the same rules. I was out of my depth. As horrific a prospect as it was, I began to think maybe Gina could be right again in seeing only one remaining viable option.

'How would we…? Do we shoot him?'

She shook her head. 'Too messy. I'm sure you don't want to be washing blood and bits of brain out of your carpet.'

She had that right. I thought I was going to throw up as it was.

'We have to be smarter than that. Even two against one, I don't fancy our chances of overpowering him, so we'll have to disable him first. Then it'll have to be done in a way where we can get rid of the body and leave no evidence tying his death to us. I've got a plan in mind. I made a phone call when I went back to my hotel room earlier and made provisional arrangements. I'll phone to confirm from the car. Come on. I'll drive.'

Gina stood to collect her coat and bag. It was escalating too quickly for me to keep up.

'What plan? Where are we going?'

She fished out her car key and smiled. Was she actually enjoying this?

'We're going to visit The Doc.'

Chapter
Fourteen

They say you should never judge a man until you've walked a mile in his shoes. I don't know who said those words, originally, but as I look back on that night I understand their meaning like never before. I walked in the shoes of a man considering murder as an option and grew far more comfortable with that, far more quickly, than I could ever have imagined.

Of course, the suggestion of taking another life should be abhorrent. Even if that life belongs to a six foot four lump of raw muscle and little brain whose place on this earth heaps untold misery on anyone caught close enough to make out the racially offensive insignia tattooed on his knuckles. Whatever depravity others prove capable of, I've always believed their punishment should reflect the higher standards of civilised society. Otherwise, you reduce yourself to their base levels, right?

Those are the values I've held through my adult life, so when Gina challenged them, I resisted. At first. It was a reflex response. But the more I began to absorb what she was telling me, the more it made sense. She said there was no option. It was the only way to be sure he wouldn't carry out his threat to harm me and my family. Otherwise, his spectre would loom over us forever. Thommo had to die. Before long, I absolutely wanted him dead too.

Is that wrong? Isn't it simply a reaction born of the most basic human instincts – to survive and to protect the lives of those we love the most? My family was in danger from an erratic force which could not be controlled except through extreme intervention. I was willing to do whatever it took to eliminate the danger. I'm not ashamed to admit that. If you judge me differently, ask yourself this:

What would you have done if you were in my shoes?

***

'Who's The Doc?' I asked as I clicked in the buckle of the seatbelt.

Gina was programming an address into the satnav. She finished spelling out the destination before answering my question.

'He's a supplier. Drugs, mostly. Not the usual recreational type of drugs. More of a specialist for people who have special requirements.'

'Criminals,' I said, like I knew she was avoiding saying the word.

'Not entirely.' She managed to almost sound offended. 'People with serious illnesses as well. People who either can't get hold of particular medication because they live in the wrong postcode or can't afford to get it by going private. The Doc is able to source the drugs and supply them at well below the rip-off prices the big pharmaceutical companies charge.'

'A saint then.' I don't normally do sarcasm but I was in a funny mood. It had been a funny couple of days, in fairness. Gina ignored me. I should've left it at that but, as I said, I was in a funny mood.

'So he sells knock-off drugs. I'm not sure taking medication of dubious origin is a great idea if you're already suffering with seriously bad health.'

'Yes, well.' Gina was losing patience with me, I could tell. 'Desperate people sometimes have to do desperate things. I would've thought you'd understand that now. Anyway, I take it you won't be complaining if he helps sort out your little problem.'

That put me in my place.

'Have you used him before?' I asked, making an effort to be less obnoxious.

'Once,' she replied and before I could follow up by asking her to explain the circumstances, she had her phone to her ear, making a call. It was quickly answered.

'Doc. It's Clarissa.'

Another identity. I wondered how she managed to keep up with whichever one she was meant to be at any given time.

'Yes please, I do. I'm setting off now to pick it up. Should be there in an hour.' She hung up and started the car engine.

'Where are we going?'

Gina put the car into gear and pulled out. 'Wakefield.'

'I've never been to Wakefield.' I don't know why I threw that into the mix. She was hardly likely to offer to take me on an introductory guided tour, was she? I kept quiet for a while after that, until we'd just passed the M1 junction for Chapeltown. I used the time to reflect on all the madness that had been swirling around me.

'Can you remember taking all that money from Thommo?'

She thought about it. 'Vaguely.'

Only vaguely? I was pretty sure if someone handed me £50,000 it would stick in my mind.

'It seems a lot of money to me.'

'Quite a lot,' she conceded in a disarmingly matter-of-fact way. 'I have taken deposits into the hundreds of thousands, but usually it's a grand or two or a few hundred.'

Jesus! Whatever planet it was she inhabited it wasn't one I was familiar with. I had to ask.

'How does it work then? This scheme of yours. Andy Hague told me it was a fake online investment company but that doesn't really tell me much, in truth. What's it all about?'

For the first time, Gina took her eyes off the road to glance at me. A hint of a smile crossed her mouth.

'Do you really want to know?'

Yeah. I did.

'I can't be much of a director if I don't understand how my own company works, now can I?'

I was attempting sarcasm again but it made her laugh instead.

'OK. It's a cryptocurrency fraud, basically. I set up a fake company, offer deals at generous rates of return to lure in the punters and they give me money.'

A fob-off. We were in a car together for at least the next half-hour and I wasn't going to let her get away with that.

'I doubt it's that straightforward.'

'No, of course not. It's got to be done properly or people are going to see through it straight away.'

'So?' She was reluctant to elaborate. It was a sort of

trade secret, so I could kind of understand that, but I reckoned I deserved more than the basics. It all came tumbling out of her then, like she'd been busting for an excuse to tell somebody all about it.

'So…' She took a deep breath. 'I set up a new limited company, registered in the UK with a UK address. Foreign investors prefer that. UK financial companies are still regarded as more trustworthy. I think it's because of the reputation of our independent regulatory bodies and our old tradition of fair play. Whatever. It works. Once you've registered your firm with Companies House, the next step is to create a legitimate-looking website and make sure you give prominence to the sort of reassurances investors are looking for. You're a new company. You're not an established name. You can get around that by inventing an impressive profile for the fund manager – former head of this, driving force behind the successes of such and such, bringing all their experience to an exciting new venture, etcetera, etcetera. It's all bullshit, of course. You can back that up by including confirmation that you're a certified United Kingdom company with an Incorporation Number, all of which is available for checking on the official UK Companies Register, which it absolutely is. You can even post a hyperlink to make it easier for them to check. I doubt they ever do.'

'Doesn't Companies House run their own checks to root out the fraudsters before they're allowed to get that far?'

Gina pointed a finger at me, as if I'd just hit on a key point.

'That's the beauty of it! Any idiot can register a new company in quarter of an hour. They never check names, addresses, anything. You need more proof of ID to get a library card than you do to register a company and once you have your registration through, you're up and running in twenty-four hours. And do you know how much you have to pay for that registration? Twelve pounds.'

'Get out!' I was genuinely flabbergasted. 'Twelve quid?'

'That's all.'

She paused, which was just as well. It was a lot to take in.

'And then what?'

'Then,' Gina added, 'you offer a particularly attractive deal, because you're a start-up and you want to make investing in your company sound like a better option than going with one of the big names, and you start to lure them in. Once you learn how to manipulate the search engine algorithms to make them push business your way, it's a doddle. Investors are soon throwing their money at you from all over the world. The US and Canada are lucrative sources. Germany, Poland, Turkey, the Middle East – and the UK, of course.'

'Buying cryptocurrency?'

'Buying crypto. The great strength of dealing in crypto is that people still don't really understand what it's all about. They read that people have made vast fortunes and that's why it's become hugely popular, but they don't really know what it is. No wonder crypto fraud is one of the biggest growth industries of the modern age. You can offer your punters outrageous growth on their money on short-term investments of six months or a year. I let the fund grow with new investors over a month to six weeks, then I pull the plug. The first the punters know about it is when they check their crypto wallets and they're empty. By then, their money is safely deposited in my offshore accounts and I've moved on to do it all again with a new fake company with a different address. It literally is rinse and repeat.'

I should've been more appalled by how pleased with herself Gina was but I was genuinely spellbound by the audacity of it all. It seemed too easy. So clean. Not victimless, though.

'Don't you feel anything for the people you steal from?'

'Why should I?' She sounded perplexed that I needed to ask. 'The way I look at it, anyone who invests in one of my schemes without doing all the necessary checks has got more money than they need and probably don't appreciate the value of it. That means they're either crooks or fools. Believe me, there are lots of both types about. I'm not going to feel sorry for taking money from people like that.'

'And the poor mugs like me whose personal details you use to set up these schemes? Which category do we fit into?'

I wasn't bitter anymore, though my anger at Gina's betrayal was still raw. That's why I wanted to get to the bottom of why she did it and how she felt about me and the others. I didn't expect it to make me feel any better, but I had to know. She took a second to choose her words carefully.

'You were *convenient*.' She put stress on the final part. 'I was working to a clear plan which required me to be extra cautious for the first two or three weeks after setting up the new companies, to minimise the possibility of arousing suspicion before the schemes began gaining serious traction. I could've just picked on any person and any address, to be honest. That's what a lot of the foreign scammers who set up fraudulent companies do, but I didn't want to do that. I wanted to be less scattergun and more targeted. Do this a handful of times, do it properly, maximise my returns.'

'Which is where the dating sites came in.'

'Exactly. The dating sites. Without wanting to sound immodest, I knew if I posted a false profile I could have my pick of the kind of man I would most likely be able to manipulate for my purposes, especially when I threw in a bit of a sob story. They had to be in their fifties, recently separated, or divorced. Not so old that they only wanted to settle for a bit of companionship, not so young as to be pushing for a physical relationship. Mature, susceptible, lonely, just a little bit desperate. No offence, Barry, but you were perfect.'

'None taken.' Charming!

'The aim was to quickly earn their trust to the point where they were willing to leave me alone in their homes.'

'The broken broadband story. I really fell for that one, didn't I?'

'Sorry.'

I shrugged. I was trying not to show how excruciatingly embarrassed I was. It was like dropping your trousers in front of a woman for the first time and provoking hysterical laughter.

'Once they allow me into their homes, I can intercept all incoming mail relevant to the setting up of the new company before the people whose identities I'm using have the chance to see it and get suspicious. It also gives me access to evidence of the personal identity I need, like date of birth, proof of address, passport number, National Insurance number, full names. Being on the inside makes it so much easier to find that sort of detail. It speeds up the whole process for such as setting up a business account with the bank.'

This was getting worse.

'A business account?'

'Yeah. You might want to get on to your bank about that. I've already moved my money elsewhere.'

'What else do I need to do to stop the Fraud Squad knocking on my door?'

I'll admit, I was panicking a bit at the thought of averting the Thommo crisis only to end up in jail for being the named owner of a company used in a con job.

'You get on to Companies House and tell them to take you off the register. It's a bit of a long process but you'll get there. Whether or not you want to report it to the police is up to you, but it's probably a good idea if you want to cover your back. It's just the bank, apart from that, but don't worry. It's a limited company, so you're not going to be held personally liable for its debts. It was never my aim to make you and the other men I used to front my companies suffer any misfortune. I leave them with a lesson in not being so easily swayed by a bit of flattery and an interesting story to tell. No harm done.'

Except emotionally.

I saw the damage caused for Andy Hague and I felt it myself. No doubt we two and the others before us would, in time, get over Gina, Diana, Clarissa – whichever alias was applicable to each of us – but there was a cost involved. Men of my generation are often accused of being afraid to show their emotions and keeping them hidden deep inside. I know that was the case in my marriage. But it doesn't make us immune to pain. And the pain lingers. I was beginning to feel I loved her and finding out that I'd been used hurt. It hurt a lot.

I was very quiet for the rest of the journey to Wakefield.

Chapter
Fifteen

I slept for most of the trip back from Wakefield. That was unusual for me. When our youngest, Lucy, was having a bad night as a baby, five minutes in the car and she was out like a light. Worked like a charm. She still often gets drowsy, even on short car journeys, though thankfully only when she's a passenger. Car travel never affected me like that before, though when you think about it I'd basically not had a good sleep for three and a half days, so it shouldn't be a great surprise that I was flagging a bit.

I stayed in the car while Gina met with The Doc, her shady supplier of knock-off medical supplies. She said it was better she went alone and I had no desire to accompany her anyway. I felt I'd been exposed to enough seedy underbelly for one night, so I waited in the warmth, on the edge of the remains of a housing estate which the ring road had long since cut straight through. I was trying not to think about anything more taxing than the sequence of traffic lights at the busy junction ahead.

She said nothing when she got back to the car, about twenty minutes later, and I didn't ask.

The urge to doze became irresistible practically as soon as we got back on the M1. Soon, I was in that strange half-world of semi-sleep; aware of still being in a speeding car but directed by my brain down odd detours of the imagination until jerked awake again by my head dipping forward like there was a weight tied to my chin or tipping sideways with a clunk against the cold glass of the door window. Before I knew it, Gina wrenched on the handbrake and switched off the engine. I stirred and realised we were outside my house.

'What time is it?' I asked, mid-yawn, stretching my neck muscles to ease out the aches from an hour of constant lolling.

'Quarter past one,' she replied, rubbing her eyes. 'I'll sleep here tonight, if that's all right with you.'

'Sure.' I might have got excited by that suggestion a few days earlier but I knew not to read too much into it now.

'While you were salivating onto your chest I've worked out what we need to do.'

I looked down. There was, indeed, a small wet patch on the front of my shirt.

'There's no point going through it now. It can wait until morning.'

A rush of chilly air blew through the car as Gina opened her door to climb out. I lumbered after her, still functioning mostly through instinct, fumbling in my pockets for the house key. In the time it took to stumble upstairs and fall out of my clothes, I collapsed into bed and was away.

The next thing I recall is fiercely bright sunlight, streaming into the bedroom with the gentle subtlety of a wet towel in the face. I'd not even had the awareness to close the curtains. I picked my watch off the bedside cabinet and blinked to bring the face into focus. Twenty to eleven.

Twenty to eleven?

I'd not slept in so late for years.

I threw back the duvet and swung my legs off the mattress. For once, I didn't ruefully reflect on the ever-expanding gut spreading over the top of my boxers as I perched groggily on the edge of the bed. Whether it was because I'd slept too long or hadn't drunk enough water, I had a banging headache. It throbbed from the sudden effort of getting up, enough to hold me still and make me close my eyes against the intrusive late-morning sunlight.

There was a noise downstairs. I prised open one eye and cast it towards the closed bedroom door but I'd quickly worked out what the cause of it was. Gina. She'd stayed over. Our first night under the same roof was not quite how I'd envisioned it a few days earlier. That wasn't the most dispiriting realisation. She hadn't only stayed because it was late. We had a job to do and not one I was looking forward to.

First things first. I creakily rose to my feet and plodded towards the bathroom. Paracetamol, then shower, then a cup of tea with a slice of toast and marmalade. Plotting a murder could wait until after then.

Gina was in the living room when I finally trudged downstairs. She was looking at something on her phone and had the radio on in the background. It was Smooth FM or some similar station that played nothing but bland crap. The kind of station my ex-wife used to listen to. I didn't have Gina down as a Smooth FM kind of girl.

'You're still alive, then,' she quipped, without looking up from her phone. In the face of everything that had been going on over the previous couple of days, it probably wasn't a statement made in the best of taste. I didn't say anything.

'You want another cuppa?' I asked as I headed straight for the kitchen.

'No ta. Just had one.'

I clicked the kettle on and made my toast. Two slices, actually, even though it was nearly dinnertime. I was hungry. Rather than join her in the living room and risk being exposed to Whitney Houston before the tea could prepare me fully for the day, I stayed in the kitchen and ate in peace. It was like we'd fast-forwarded from love's young dream to thirty-five years of age-wearied wedlock in the blink of an eye. I suppose I was making a point about who was clearly to blame for the mess we were in. I was making her wait until I was ready.

In my own good time and having poured a refill, I deigned to join my soon-to-be accomplice.

'Are you ready to get down to business now?' She glanced towards me from the top of her eyes with the tolerance of a mother who had allowed a toddler to scream itself out of a tantrum.

From the coffee table beside her she picked up one of five boxes. Four of them were identical and the other was a different design, but they all looked like they should contain small bottles of medicine.

'This is midazolam. Have you ever heard of it?'

Of course I hadn't.

'It's a drug they give patients before they go into surgery. It calms them down when they're anxious, to the point where you can do what you need to do and they won't remember a thing. It's not designed to take their pain away, but in a big enough dose it'll make them highly compliant and very sleepy. Combine it with this…'

She picked up the odd box.

'This is ketamine. Another fast-acting, very efficient anaesthetic and also a painkiller. Mix it with the midazolam and you can induce unconsciousness. We've got enough on this table to knock out a bull elephant.'

I took one of the boxes and opened it, allowing the small glass ampoule it contained to fall into the palm of my hand. I picked it up between the thumb and forefinger of my other hand. It was a sealed bottle. No cap or lid. I shook it and wondered how you were meant to get the clear liquid out with breaking the bottle. Maybe the box offered a clue.

Solution for injection or infusion, it read.

Injection?

'You're not seriously suggesting we try sticking a needle into this guy?' The thought was positively horrifying. I've never been good with needles. I fainted once having a blood sample taken.

'No need,' said Gina. 'It can be slipped into his drink.'

'Oh, yes! That's much easier. Cup of tea, Thommo? Do you take it with milk or mizodapam?'

'Midazolam.'

'Whatever. How are you going to get him to drink it?'

'He wanted you to give him whisky yesterday, didn't he?'

'Yes....'

She waited for me to work the next bit out for myself but I wasn't playing ball.

'So you put it in the whisky.'

'All this in one whisky?'

'In the bottle. You pour a measure into a glass for yourself. Put the rest in the bottle. Offer him the bottle. He drinks it. Jesus, Barry, it's not complicated.'

She was losing patience with me. I was being deliberately obstructive, so I deserved the scorn. The plan actually made perfect sense. So far.

'What then?' I asked.

'You give him the whisky to drink while he's waiting. You tell him I've been delayed. I had to go to Switzerland to collect the fifty grand in cash and my flight back was late departing. You tell him I've called and I'm on my way but it's going to be another half-hour. That's when you ask him to join you for a drink.'

'Very cosy.'

'When he passes out, you call me from upstairs and we get him ready to transport.'

'So we're not going to do it here?'

That was a relief. I didn't fancy the thought of having a dead body in my house, no matter for how short a time.

'No. We're going to load him into his own car and drive him along the back roads as much as we can, to avoid cameras, to a secluded spot where we can kill him and make it look like an accident. I thought that reservoir you drove me to when we had the day in the Peak District.'

'Ladybower?'

'That's the one. I recall quite a few pull-in places off the road where we can park the car, drag the body to the reservoir and put him in the water, still unconscious. He drowns, job done.'

It did, indeed, sound like a decent plan, but I felt it my duty to try to expose a flaw.

'Yeah, until they do a post-mortem and find out he's full of meza, miza-whatsitsname.'

'Midazolam.'

'That. They're bound to work out he was drugged.'

'Sure, but how could they possibly link that to us or to here? That's why we're going to put some distance between your house and the place they're going to find him. I dare say a guy like Thommo has a long list of known enemies and working down that is going to be more than enough to keep the police occupied until they give up bothering about the death of a psychopath from Skelmersdale. Let's face it, he's not going to attract a huge amount of police sympathy at his passing.'

I could see that. Gina had clearly put some effort into thinking this through.

'OK,' I said. I was beginning to buy into this more. 'I think I know of a little car park by the reservoir that might be ideal.'

'Good. That's settled then.' She was pleased with herself. I could tell.

The whole scheme still left me very uneasy, but something had to be done and I could think of no better option.

'Right.'

The clock on the wall said almost quarter past twelve. Thommo had threatened to be here at five. That was an awfully long time to wait. How are you supposed to pass the time when you're waiting to drug a large scary man and drag him off to kill him?

'Are you ready for that cuppa yet?' I asked.

Twenty-five to four. Even I'd had enough of drinking tea and I was getting so nervous I didn't trust myself to eat anything without risking bringing it straight back up. There was nothing on the telly and I didn't want to watch anything anyway. I was staring blankly at a book on the Dambusters raids of 1943, attempting unsuccessfully to take in even some of the information on the pages. In fact, the only part

I did properly absorb was the bit about how 617 Squadron practised for the raids at Ladybower Reservoir, which kind of defeated the object of trying to take my mind off what I would soon be required to do.

Gina was still on the sofa, fiddling with her phone. The only relief was that she'd allowed me to turn off Smooth FM without objection. I think four more hours of that might have tipped me over the edge.

Such was my heightened state of tension that a knock on the door startled me much more than it should. I looked at Gina. It was far too early for Thommo and, besides, it wasn't his usual method of announcing his arrival. She gazed back at me quizzically, wondering if I was expecting a caller or somehow knew by mystic powers who it might be. I gave her an answer by staring gormlessly.

'Get rid of them,' she hissed and jumped off the sofa, heading for the stairs. I waited for her to disappear from sight and for the sound of her footsteps to cease before warily opening the door.

I could've died.

'Hello Barry.'

Chapter
Sixteen

She was the last person I expected to see on my doorstep.

That's not strictly true, I suppose. I would've been even more astonished if I'd opened my door and there was Mick Jagger, or the Dalai Lama, or the Yorkshire County Cricket Club first eleven, in full whites. But it's fair to say if I had been expecting anybody on my doorstep at that time, I wasn't expecting her.

She was much more deeply tanned than the last time I saw her. Not one of those orangey fake tans, either. Her skin almost matched the colour of her eyes. Her hair was worn longer and in a different style. She'd also had pink and blonde streaks put in, for whatever reason. She was wearing a large, padded coat, even though it wasn't a cold day at all, but beneath it was a yellow dress cut to mid-thigh length, revealing a lot of exposed brown leg above strappy white sandals. She looked younger.

I'd barely seen her in the eleven months or so since she told me she wanted a divorce. Most of our conversations during that hellish period had been conducted through lawyers. Because of time elapsed and the changes she'd made to her appearance, it actually took a couple of seconds to recognise her, like when you bump into a person you know somewhere you didn't expect to see them. Maybe the surprise element also played a part, but there was far too much gawping involved before my brain could get my mouth to work.

'Louise!'

It really was her! She managed to form a timid thin smile while I just stood there, frozen in an expression of stupefied bewilderment. This was clearly an awkward enough situation for her as it was and I wasn't helping.

'Can I come in?' she asked.

'Yeah, yeah! Of course!' I opened the door wider and took a half-step back. Louise, instead of coming straight in, turned to collect the pink suitcase and matching cabin bag behind her, which I'd not noticed up to then because I was too preoccupied.

'Here, let me help you.'

I grabbed the big case while she lifted the smaller one over the threshold. When I'd lugged it in to join her in the living room, she was waiting stiffly, as if seeking instruction before moving, like a nervous interviewee.

'Thank you,' she said, without warmth. It was all a bit odd. I tried to cut through the wall of her obvious discomfort.

'You're looking really… well. I wasn't… This is so… How are you? What are you…? What are you doing here?'

I didn't make a very good job of it.

Large blobs of tears began to well in her dark eyes.

'I fucked up, Barry. Really badly.'

That was it. The dam wall burst. She broke down. Instinctively, I wrapped her in a protective hug while she sobbed against my shoulder. I couldn't think of what to say, so I just let her cry herself out.

'Sorry,' she said, pulling away to retrieve a tissue from her coat pocket. She dabbed at her eyes, bowing her head in hooded embarrassment.

'Come and sit down.' I gently touched her elbow to guide her towards the sofa, sitting close enough to be on call to provide further support if needed but not so close as to make her feel crowded. 'What's this all about? You can tell me.'

'I've been such an idiot.' She blew her nose. I leaned to the coffee table for the tissues to offer her another. She took the whole box.

'I made such a fool of myself and got tricked. I've lost all my money.'

'All of it?' I spluttered. Even after paying the legal fees for her end of the divorce I reckon she must have had the best part of a hundred grand in the bank as the settlement for her half of the house.

She nodded. 'I had to borrow just to have enough for the flight home.'

I needed a few moments to take that in. Blowing a hundred grand in six months was going some.

'Where did you get to?' She had never let me know where. If she'd told the kids, they'd not let on.

'Mexico.'

'Mexico?'

'I'd always wanted to go there.'

I couldn't recall her ever mentioning that, but it wasn't the time to discuss the point.

'I rented a flat in Cancun. I figured I'd spend a few months there at first and then maybe move on to somewhere else in the world. It was wonderful, at first, and then I met this guy.'

She plucked another tissue from the box.

'His name was Antonio. He was a bit younger than me, tall, dark hair and very handsome. Kept himself in great shape. Owned a bar just outside the main tourist area.' A hint of a sparkle returned to her eyes ever so briefly in memory of happy times.

'Me and Antonio started seeing each other. He made me feel like a real woman again. We were great together. I stopping planning out where I wanted to fly to next and began to want to stay with Antonio. Then one day he offered me the chance to invest in the bar. He said it was making good money but he had such plans to make it even better, only he couldn't raise the capital. The banks over there don't work like ours, apparently. He said we could share the profits fifty-fifty if I'd finance the expansion, so I said I would. He made it sound like such a golden opportunity.'

Tears welled again. It was time to deploy the second fresh tissue.

'I asked him time and again when work was going to start on the expansion but he kept fobbing me off. Said he was waiting for the right permissions. Then one day he told me he was being leaned on to pay off the local mafia bosses but that everything he had was wrapped up in the project. He asked me to lend him more money. I gave him all I had left. He looked genuinely frightened. The next day, I went down to the bar and it was closed. No sign of Antonio. A couple of the bar staff showed up and they were no wiser. His phone was dead. I went round to his flat. I could see through the window he'd cleared it out. I went to the police. I didn't know what to think. I didn't know if the mafia had got him or what – but then why would they empty his flat? I told the police what had happened but I could tell they were practically laughing in my face. I knew what they were thinking. Stupid old English woman gets tricked out of all her money after falling for a younger guy. They weren't interested in helping me find him. Probably knew full well there was no chance, so why bother? I got to know later Antonio didn't own the bar after all. It turned out he was just running it for somebody.'

She sighed. I reached out and gently laid my hand on hers. She appeared startled by the move at first and then pleasantly relieved. I don't know if she was expecting me to go mad at her for being so irresponsible, but I was hardly in a position to judge on that score, now was I?

'The rent on my flat was paid up for another week or so and all I had left was the money to live on until then. I had to phone our Penny to ask her to transfer me the money for a plane ticket. Of course, she didn't hold back on telling me what an idiot I'd been.'

Her sister, who I'd never got on with especially well, turned out to be a bit of an ally when Louise announced she wanted a divorce.

'I sold what I could to raise a bit more cash and the rest of my stuff is in these two cases. It's all I've got left.'

The crying started again. I wrapped my fingers around her hand and squeezed.

'I've nowhere to go, Barry. Can I stay here, just until I sort myself out again? I can sleep in the girls' room. It won't be for long.'

Of course I wanted to say yes. You can't spend so many years of your life with one person and feel nothing for them. Ordinarily, I would definitely have offered all the help I could give. No question. But these were not ordinary times.

'I don't know if I can do that,' I admitted.

I turned my head away but I could feel the hurt in her eyes as she looked at me.

'It's complicated. Not good timing.'

'What do you mean?' The edge of desperation in her voice had become even more pronounced.

'It's just that…' I stalled there. How could I possibly explain the rest? Thankfully, I was saved from having to face that by the sound of singing from upstairs.

Louise's gaze switched in the direction of the stairs. Mine followed. Down came Gina, humming the chorus of a song I vaguely recognised as one of Adele's. That wasn't the most striking aspect of her sudden appearance.

All she had on, as far as I could tell, was the old white T-shirt I bought when I went to see Springsteen at Bramall Lane in 1988. It was long enough on her to cover to the top of her legs but she plainly wasn't wearing a bra underneath. For certain. I watched her jiggle down every stair, transfixed. I couldn't help it.

I'm sure Louise must've noticed, too, but I didn't dare look at her to confirm that. We did, however, both rise to our feet virtually in unison.

'Oh,' said Gina, feigning surprise. 'I didn't realise we had company. I thought you were taking a while with that bottle of champagne.'

I was dumbfounded for the second time in a matter of minutes. By the time Gina padded barefoot to right in front of us I was completely numb. I think I'd stopped breathing.

'Aren't you going to introduce us?' she said with a sugary sweet smile.

'Sure!' I snapped myself out of the enchantment. 'Gina,

this is Louise. Louise – Gina.'

Gina held out a hand and Louise, hesitantly, accepted it.

'Your ex-wife! How lovely! I've heard so much about you – but don't worry, I didn't believe all of it!'

She laughed with a bit too much enthusiasm. I attempted to join in. Louise didn't laugh at all. I think she was still a bit stunned.

'Actually, I've so much to thank you for, for giving up this gorgeous man.' She sidled closer to me and hugged my arm. 'I feel as if we've known each other for ever. We've become so close. I won't lie, the sex has been a-mazing, but we mean so much to each other beyond the incredible physical pleasure. We're proper soulmates, isn't that right, hun?'

The best I could muster in response was an inane grin. I flicked a glance at Louise in search of a clue as to what she was making of this. Honestly, I don't think she could've appeared more shocked if she'd caught her granny doing a line of cocaine.

'Where are my manners?' Gina slapped her open palm to her forehead. 'This calls for a celebration. Would you like to join us for a teeny sip of champagne, Louise? Barry, go and get three glasses.'

I don't know what Louise imagined the invitation might lead to but I'm sure I saw raw terror in her eyes.

'No. No, I'd better be going. I need to…' She picked up her pink cabin bag and wrestled to try to extend the handle of the suitcase so she could pull it away.

'Let me help.' I was stung into action. Louise reluctantly gave up trying to get the handle to conform and allowed me to pick it up as she beat a hasty retreat to the front door. She was almost at the end of the drive by the time I'd manoeuvred the case outside.

'Louise!' I called, attempting to catch up. 'I'm sorry. It's just that…'

'So I can see,' she snapped, disapprovingly.

'Where will you go? Let me give you a lift.'

'It's all right, I'll get a taxi.' She stopped at the end of the drive for me to reach her and took the handle of the case from me without attempting eye contact. 'Goodbye, Barry.'

She bustled away up the road, struggling to manage the two cases. I felt awful. Weighed down by shame, I headed back to the house.

Gina was still in the living room, arms crossed.

'That was cruel,' I said.

No apology was forthcoming. 'Crueller than the way she treated you?'

Fair point, but it didn't make me feel any better.

'You would never have got rid of her if I'd left you to it. She couldn't have been here when Thommo arrived, you know that. Get over it, Barry. We've got a job to do.'

With that, Gina strode across the floor to the stairs. I didn't even have the heart to catch a last glimpse of how good she looked in my T-shirt.

Chapter
Seventeen

When Gina came back downstairs – fully clothed – her attitude had mellowed. Maybe, while she was getting dressed again, she'd reflected and realised she might have come across as a bit harsh.

'I'm sorry, Barry. That must have been tough for you.'

I acknowledged the concession with a slight raising of the eyebrows but no words. I was properly conflicted, if the truth be told.

On one hand, my ex-wife was back. She was in a deep mess and of all the people she could have chosen to turn to in her hour of most desperate need, she turned to me. This told me that the bond between us, forged through thirty-five years together, was still as strong as tempered steel, despite bearing the strain of our separation and divorce. It reminded me that, through it all, my love for Louise had never died and made me believe that, in spite of every hurtful word she had said, she felt the same way deep down.

I suppose I had the right to be bitter towards her for what she put me through in the last eleven months or so, but I couldn't be. I never gave up on her. I just tried to accept that she'd given up on us and that made me sad, rather than angry. Now I knew she still needed me. Me. Above all others. Me.

On the other hand, I'd sent her packing. Louise had returned, wanting comfort and guidance as she tried to piece together the shattered fragments of her life, and I'd turned her away. Humiliated her. Rubbed her nose in it by taking part in some sort of better-off-without-you charade, then I'd turfed her out on the street with nowhere else to go.

What a twat!

Of course I realised Gina was right. Louise couldn't be in the house when Thommo arrived – and he was expected in less than an hour. It would be too risky. The situation was potentially volatile enough and if one of the many things that could go wrong did go wrong, it would be cruel to run the danger of Louise becoming another innocent victim. Even if it all went to plan, it would be wrong to make Louise an accessory to murder.

No. That wouldn't do. She had to be kept out of the firing line. It was the only way.

But I still felt like a twat.

'Will you be OK?' Gina asked.

I nodded, not trusting my ability to reply in word form.

'Good. Let's go through the plan again.'

She did all the talking. I did listen. I found it useful. I had grasped what was required of me from the first run-through but the second briefing helped me regain my focus. After all, the stakes were high. I had to get this right.

'Now, the whisky,' she said.

I stood up to fetch the half bottle of Glenmorangie from the sideboard. There was just over half of it left.

'Will this be enough?' I asked, tipping the bottle to

demonstrate how much of the pale amber liquid it contained.

'That'll be fine. Don't forget to pour some for yourself first.'

I stepped through to the kitchen to get a couple of glasses. Normal ones. He wasn't getting my best ones. I brought them and the bottle to set them down on the coffee table, which Gina had lifted out from its normal place to stand between the sofa and the armchair.

I poured myself a good measure and downed it in one. It made me shudder but I didn't care. I needed that.

'Careful,' Gina chided. 'You'll have none left and besides, we need you to stay sharp.'

I poured another and left it on the table this time. 'I'll be fine. Don't worry about that.'

Gina had also brought over the five small boxes containing the drugs. She took out the first ampoule, gripping it in the material of her open zipped top and snapping the glass neck. She tipped the contents into the bottle and repeated the procedure with two more of the midazolams and the one of ketamine. That left one ampoule unopened. She hesitated, calculating.

'Might as well put it all in. We can't tell how much of the whisky he'll drink.'

She snapped open the fifth and swilled the mixture around in the bottle. God knows what it must've tasted like but I suspect anyone who knew their whisky would've known something was amiss. We could only hope Thommo was no connoisseur.

'Now we wait,' said Gina. We both looked towards the wall clock. It was almost twenty-five past four. In theory, there was only half an hour or so to go, but we were both aware the timing was not in our hands and it could be anybody's guess when he actually turned up.

'I'd better take myself upstairs, just in case. Are you sure you know what you need to do?'

I attempted to present a face full of flinty confidence but, to be honest, I was absolutely cacking it. Gina cast me one last you-can-do-it assuring smile and then I was left alone. To wait.

He didn't keep me waiting as long as the last time. Only forty-three minutes behind schedule. For the sake of my frazzled nerves, that was a small blessing.

But it was no consolation when he did burst through the front door with his now customary crash and clatter. There was no getting accustomed to having that in your front room. Large as life and twice as ugly, as my mother used to say.

Thommo stepped to the centre of the room like the king of the beasts, fiercely alert eyes darting, surveying. Practically sniffing the air for the scent of fresh meat.

'Where's your girlfriend?'

I attempted to portray as close to a picture of calm as was possible. Nothing out of the ordinary here. Just a normal night in, sipping a glass of whisky while waiting to drug and then murder a dangerous psychotic.

'She's on her way but she got held up. Delayed flight from Zurich.'

He considered that information.

'Zurich? Where the fuck's that?'

'Switzerland.'

'Switzerland? What the fuck's she doing in Switzerland?'

'Getting your money. Fifty thousand pounds isn't the kind of sum you can take out at the cashpoint, you know.'

He appeared to want to find a reason to object but could not.

'She called not long ago. The plane's landed and she's driving up from the airport. She should be with us soon.'

On cue, my phone pinged. I opened the message, as if I didn't already know what it was going to say.

'There's been an accident on the M1 near Derby. She reckons another thirty to forty minutes.'

Thommo's eyes narrowed. 'If this is some kind of trick….'

'What on earth would I stand to gain from that? She's on her way. Look at the text yourself if you want.' I held out the phone. He didn't take up the offer.

'Look, Gina's travelled across Europe to get this money for you. I'm sure you can wait a bit longer. Why don't you just have a sit down?'

He held his ground for a short while longer, possibly out of reluctance to be seen to be taking advice from the likes of me. Then he worked out nobody else was in the room to give a damn and relented. He practically overwhelmed my armchair.

The table with the whisky bottle had been placed in his direct eyeline. I leaned forward to pick up my glass and had a sip. I could tell he was watching.

'Do you want one?' It was unlikely he was waiting to be asked but I asked anyway.

He stared at the bottle. It was not as straightforward a decision as I expected.

'Nah,' he said. 'I had too much yesterday. My guts are off.'

I tried not to show outwards signs of panic but, inwardly, I let out a silent shriek of alarm. If I couldn't get him to drink the drugged whisky, the whole plan would fall apart. What was I supposed to do then? Hit him with the bottle? I'd have to come up with an alternative fast. I could only delay for so long before he's start asking awkward questions about Gina's imminent 'arrival' – and then what?

'Are you sure?'

'I just said, didn't I? You deaf?'

This was serious. I had to find a way.

'It's just I always thought if you'd had too much the day before and felt a bit ill, then a drink can sometimes, you know, perk you up a bit. There was this time a few years ago – quite a few years ago, actually – I got very drunk on rum and I was really rough the next morning, but a mate of mine persuaded me to have a little tot of rum because he said it would do me good. I mean, just the smell of it made me want to throw up but I did what he said and, you know what, it did help. What's the expression? Hair of the dog?'

'What dog?'

'It's just an expression.'

That went OK, I thought. Still no result, though.

'Perhaps I could get you something else?'

Thommo stirred in his chair. I was getting to him, just not in the way I wanted to.

'Don't you ever stop fucking talking?'

'I've got some elderflower presse which is quite refreshing. Or chamomile tea. That's good for you when you're feeling a bit delicate.'

I took another sip of whisky and waited for a reaction.

He was wavering. Gazing at the bottle. He cracked.

'Do you want a glass?' I offered.

'Fuck off,' he replied, taking a long swig.

'Fair enough.'

I was so relieved I thought I was going to collapse.

Thommo took another long gulp and paused a second before swallowing. His brow knitted. He inspected the label.

Jesus! If he suspects!

'Glenmorangie,' I said, mustering all that remained of my calm. 'My favourite. Quite a distinctive flavour, don't you think?'

He held the pose for an agonising moment more. I held my breath.

'S'allright.' He wrinkled his nose and drank some more.

I wasn't sure how much more I could take.

One question I forgot to ask when Gina and me had our strategy meeting was about how long it would take for the drugs to work.

Would it be obvious? All I could think to do was to sit quietly and occasionally try to pick up signs through surreptitious glances out of the corner of my eye. How long would it take to work? It turned out the answer was 'not very'.

For the first time in my short experience of being in his company, Thommo appeared less potentially explosive than a volcano full of dynamite. His posture changed. Not so stiff, intense, ready to strike whether with or without reasonable cause. I'd hesitate to use the word softened in his case, but he was kind of chilling. Visibly.

As he eased back in the chair and swigged at the whisky, gazing away into nothingness, you could almost have said he was becoming reflective.

I was happy just to sit quietly and observe. Wait to see when he reached the next stage. Hopefully, the catatonic stupor stage.

'I've got a kid, you know,' he suddenly announced.

'Really?'

'She's called LaGucci. Shit name, int it?'

'No, I think it's… lovely.'

'Her mother's idea. Me and her split up. The kid's nearly three. I don't get to see her much.'

The stare drifted further away again. I preferred this mellow version. Less likely to inflict grievous harm. Then he shot to his feet without warning and I almost jumped out of my skin.

'Do you want to see a picture?'

'Yeah,' I said, attempting to becalm the excessive thumping in my chest. 'Sure.'

I assumed he must mean a picture on his phone. I didn't expect him to begin unfastening his jeans. As he unzipped and lowered them to his ankles, revealing a surprisingly colourful pair of boxer briefs, it became apparent why. He had to point it out, among the mass of other inky shapes, but eventually I could see it clearly, on the side of his right calf. A baby's face.

'She was younger then,' he clarified, just in case I hadn't worked it out for myself.

It was a nice bit of tattoo portraiture. Not my style, but still.

'I see. She's very pretty.'

'Yeah,' he said, proudly, as he began to pull his jeans back up. Thankfully.

He sat down again and took another long drink of whisky.

'That's why I put my money into your girlfriend's scheme, y'know? I don't normally trust banks and such, but I saw the write-up and it looked like a good idea. Discreet. Not somewhere the law would go looking for it. I reckoned if it was as good as it promised, by the time my little girl was older, it'd be worth enough to make sure she never had to struggle like I did. It'd be a way for her to remember me for ever. But then it got stolen and…'

His mood darkened. I couldn't afford to allow him to become too worked up.

'But you'll have it back again. Very soon.' It worked. He calmed.

'Yeah. Soon.'

'So let's have a drink.' I raised my glass. 'To your daughter.'

'To my LaGucci.' He brought the bottle to his lips and had to tip it high to drain the final drops. 'My beautiful little girl.'

Thommo's arm dropped limply to the side of the chair and the bottle slipped from his fingers to the floor. He was becoming ever more benign.

'Y'know, you're not a bad bloke,' he slurred. 'I didn't mean nothing personal when I said I'd kill you and kill your family. It's just I couldn't…'

He was floating further away.

'I understand,' I said. 'It's OK. Why don't you just close your eyes and have a little sleep? Gina will be here in a few minutes. Just relax.'

His chin slumped to his chest. Before long, his breathing became deep and regular.

Chapter
Eighteen

For a while, I just sat there. I dare say if I had needed to move, I could've, but at that moment the effort demanded to do anything, even something as minor as lifting my hand off my knee, seemed too much. My whole body felt heavy, unresponsive. It was as if the emotional strain of holding myself together through the previous fifteen, twenty minutes (was it even that long?) had emptied everything I had. I was drained.

All I could do was stare at the unconscious mass of a man filling the chair opposite me. Thommo was still alive. Though it was only slight, I could see the movement of his tattooed head, slumped limply forward, as it rose and fell with every breath of his drug-induced slumber. The midazolam/ketamine cocktail had not killed him. It had sent him into a docile state in which he could no longer threaten harm and so it had done its job. The rest was down to us.

As we sat across from each other – one of us starkly awake and the other deep in sleep – I knew the time when we had choices to make had passed. Gina and I had not yet taken a life, but we had reached a point from which there was no turning back. We had shown our hand. Even if we did change our minds, lose our nerve or whatever, there was no bluffing our way out of this one. Should we wait until he regained consciousness and try to claim it had all been a big mistake? I couldn't imagine that going well.

So while Thommo had not yet drawn his final breath, I believed then I had seen his last waking moment. Heard his final words.

It had to be done. It was him or us. I understood that. It still didn't make it any easier to deal with the words whispered from deep within my soul as they burned into my brain.

This is something you'll have to live with for the rest of your life.

I didn't notice Gina as she crept cautiously to the top of the stairs, seeking confirmation before giving up her cover.

'All clear?'

Without being able to take my eyes off the man in the chair, I nodded solemnly.

Her descent became quicker and more confident with every step. She still approached Thommo with the light-footed hesitation of a small creature hardly daring to believe the predator was tethered and caged. She prised open one of his eyelids and allowed it to drop shut again. Then she drew her hand back and launched it into a hard slap across his cheek.

'Jesus!' I yelled, recoiling almost as if I too had felt the force of the blow. Thommo remained entirely oblivious to it. I could see why Gina would want to be certain he was so out of it that there was no danger he would wake if we tried to move him, but I wished she'd found a better method. That was like unearthing a wartime bomb and giving it a big whack with the spade to see if it was still live.

'Away with the fairies,' she pronounced and turned to face me. 'Good job, Barry. Now help me get him on the floor.'

The coffee table had to be moved out of the way first, to make space. I finished the last drops of my whisky and lifted the table back to its usual place, next to the sofa. I was about to grab the ankles of Thommo's heavy boots when a thought struck.

'Shouldn't we wear gloves?' I asked. It had become automatic over the years with my job to put gloves on before attempting heavy lifting but this time I was thinking more in terms of protecting our identities, rather than our hands.

Gina, poised to cradle his head while I dragged Thommo's body off the chair, nodded. 'You're probably right.'

I always kept gloves in the shed in the back garden and went to fetch them. My spares were too big for Gina, so I knocked the dust off an old pair Louise used to use for gardening. They would have to do.

'They'll be fine,' she said. 'Ready?'

I pulled, she cupped her hands around the back of his skull to stop it cracking against the floor. It seemed a bit daft to take such care, bearing in mind what we were about to do, but it made sense, if you think about it. The last thing we wanted was to have to deal with his blood on the carpet.

When he lay flat, Gina began going through his pockets. She produced a bunch of keys from his hoodie jacket.

'Got them! Where are yours?'

I pointed to the sideboard.

'Right. I'll move your car out of the way first, then find whatever it is he's driven here and back it onto the driveway.'

We'd already decided it would be smarter to do it that

way, both so we didn't have to carry this considerable weight as far and to reduce the chances of being seen. We were going to take him to the reservoir in his vehicle.

While Gina was sorting out the cars, my job was to make Thommo a little more easily transportable and, in case of prying eyes, make it look a little less like we were moving a lifeless body. I had a roll end of a decent quality deep pile carpet I'd intended to put down in the small back bedroom. We were going to wrap him in that. As I was creating more space to lay the carpet out beside Thommo, I could hear the throaty rumble of a vehicle being reversed onto the driveway. It definitely wasn't mine.

'You found it then?' I asked as Gina came back into the room.

'Yeah. Vulgar and shouty, as you'd expect. Plenty of room in the back, though.'

Together, we rolled the unconscious bulk into the carpet. When we'd finished, I used almost a full reel of heavy duty tape to try to make sure he didn't unravel on us. This part of the job was physically demanding enough in itself, but it was easy compared to what had to follow. We needed to load him into the back of the car.

Now I've been lifting and moving stuff all my working life. Some of those big rolls of carpet are pretty heavy – and damned awkward to manoeuvre up a flight of stairs, let me tell you. Years of doing that for a living shapes your physique. You probably wouldn't think that to look at me, because I'm five foot nine and could do with losing half a stone, but it's left me pretty strong. What I'm saying is I knew I could handle my end of the deal, as regards the moving and lifting, and if my mate Charlie had been with me, there would have been no problem.

Gina, though, was not made for manual labour.

'It's no good. I can't pick him up,' she cried despairingly, allowing the feet end of the Thommo-filled carpet to fall to the living room floor for the fifth time in barely three yards of progress.

I had my arms wrapped most of the way around roughly at his chest level, arching my back against the strain. It was as much as I could do to peek behind me to try to navigate a path to the door without bumping into furniture. I couldn't see anything that was going on at the other end of the operation.

'It's OK. Just try to hold him a little bit off the ground and I can drag him most of the way.' I was attempting to be calm and encouraging, which isn't easy when you're speaking through a faceful of rough hessian carpet backing.

We managed to haul him a few more feet before the next heavy thud from the other end.

'Oh, this is impossible! I think I've pulled a muscle in my back now.'

I swore under my breath. Sometimes, in my line of work, you get customers who decide they want to make themselves useful instead of standing back and letting you get on with the job. Almost every time, they turn out to be more hinderance than help. There is a knack to moving bulky heavy goods and most people just haven't got it. To prevent them doing themselves an injury, you have to gently persuade them to stay out of harm's way. Theirs and yours.

'I tell you what, how about you get the doors for me and make sure I'm not about to knock stuff over?'

Even though it put all the strain on me, this was a much more efficient arrangement. Until we reached the part where we had to get him into the car.

I say car. It was a big chunky lump of 4x4, like a Jeep or a Land Rover. The kind of vehicle that looks as if it was designed for people who live half way up a mountain and have to cope with the roughest terrain but which are usually driven by knobs from city suburbs who like to charge to within three inches of your exhaust pipe if you stay in the outside lane without getting out of their way immediately.

It was at least, as Gina said, roomy, but the tailgate was pretty high. The only way I could see to get the load in on my own was to climb backwards into the rear of the car first, still holding on to the Thommo carpet, and then heave with all the strength I could muster until most of him was in and he wouldn't slide back out again. Easier said than done, but it was going OK until Gina hissed a warning call.

'Someone coming!'

She closed over the rear door as far as it would go and I had to slide out of view, under the carpet. Most of the weight, it seemed, was being borne by my testicles. Finally, she opened the door again to give the all-clear.

'Just somebody taking the dog for a walk.' She stared down at me, legs and arms straddling a large roll of carpet. I must have looked like someone who was hugging a tree trunk just at the moment it was being felled.

'You OK there?'

I was anything but. 'Chuffing marvellous,' I grunted as I tried to extricate myself.

With plenty more effort and a little more swearing, I got him fully in. Gina closed the rear door while I attempted to get my breath back.

'We should get going,' she said. She was right. It was nearly dark. By the time we reached the reservoir it would be properly dark, which was good. But it was going to take us at least an hour to get there and we didn't know how long the drugs were going to keep Thommo unconscious.

I made my way to the driver's side door and took a first proper look at our transport.

'Not exactly unobtrusive, is it?'

Gina walked up beside me and dangled the keys for me to take.

'That's why we need to stick to the back roads as much as possible, to avoid being picked up by traffic cameras if we can. If they come looking for the car after they find the body, we don't want to leave a trail leading them back here. Are you sure you can get us there without hitting the main roads?'

I'd driven to Ladybower many times. I knew the more scenic route. I grabbed the keys.

'Let's go.'

We headed out of Woodhouse through Hackenthorpe and on towards Ridgeway and Dronfield, then in the direction of Grindleford and Hathersage. It wasn't the way the satnav would've sent us, but that was kind of the point. Soon, I began to relax just a little. Simply being in the heart of the Peak District usually has a calming effect. I was also enjoying the drive. The car may have been obscenely over the top in so many ways, but it was really comfortable.

'What are we going to do with the car after... you know? Should we set it on fire to destroy any evidence?'

'No.' That was emphatic. She'd clearly thought this through already. 'Torching the car would only attract attention. If there's a chance the police might treat the death as non-suspicious, once they find the body, we don't want to offer them a big clue that somebody's covering their tracks. I've got a better idea. We'll drive it to Manchester. I know places we can dump it with the keys in the ignition and, within half an hour, I guarantee it'll be sold on with different plates or be in the chop shop being broken down into component parts.'

'Manchester?'

'That's right. Then taxi to Piccadilly Station, late train back to Sheffield. Sorted.'

Who was I to argue? After all, I'd been nothing but a bit-part player throughout this whole wretched mess. A few weeks earlier, I was no more than a lonely bloke living out a boring life a million miles away from the world of glamorous con artists and oversized Lancashire hoodlums. Now here I was about to assist one in the murder of the other.

Maybe there was still time to take a breath.

'You know when I was downstairs with Thommo, just before the drugs kicked in?'

Gina stretched her back and rolled her shoulders. 'What about it?'

'Well he started acting a bit more, you know, mellowed out. He started telling me stuff.'

'Oh yeah?'

She didn't sound that interested but I pressed on.

'He's got a kid. She's a similar age to my granddaughter. He took his trousers down to show me a tattoo of her on his leg.'

'Nice.'

'Thing is, he said that was the reason why he put money into your crypto scheme. He was setting money aside for her. A kind of trust fund, I guess.'

Gina fell quiet for a second before turning in her seat to face me.

'What are you saying, Barry?'

I suddenly felt on the spot. In truth, I wasn't entirely sure what I was building up to.

'What I'm saying is, we kind of struck common ground. I saw another side of him and I could relate to it. He was trying to do his best for his daughter and, I don't know, maybe that was why he was so angry when the money disappeared. Who wouldn't be, you know? In the circumstances.'

She was annoyed by this. That was understandable. In not so many words, I was suggesting she should be ashamed.

'So all this is my fault, is it?'

'Well, not *all*…'

'But mostly.'

Time to bite the tongue. This was not the path I wanted to go down.

'The point I'm trying to make is, we connected. Sort of. It might be a basis to get out of this mess without anyone, you know… dying.'

And there we had it. We got there eventually. I just wasn't at all comfortable with the concept of being an accomplice to murder.

The closer we came to reaching our destination, the more the weight of that responsibility scared the shit out of me. I didn't know if I could handle it. In fairness to Gina, she seemed to recognise this.

'I get it, Barry. I do. This is a drastic solution, but don't lose sight of what led us here. We are in a dire situation. You cannot negotiate with people like Thommo. He'll take everything you have and when there's no more for him to take, he will kill. He won't take a backward step. He plays to a different set of rules to the rest of us and that means we have only one shot at stopping him taking his retribution in the only way he knows how. If you think he'd hold back from harming your granddaughter to get what he wants, just because she's the same age as his daughter, you're fooling yourself. You can't allow even the remotest possibility of that happening. It's him or her, Barry. Which are you going to choose?'

It was a proper dressing down. She allowed a short time for her harsh summary to sink in.

'You know it was the drugs talking, right? When he was opening up to you. Midazolam does that. Remember what I said? It's used to relieve anxiety in people facing surgery and it will release inhibitions as well. Makes them say things they might ordinarily not tell a soul. It also makes them entirely amnesic, so if you tried to re-establish the connection you think you forged with Thommo when he regains consciousness, he'll have absolutely no recollection of it. More to the point, he'll be profoundly pissed off that we've drugged him and dragged him to the Peak District, in the dark in the middle of nowhere. How do you think that's going to play out with him?'

She was right, of course. I'd already realised for myself we were past the point of no return.

Shortly after, we also reached the point of the A6187 directing us right towards Ladybower. There was no heading back then.

Chapter
Nineteen

Ladybower Reservoir has always been a special place for me.

My earliest memory goes back to when I suppose I must have only been five or six, when I was lured into my parents' Morris Minor and told that where we were going was 'just like the seaside'. This was a very exciting prospect because we only ever got one week by the seaside every year – and always at the same static caravan in Chapel St Leonard's owned by a man my parents only referred to as Mr Tipper.

Well, it wasn't just like the seaside. There was no beach to play on, for a start. Neither were there shops piled high with sticks of rock or amusement arcades or donkey rides. But there was ice cream from a van and when that had helped to mollify my initial noisy disappointment, I started to quite enjoy myself. I had never seen such a large, enclosed body of water – flat and calm like a sheet of glass on that sultry autumn day. The spectacular rising hills which hemmed in the reservoir climbed impossibly high and promised a world of strange creatures, adventure and danger. I ran free through woods like a dog off the leash, swishing at invisible foes with a broken tree branch and collecting pine cones from the ground to present to my parents like they were precious exotic fruits. It might not have been the seaside but it was also so unlike busy built-up Sheffield and I grew to love it. It captivated me then and it's held me in its thrall ever since.

The other visit with my parents that really sticks in the mind was during one long, dry summer. I was still quite young, so it might well have been during the bad drought of 1976. The water levels had fallen so low that the remains of one of the two villages that were evacuated when the valley was dammed and flooded were visible again. All you could make out among the mud were the low ghostly stumps of demolished stone buildings long since abandoned but it was possible to imagine what it once might have been when a small community thrived there. I thought that was awesome.

A few years ago, I went to watch a Lancaster bomber flying low over Derwent Dam to mark the seventy-fifth anniversary of the Dambusters raid. Even more than this extraordinary sight, my most vivid recollection is of the low roar of the four mighty Merlin engines vibrating against my chest as the old warplane swept through, barely high enough to clear the great stone towers. What a sensation it must have been when the full 617 Squadron swooped down the valley to practise for their audacious 'bouncing bomb' attack on the Ruhr Valley in Germany in 1943.

Over the years, there have also been so many great days out there walking – sometimes as a family, other times just with Louise and occasionally on my own.

As I said, a special place.

This latest trip was set to be another memorable one, though not for the right reasons. Perhaps it would prove to be the most unforgettable of all. As I drove over the

Ashopton Viaduct across the water and took the right turn towards the dams with a rising sense of foreboding, all I could only hope was it would not leave an immovable blot on all those happier times and tarnish special memories forever.

The road became more gloomily secluded as we rattled over the cattle grid and followed the narrowing asphalt track, between thick lines of trees to our left and a grass bank sloping away to the reservoir to our right. Only the bright shafts of our headlights pierced the blackness, with no moonlight able to break through the heavy cloud and dance on the dark water that night. The last of the day's walkers had long since left. We appeared to have the whole place to ourselves, which was eerily comforting in a way.

Almost there. Almost time.

The spot I had in mind was maybe two miles down the road, the last of the pull-in car parks shortly before the trail reaches its end at the visitor centre. Normally, on weekends, you needed to arrive pretty early to find a parking place there. As we neared it on our right, it was confirmed we were to have no such problems this time. It was deserted. Much as part of me was still wishing for an excuse to give up our deadly plan, I was relieved not to have to deal with an additional complication.

I pulled in, cursing myself for absent-mindedly flicking on the unnecessary indicator signal that benefitted nobody. At least my reflex error drew a small, nervous laugh from Gina, which probably helped her. She must have been feeling the tension too.

The car park was around a hundred metres long and maybe two and a half car lengths wide. I'd chosen this spot because it was pretty secluded and on the right side of the road for access down to the water. I stopped the car and turned off the engine. The sudden silence was striking.

'OK, let's get to it,' said Gina, opening the passenger door. I followed her lead, reluctantly.

She had the rear door open by the time I got there. I took a deep breath, hoping our load was easier to get out of the car than it was to get in. It was. I hauled the head end of the carpet towards the tailgate and spun it round until I was able to grip my arms around it and pull. Momentum and gravity helped with the rest. Then I dragged him so that the large car shielded us from sight from the road. Just in case.

I'd brought my retractable knife to slice open the tape I'd wrapped around the carpet to stop it from unravelling. Gina helped me unroll the carpet to get to its human core and I spooked myself, as we reached the last layer of the deep pile covering, imagining a wild vision of Thommo suddenly springing into wide-eyed life, like a maniacal ghoul in a cheap horror flick.

Thankfully, he remained peacefully still when we finally exposed him to the night sky. A little too peacefully still, if anything. We'd not really considered the possibility he might suffocate.

'Do you think he's....' I asked.

'Hard to tell,' Gina replied, warily keeping her distance. 'It's so dark. Can you check?'

My knowledge of medical examination is strictly limited, but Louise once showed me how to take a pulse. She said it was a skill that might come in handy some time. Well, the time had arrived.

I removed my glove and lifted Thommo's wrist. I could feel the beat jumping under my middle and index fingers, strong and regular.

'Yeah, he's alive.' There was more than an edge of disappointment in my tone. A different outcome might have saved us some bother.

'There's a steep bank leading straight down to the reservoir,' I added, gesturing in the direction. 'Have you got a torch on your phone? It should be fairly easy to get him down there but I'll need you to guide me.'

Gina retrieved the phone from the back pocket of her jeans and turned on the torch, shining it down the hill to gauge the descent. The dirt bank dropped away quite sharply through a slalom course of mature trees which had deposited the additional hazard of fallen twigs and branches. Around forty metres down was the path well-trodden by so many ramblers over the years and then the bank declined for a similar distance again to the water's edge.

'What's that bridge?' she said, peering beyond the furthest reach of the torch's light at the shape of a structure stretching out across the reservoir.

'Some kind of a pipeline, as far as I remember.' I must have walked past it many times without really taking notice but I thought I understood why Gina was pointing it out now. 'It's not a solid structure, like a dam. Objects can get through it.'

She gazed out, not quite convinced as far as I could tell. I shared her concern that Thommo might get stuck close to the shore. We wanted him to drift well out and, preferably, sink without trace.

'Right,' she said. 'I suppose we can take a better look when we get down there.'

I pushed my hands under Thommo's armpits and started to manhandle him into a position from where I could get enough purchase to drag him towards the hill. As far as

I was concerned, we were getting him down there, getting him in the water and getting away as quickly as possible. I said nothing but I was ready to stand up for myself if I needed to. If Gina thought I was going to haul him around the reservoir half the night until she found the perfect place to cast him adrift, I was going to tell her she had better think again.

The new resentment fuelled my efforts to get a good grip on the huge body of our adversary. Soon, I had him on the down slope.

Moving Thommo was not the problem then. Not moving too quickly was the issue. Even with Gina's torch to provide some light, picking a way backwards through the debris so I could keep my feet and avoid being steamrollered by the bulky deadweight was not easy. We inched towards the path without incident but the effort took more out of me than I expected and I had to rest before we pressed on, encouraged by the sound of the water drawing closer.

We picked up the line of a small stream until we reached a shallow bank and the edge of the reservoir. I lay the unconscious body down again as we worked out the best way to approach the next part.

'You're going to have to get in there and tug him towards you,' said Gina.

I stared at the water, hands on hips, still breathing heavily from the exertion.

'We could roll him in.'

'We still need to get him into the deeper water for him to float out. You won't be able to do that without getting in there yourself.'

I didn't want to have to agree. The prospect wasn't hugely appealing.

'Why don't you get in there with him?' It was the best counter-proposal I could come up with.

'I'm not as strong as you.'

'The water will take most of the weight.'

'You're taller than I am. You can take him further out.'

Clearly, this was an argument I could not win. 'All right then,' I muttered, resentfully, and began to remove my shoes and socks. I rolled up the legs of my jeans but could get them no higher than mid-calf.

'Why don't you just take them off?' I peered sideways at Gina to see if she was taking the piss. There was a hint of devilment in her eyes but she was being serious. 'Go on. I promise not to look.'

She raised one hand to cover her eyes, then stretched a deliberately large gap between her middle and ring fingers to show she intended to take a not-so-sneaky peek.

'Fuck's sake.' In a tense situation, it was a welcome lighter moment. I cracked a smile and unbuckled my belt.

By Christ, the water was cold!

We rolled Thommo as far as we could until he was in the shallow edges of the reservoir and tried to push him out, with limited success. It was time to bite the bullet and wade in. I trod gingerly over the slippery stones beneath my feet, feeling the paralyzingly freezing water rise past my ankles and up my shins. Soon, Thommo's passive body was fully immersed. I guided him deeper until I reached my unspoken limit. Mid-thigh. I wasn't willing to take it further and risk the icy depths touching my scrotum. I spun him around so he was pointing out towards the open water, head first, turned him onto his front and launched him out into the blackness with a firm push on the soles of his boots.

With a gush of his own bow wave, Thommo was soon

out of reach and drifting deeper, bobbing out, out and out towards his intended oblivion before slowly beginning to disappear below the surface. It was done.

I didn't stay for long to watch him go. I had to get out of there. My teeth were chattering by the time I waded back to the bank. Though I was no longer in the water, I could still feel its frosty grip on my legs below the line of how deep I had allowed myself to go.

Gina had gathered up my jeans and shoes.

'Come on. We need to get you dry and warm.'

We scrambled up the bank towards the car. Twigs snapped and stabbed the soles of my bare feet with every step but they were so numbed I hardly felt a thing.

I had to get dry and try to coax life back into my legs. I used the carpet as a makeshift towel while Gina started the car so the heater could warm the cabin ready for me. I climbed into the passenger seat to get dressed, grateful for the change of temperature. Gradually, my shivering began to abate and a tingling sensation started to return to my lower body.

'Better?' she asked.

'Yeah,' I replied, still vigorously rubbing my legs through my jeans. 'Let's get out of here.'

We both clicked on our seatbelts and Gina switched on the headlights.

'Oh, my Christ!' she screamed.

Spotlighted by the headlamps, a vast, soddened creature was lumbering slowly towards us, maybe fifteen metres away and not closing the gap especially quickly. He lurched forward as if only through instinct, blank wide-staring eyes seemingly unaffected by the glaring brightness of the car lights, dripping a trail of water as he trudged mechanically on. It was like a cross between swamp monster and zombie apocalypse. If I'd taken a moment to hazard a guess, I would have said Thommo was still mostly under the influence of the drugs we had given him and was not particularly aware of where he was or what was going on.

What was for sure was that he wasn't at the bottom of the reservoir. That was all that really mattered right then.

Gina jammed the car into gear and stamped down on the accelerator. The engine roared and the wheels spun, spitting stones from the loose surface until they found the traction to send us shooting forward fast enough to press our backs against the seats.

Thommo made no effort to dive out of the way. His drug-addled brain could not react quickly enough. Intuitively, he managed to crouch and turn, so his right side felt the full force as the car struck him with a pounding thud. The impact threw him up as well as forward. Our momentum drove us under him and his body cracked against the windscreen. The front seat airbags exploded in our faces as Gina jumped on the brakes. We screeched to a skidding halt and Thommo rolled over the bonnet to land heavily, lifelessly, on the ground in front of us.

Neither of us could speak, move or breathe until we had allowed a moment to absorb the blinding flash of what just happened. We turned to look at each other practically simultaneously.

'You OK?'

She nodded. 'You?'

I was fine, but that wasn't my main concern.

'I'd better check.'

She nodded again.

I unclipped the seatbelt and opened the door, reaching

into my jacket pocket for the retractable carpet knife. I might need its protection.

Edging around the side of the car, I could see Thommo's legs, the right one twisted awkwardly under the left where he had fallen. I nudged closer, shakily holding the blade in front of me. The nearside headlight was smashed but the other was intact. He lay a couple of metres in front of the bumper and was not moving. His head tilted to one side, showing a red gaping wound above his right ear from which a trail of blood was trickling down to his neck. I removed my glove again and held the back of my hand in front of his nose and mouth but could not feel the touch of his breath. I lifted his limp arm to take his wrist and check for a pulse. His skin was ice cold. I pressed my two fingers along the inside of his forearm, trying to trace the artery and pick up a sign of life. I couldn't find one.

By this time, Gina was out of the car and was looking down on me, hugging herself against the chilling effects of shock.

'I think he's dead,' I said. She remained silent and we held our postures like that for half a minute. I think we were both trying to figure out what to do now.

'Should we get him back in the water?' I suggested.

'We might need a change of plan,' said Gina after a while. 'The car's no good now. Even if we cut away the airbags, the windscreen's smashed and the headlight's broken. We can't drive it to Manchester like that. We'd be pulled up for sure.'

It was hard not to feel incredibly isolated just then. Miles from anywhere and with no means to get away. But we still had a more urgent problem to resolve.

'So we abandon the car and make it look like an

attempted car-jacking,' I said. 'He gets out of the car, someone else drives up and tries to steal it, but he comes back to stop them and gets knocked over in the attempt. They scarper in their car.'

Gina was thinking it through. 'But why would he drive out here and get out of the car with the engine running?'

'I don't know. Taken short? Perhaps we leave the carpet. Make it look like he was dumping it. People do dump their rubbish in the middle of nowhere.'

'So it was a fly tipping-related murder?'

'No… I was just...'

She didn't have to be sarcastic.

'Anyway,' she added. 'We should take the carpet with us. It's a potential clue that might lead the police to us otherwise. Batch numbers or something. I don't know, but I think we should take it.'

'OK.' Overcautious, maybe, but I wasn't going to argue against overcautious. 'We leave the scene as it is, without the carpet or anything else that might connect us, and it's up to the investigators to work out what they think happened. We just need to get away from here now.'

Gina nodded. 'Agreed. Head back towards the main road but stay out of sight.'

'Find somewhere to hide out until morning, I say. He'll be found well before the first visitors arrive and it'll be a madhouse then, but when the area around the reservoir starts getting busier we can emerge and blend in, then catch the bus back to Sheffield.'

'Do you know somewhere we could hide?'

I didn't. The need had never cropped up before. We were going to have to improvise.

'We head into the woods.' I pointed to the dense mass

of trees on the opposite side of the road. 'No chance of being spotted by a random passing car. We follow a trail through the woods until we reach the Snake Pass and then stay under cover until it's safe.'

I could tell Gina didn't much care for the plan. In truth, I wasn't convinced it was a good one myself. But it was the best we had.

So we made a last check, to be sure we were leaving nothing behind, and headed for the woods.

A man, a woman and a roll end of luxury deep pile carpet.

Chapter
Twenty

'Are you sure we're going the right way?'

We'd been walking for well over an hour and still all we could see were trees, trees, and more trees. We were constantly tripping over roots and snagging our hair in low branches, making progress pitifully slow even if we hadn't been carrying a long roll of carpet between us. We'd jumped out of our skins at every small crackle, creak and groan stirred by the wind or whatever nocturnal creatures were going about their normal business. We were mostly operating blind because the phone torches ate up battery power and both of our devices were running low on charge. We'd not been able to pick up a phone signal since we first entered the woods, so there was no way of using Google maps to help navigate a way out. My mood had not been helped by slipping into a brook and getting a left shoe full of water about three-quarters of an hour back. For all I knew, we'd been stumbling, sliding and squelching round in circles since then. Even setting aside the fact that I was still considerably freaked out from my part in the drugging, attempted drowning and knocking down of a man who lay dead in a nearby car park, I was exhausted, cold and frightened. I wanted nothing more than to be home in my lovely, safe, warm bed, but that prospect appeared as remotely inaccessible as the moon, which was currently hidden behind a thick blanket of cloud. In short, I have rarely been so pissed off with my situation as at that precise moment.

And Gina wanted to know if I was sure we were going the right way.

'Nope. Not at all.'

She stopped dead at my frank admission and dropped her end of the carpet.

'You don't know?'

'I do not have the slightest fucking clue.'

'You mean we could be heading the wrong way?'

'Correct.'

I can't imagine how she didn't already suspect this to be the case. Clearly, she had more faith in my sense of direction than was justified.

'I thought you said you'd been here lots of times.'

'Here, as in Ladybower, yes. Here, as in the middle of a forest next to Ladybower in the middle of the night, not so much.'

She slumped to the floor and sat. 'So we're lost. Great.'

I set down my end of the carpet and sat on it.

'Yes we are. Totally.'

We stayed that way for a while. Two people together in the dark woods, both contemplating the many places they would rather be and, probably, how many other people they would rather be there with. If ever there were circumstances for giving in to a range of negative emotions from despair to panic, that was it, but neither of us went there. Strangely, without the marching soundtrack of our footsteps and laboured breathing, the woods became an oddly tranquil place. Our attempts to find a way out had proved hopeless and accepting that as fact actually had quite a calming effect.

We were lost. There was nothing to gain by getting in a flap about it.

'Look, why don't you come and sit on the carpet with me? I'm sure it's more comfortable than the ground.'

It was meant as a peace offering. We're in this together. Reluctantly, she took up the invitation, though keeping her distance.

'We can't be so badly lost,' I suggested tentatively. 'It's not that big a forest. It's just disorientating in the dark. Look, we said we were going to stay under cover till morning anyway. I guess here's as good a place as any for us to settle down for the night. It's dry, it's safe and there's nobody else around. When it gets light, we'll find the way out easily.'

'You think so?'

'Sure.'

I hoped so. We fell quiet again.

'Not heard anything yet. You know, sirens,' she added.

'Maybe a bit soon. I don't suppose they have night patrols at a reservoir.'

'Probably not.'

'No. Probably not.'

As we drifted into our own thoughts again, I pictured Thommo lying where we left him. For whatever reason, I started imagining his corpse being nibbled by creatures foraging for food. Nothing major like bears, of course. Not many of them in Derbyshire. Rats. Stoats. That sort of thing. It made me kind of sad for him. It wasn't a nice thing to happen to anybody.

Gina was thinking on more practical lines.

'You do realise we can never say a word to anybody about this, don't you?' she said.

To be honest, I couldn't even contemplate *trying* to tell anybody about it. Where to start?

'Absolutely. I know that.'

'I'm thinking particularly about your ex-wife,' she added, staring meaningfully at me. 'If she's back on the scene, you might be tempted to talk to her about it one day. But you can't.'

I'd almost forgotten about Louise's sudden reappearance, only a few hours earlier. Ordinarily, I wouldn't have been able to think about anything else. Other events had commanded my full attention since. When it happened, I'd felt bad about ushering her away so abruptly but I'd not even considered how I might react if she was, truly, back for good.

I couldn't foresee a scenario where I'd be in a hurry to tell her about all this, though.

'I won't.'

'Good.'

She paused. 'How do you feel about seeing her again, though? It must've been a shock.'

I'd purposely tried to avoid going on too much about Louise and the break-up and the reasons for the break-up while I was still under the misapprehension that I was nurturing a new relationship with Gina. Heartbreak tales about exes isn't a smart subject for conversation when you're in the early stages of getting to know another special someone, I would say. But I did confide a little to Gina about how hurt I was by the divorce. It had shaken me to the core, in truth. I was very much still dealing with that. I didn't just blurt it out, though. She'd asked. It was during one of those wonderful post-meal cosy evenings on my sofa when everything was so magical and all possibilities for a future together were open. Or so I believed at the time.

'It was,' I said. 'I thought I might never see her again and then there she was. She was so… desolate. Crushed. I felt sorry for her.'

'Do you still love her?'

Now *there* was a question! I'd spent the last year desperately wanting not to love Louise anymore because to do so only made breaking up more painful and, at times, I'd sort of persuaded myself that I no longer did.

But then she turned up on my doorstep and, in an instant, I knew.

'Yeah. I think I still do.'

'Even after all the shit she put you through?'

'Yeah. Strange, isn't it?'

'Huh!'

Then Gina leaned to me and patted my hand.

'Good for you. I hope it works out.'

I smiled. 'Thanks.' I didn't see it as condescending. I think she was genuinely happy for me.

We sat still a while, reflecting on the complexities of human emotions, until I asked: 'What about you? Have you ever been in love?'

It occurred to me I knew hardly anything about Gina. Not the real Gina – or whatever she was actually called – anyway. All I'd been told was the cover story.

We had all night. Maybe it was time to get to the truth.

'I have,' she said. 'I was married and madly in love with a guy but it turned sour. You know why. Sort of.'

I was puzzled. 'Do I?'

She waited for me to figure it out alone.

'You mean the abusive guy in Bristol? The one who kept you locked up and got obsessive about making babies? Him? That really happened?'

'Pretty much,' she said. 'Only the names and places were changed to protect the guilty!'

Gina laughed at her own joke but it was the kind of laugh people sometimes use to mask the hurtful seriousness of a bad situation. She fell quiet again. I decided to risk it and probe a little deeper.

'So all the controlling behaviour and the isolation and the violence – that was all true?'

'Yep!'

'Until one day you found the courage to just walk out and start a new life.'

'I did. Well… I altered that part of the story to suit my purposes, to be honest. The actual way I brought it to an end was far more satisfying.'

There was that mischievous smile again!

'Go on…'

'He hit me one night, like I said when I told you the story first time. He'd threatened me before. Threats were a big part of his way of "keeping me in line", as he saw it, but this time he went further. A proper punch. Caught me on the side of my head. I must have been unconscious for a short time because he wasn't in the flat when I came to. Curiously, though, it was that punch that brought me to my senses. I knew then I had to escape or it was only going to get worse, but I didn't know what to do, where to go. The only person I could think to turn to was Christine, who was my best mate before Peter – that was the bastard's real name – stopped us seeing each other. I no longer had a car and I had no means of paying for a taxi, so I walked four or five miles to her place and told her everything. She was great. We cried together, she listened, she comforted me. She said I could stay with her for as long as I liked and we had a glass of wine. Then we had another. Then we started to talk about what might happen beyond the immediate future. I'll always remember what she said.'

She stalled, lost in the memory as she ran it through in her mind.

'She said: "Do you want to do this the proper way and risk becoming just another forgotten domestic abuse victim in the police files, waiting years for justice, or do you want to do this the sweet way?" Maybe it was the wine, maybe I was just intrigued to find out what she meant. I said: "The sweet way, of course!" We started planning. We talked for hours.'

I got the feeling it wasn't going to end well for the husband. I hoped not.

'What did you come up with?'

'She told me she could put me in touch with a guy who could fix us up with a drug to help us get revenge on Peter. She called him The Doc.'

'The medizolene man?'

'Midazolam. Yes, him. I told him what we had in mind, thinking a couple of strong sleeping tablets would do the job, but he recommended the midazolam. He said it was safer and more reliable for doing what we required.'

'So that must have been the time you used his services before, like you told me on the way to Wakefield. What plan did you concoct between you, then?'

'Well.' You could tell she was relishing the opportunity to share her tale of success, just as she had when she was telling me all about her crypto scheme for the first time.

'I stayed with Christine a couple of weeks, keeping a low profile. We reckoned that was long enough to leave Peter stewing in his own juices, wondering where I'd disappeared to. Christine made the first contact with him, saying I was prepared to go back, but only as long as he promised things would be better from now on. He came out with all the pathetic bullshit you'd expect – how deeply sorry he was, how he loved me so much, how it'd never happen again, blah, blah, blah. I didn't believe a word of it, of course. Sure, after I moved back in he was falling over himself, trying to convince me he was a reformed man, but I knew it wouldn't last. Coercive controllers don't change personalities that easily. I had no intention of putting his promises to the test anyway.

'It was on the third day back that I did it. A Sunday. He'd been to the gym and he liked to have one of those foul-tasting whey protein shakes after doing his work-out. Being the good wife, I offered to mix one up for him while he was in the shower. Plus a little midazolam, naturally. It took effect a lot quicker than I thought it would. He really chilled out, like he'd had a bit too much alcohol. The Doc had said I'd be able to make him do whatever I wanted and that he wouldn't remember a thing, but I didn't think it'd be that effective! He was totally compliant. It was getting dark but I told him we were going to take a little drive. He walked with me to the car without even asking where we were going. I drove him to a place out in the sticks in the Mendip Hills, three or four miles from the nearest village. After I'd helped him out of the car, I told him to take all his clothes off because I was going to do something special for him. That got his interest. When he'd stripped off, I gathered up his stuff, told him I was going to get a blanket from the car and drove off. The last I saw of him was in my rear view mirror, totally naked, chasing the car down the road. I left him with no phone, no money, nothing.'

'Remind me to never get in your bad books,' I said. 'I can see why you came up with a less potentially disturbing version of the ending to tell your dating site people.'

'That was only part one of the plan,' she added, eagerly. 'I drove home and fired up his laptop. I wasn't supposed to know where he kept all his passcodes and log-in details, but I did. I emptied as many of his accounts and investment funds as I could, diverting the money into a holding account I'd already set up for myself so that I'd be able to move it on and make sure he was never able to trace it. Then I accessed his mailing lists of friends, work colleagues, clients – everybody I could think of – and sent them an email detailing the appalling ways he'd treated his wife and making sure they knew precisely why I was leaving him. Oh, and then I gathered up his laptop, phone, fancy expensive watches and a few other bits I was able to get my hands on and set them going on the heavily soiled programme on the washing machine. That was me done. I packed everything I needed, drove Peter's car to the train station and parked it on double-yellow lines, then I caught a train north to start a new life.'

She looked very pleased with herself. Why not? It was revenge on a magnificent scale, beautifully executed. I'd have loved to have known how the husband got his head around his predicament as the amnesic effects of the drug wore off.

'Did you ever get to know what happened later?'

'Some of it, from Christine,' she said. 'She told me he

had to sell up and move on. It ruined him. I'm glad. He deserved it.'

'So how long was it after that you came up with your crypto fraud scheme, then?' I spat out the words 'crypto fraud scheme' in a scathing tone to show I still disapproved.

'A week or two. I could never go back to being a full-time web designer for fear that one day Peter might be able to find out where I was, through a contact or a client who hadn't completely severed links with him. Maybe the police were after me as well. I couldn't be sure. The money I syphoned off wouldn't last forever and a girl's got to make a living somehow! I never wanted to be reliant on anyone else ever again, so I set out to devise a plan that would allow me to operate for short spells, make big money before anybody could figure out what was going on, then move on. I'd read an article from a newspaper online about one street in London where something like a hundred fake companies had been registered by criminals taking advantage of how ridiculously easy it is to exploit the loopholes in the system at Companies House. One guy found he apparently owned twenty companies he knew nothing about. The simplicity of it appealed to me. It was perfect.'

'Perfect?' I asked with a scornful snort. I hardly needed to spell out how obviously a flaw had been exposed.

'Yes, well,' she conceded. 'Perfect up to a point. We've dealt with that now though, haven't we?'

'I suppose so.' I could've also pointed out that some of us had been left to deal with another set of consequences that hadn't been budgeted for in Gina's 'perfect' plan, but it somehow didn't seem worth bringing up again. Not right then, anyhow. Nevertheless, it stung a raw nerve. I'd embarrassed myself with how easily I'd been suckered. A little self-conscious shame might not amount to much in light of the more serious stuff that had been going on since, but the bruise was still tender to the touch and Gina had prodded it again.

'One bit I don't get,' I added. 'Why twenty-three days?'

She looked puzzled. 'In what context?'

'As in the time you stay around. Why specifically twenty-three? Why not twenty-two, or twenty-four, or thirty-three?'

If she was playing the innocent, she was playing it well. She shook her head, apparently mystified.

'I'm sorry. I'm really not sure I understand.'

'Well,' I explained, 'when I met with Andy Hague, the guy from Manchester, he told me you were with him for twenty-three days and then disappeared. He said he contacted another guy in Peterborough and it was the same. Twenty-three days and off.'

'I see,' she said and sighed. 'I've done this seven times now. You're my seventh. What I've found is it takes three to four weeks to develop the new company to the point where it's legally up and running and attracting a good flow of investors. At that stage, I don't need to do much more because it begins to generate its own momentum as investors who think they've hit on a good thing recommend it to other investors and so on. I give it a further two, three, four weeks after that to keep drawing in the cash and then I pull the plug. Move the money somewhere safe and start again. I've explained this to you before. As to specifically the number of days I stay in one place, I don't have a particular number in mind. I stay for as long as it takes. If those two said that time was twenty-three days in their case, then that's how long it took with them.'

'So it was a coincidence.'

'Just a coincidence.'

That explained that. Not quite the mysterious calculation I'd been led to expect.

The wind was getting bolder. I turned my eyes to see how the tops of the trees were stirred by it and, beyond, to watch the clouds being broken and chased across the night sky. A freshening breeze made me hunch my shoulders against the chill. Beside me, Gina let out a small gasp as she, too, felt its cold bite.

'You're shivering,' I said. Her hand were thrust deep in the pockets of a jacket that wasn't designed to offer protection against conditions such as this. Neither of us were dressed appropriately for facing a night in the open air. It wasn't what we had in mind when we set out. Now we were no longer on the move, the falling temperature was getting to us.

'I don't know if I can stand this all night.' She drew up her knees, to conserve heat. Even more so than usual, she appeared so small and fragile. 'Can't you make a fire?'

'Not unless you've got a lighter or something. I wasn't in the scouts.'

Nevertheless, I felt duty-bound to do something to help. I rose to my feet, with the noble intention of offering her my jacket, even though I could also have done with more protection from the elements myself. Then I had a thought.

'Hang on. Stand up a sec.'

She did as I asked. I picked up the carpet. It was rolled with the backing on the outside, to protect the pile. It probably wasn't in any fit state to be laid in my small back bedroom anymore. All the same, I could see it might still have its uses.

'How about we turn this into an improvised sleeping bag?'

I began to roll it out. It was the standard four metres wide and about two-and-a-half metres in length. Good enough for my little bedroom and also potentially good for keeping a couple of stranded campers warmer through a chilly night in a forest.

Gina watched, uncertain but keen enough to hope it might work.

'Come on. Lie down.'

I sat in the middle and she lowered herself next to me. I folded the excess carpet from my side over us and tucked it under her, then folded over the other end of the carpet and secured it under both our bodies, until we lay there like two strips of chicken in a tortilla wrap.

Though I say so myself, it was quite snug.

'Better?' I asked.

'Better,' she confirmed.

We lay still for a ten minutes or so, allowing our combined body heat to build.

'Hold me, Barry,' she whispered.

I extended my arm so she could shuffle closer and rest her head on my chest, with her arm around my belly. I drew her tight, laying my hand on her hip.

I felt her relax, sinking slowly with the rise and fall of my chest until her breathing became longer and deeper as she slipped into sleep. Gradually, I also felt my eyelids grow heavy, lulled by the warming woollen fibres of our makeshift covering and the exquisite intimacy of our embrace.

Chapter
Twenty-One

Trotting close to the line of the trees, a hunting fox – a lone vixen – patrolled the edge of her territory. Pickings had been thin so far. Only a half-eaten discarded apple. Scent trails had yielded nothing. It was still early. A proper meal would surely be located and eaten long before first light.

She stopped, smelling the air. She had scented something. She watched but picked up no movement. But her nose never let her down. It was close. Nearer the water.

She was wary. She'd seen the car. Cars meant humans. Humans were to be avoided. She always stayed well out of the way while the humans were about. It was safer to remain in the den. Sleeping, mostly, but always alert to potential danger. By hunting time, the humans and cars had usually all gone. This car wasn't moving, but she was suspicious. Curious, though. Cars meant humans and humans often left food. Their food. Spilled or thrown away and left. An easy meal. She was wary of the car but it was worth checking out if it meant an easy meal.

She padded quickly, keeping low and silent, across the road. The car was shelter, shielding her in case any predators were about. Or if a rival fox had detected an intruder on their territory. She didn't want a confrontation. Just to see if there was food. She sniffed the air again, stalking slowly. Constantly vigilant. She stopped, completely still.

Human. Flat on the ground. Unusual. Not moving. Unusual. A human, though. Humans meant danger. Her instincts told her it was probably safer to leave it alone. Scurry back across to her territory. She was curious, though. What was it doing here and why wasn't it moving? Was it dead? Was it edible?

Though it was much bigger than her usual prey, it was worth a closer look. Carrion was still a meal. She stepped timidly nearer. Not making a sound, watchful, until it was right in front of her. She sniffed. If it was a kill, it was a fresh one.

It had been wounded. It was bleeding. She could smell it. There. On the side of its head. She stretched her neck to reach it and licked.

She recoiled. It had moved. Its eye was open. They stared at each other. Her heart was beating faster. She was rigid. It had not moved much. Just the eye. She watched, waited. It made a sound. A throaty growl.

'Fuck off!'

She ran. There were easier meals to be had than this.

The human still did not move. He was not certain he could. He was not certain of anything. Until he was stirred by the rough sensation of the animal's tongue on the side of his head, there had been nothing beyond the small light of consciousness in his brain. The animal had stimulated a response. His brain wanted to find out what had caused it. The eye had identified the blurry outline of a nearby creature in the dark and the brain had reacted to that by instructing the voice mechanism to issue a warning to keep it at bay. It had worked, but nothing else was working yet. Just the one staring eye, taking in whatever information it could see until the brain began to function more efficiently and could process what it was being told.

A large, solid shape filled the eye's scope of vision. As the eye adjusted to the low light and the brain emerged from its shut-down state, he saw that the shape was a vehicle. It was all he needed to know for now. It was a vehicle. Anything else was not his priority. The brain had more fundamental duties to perform first.

Body first. I'm breathing. I'm alive. Is there pain? I can't feel pain. I can't feel anything. Not below the chest, not beyond the shoulders. Can I reach beyond and reconnect? Frantic signals to nerve endings, beseeching movement. A finger twitched into life. Stiffly and only slightly but it moved. Progress. Another finger curled, then all five gradually clenched into a loose fist. Good.

Legs next. No sensation at all, like they didn't belong any more. Come on! Move! He screamed inside to make them respond. It took a lot of effort but, finally, both ankles creaked and bent. Only a little, but he heard them scrape across the loose stone ground. They still felt numb. His whole body was numbed, as if he had been deep frozen. Every small action demanded a surge of willpower.

He lay there for an age, bullying his body. Making it comply. He needed to get up. Eventually, he had enough control over his right arm to force it into a position to lever his upper body off the ground. One deep breath. The air was released from his lungs with a low moan as he put everything into the lift, twisting and raising his torso until he sat upright. It took so much out of him. His head, pock-marked with grit on one side and stained by a trickle of blood from a gaping wound on the other, was sent swimming by the adjustment in posture. He breathed heavily to clear it. His body still didn't properly belong to him. His left arm, which had taken his weight while he lay, was lifeless. He stretched and flexed some more. He was able to draw up both knees. The left arm came alive again. Every small movement demanded so much more effort than usual, but at least the numbness was gradually easing. That was when he realised his clothes were soaking wet. Somehow.

It was time to get up. He knew he had to. It was the only way to get back to normal. He assessed. The vehicle could be used to help him get back to his feet. It was only a couple of metres away. He turned onto his hands and knees to be able to crawl up beside it. A stabbing pain in his right hip, as he put more weight on the joint, held up his progress. A sharp, unfamiliar pain. He couldn't understand why it hurt so much. He had to block it out. He reached the car and raised himself to a kneeling position with his powerful shoulders and arms. Then he leaned against the bumper again and clambered until he was on his feet, resting against the bonnet. The hip was throbbing. It was damaged but he could still move. Only with difficulty, though. He didn't have full control of his limbs. He was struggling to think straight. So he waited.

The recovery was on. For the first time, he began to take in his surroundings.

Where the fuck am I?

There were not many clues. Trees on either side. A road. None of it was in the least bit familiar. Through the trees and down to his right he could make out something else. In the low light and with a still-scrambled brain, he couldn't be sure but it might be a big lake. That would explain the wet clothes. It didn't explain much more.

How the fuck did I get here?

With the return of sensation came the realisation that he was cold. So cold. The shivering had started. His body was trying to warm up. He had to do something to get warmer. Get in the car. Inside is usually warmer than outside. He leant against the bonnet and swung his legs to propel himself towards the passenger door.

This car. It's my car.

He remembered then. He'd claimed it. Someone had taken liberties by selling drugs on his turf, so he'd taken physical retribution on them and then took their car. He liked it, so he took it. It had status. He had status. He felt good driving it. Taking it also sent a powerful message. Don't fuck with me. The previous owner wouldn't fuck with him again. He wouldn't be driving nice motors again for a long time either. It's not easy to drive when somebody has shattered your kneecaps with a lump hammer.

He reached the passenger door. It was unlocked. With another surge of effort, he hauled himself into the cabin and closed the door. It was still cold.

Turn the engine on. Get the heater going.

The inflated airbags hampered him but eventually he was able to stretch across to the far side of the steering wheel column. The keys were in the ignition. He turned them and the motor ticked into life. He set the heater to full and the temperature to the maximum, but the initial blast of cold air chilled him even more.

These wet clothes. Get out of these wet clothes.

He had other clothes. Dry clothes. He'd brought a holdall because he was away from home. He'd thrown it on the back seat. He reached around and fumbled until he could locate it and drag it to the front. He unzipped it eagerly. A hoodie top. A tee-shirt. Underwear. That would do. He tore off all the wet stuff and immediately felt better for being able to put on dry clothes, even though it left him only partly dressed. He was still convulsed by shivers but the heater was starting to do its job. As he rubbed and smacked his limbs to full life again, so his head began to clear.

So how the fuck did *I get here?*

He tried to piece the fragments back together. He could remember the room at the pub. He'd been staying there. He remembered the bar. Drinking and doing lines and dropping a few pills with a couple of the locals. Good blokes. They had a laugh. He remembered waking up in the morning feeling like shit, getting up and puking his guts up, then going back to bed. What happened after that? He went to get his money back. That was it! The fifty grand that bitch stole. She was supposed to show at the boyfriend's house, so he went there to collect his money and… What? She wasn't there. The boyfriend was there. Why wasn't she there? The money wasn't there. What happened? He told me to wait. The boyfriend said I should wait, so I waited. There was a bottle of whisky. I had a drink and… What happened? Nothing after that. No memory of anything after that. Until I woke up here freezing cold and soaking wet. Here. Where the fuck's here?

He reached for his wet clothes in the driver's side foot well, looking for his phone in the zip pocket of his top. It was still there but it wouldn't turn on. It must be full of water. He tossed it onto the driver's seat. The car satnav. He usually did it through his phone but there was one built in. He tried to get it on the dashboard screen. No signal available. He tried again. Same message.

Useless piece of shit.

Wherever here was, the big question was how? How the fuck did I get here? There could only be one answer. It was all coming clear now. That bitch and the boyfriend. They drugged me, jumped me… however they did it, it must have been them. They brought me here to kill me, to get out of giving me my fifty grand back. It must have been them.

His blood was properly running hot now and that wasn't all down to the heater.

Nobody gets to do that and live. They took one shot and failed. They don't get a second. They're going to be made to regret that. Suddenly, it was about so much more than the money. They were dead. So dead.

He dipped his hand into the holdall to make sure it was still there. He felt the cold metal of the Glock 17 and drew it out to reassure himself it was fully loaded and ready. It was, but he wasn't just going to find them and shoot them. Oh, no. He wasn't going to make it that easy. That painless. They were going to suffer first. They were going to pay for what they did.

He sat, planning, as the car heater blasted out hot air to progress his steady thaw. Soon, the shivering ceased. Body and mind were functioning again. It was still dark but he wanted to leave. Find out where they had dumped him and find his way back to the boyfriend's place. Pick them both up. Make them pay.

The jeans and boots were still wet but he'd have to put them back on. He stuffed the other wet things and the waterlogged phone in the holdall, concealing the pistol.

The car. The airbags could be ripped out but the windscreen was a problem. It was practically shattered on the driver's side, distorted by a concave bulge where something heavy had hit it from the outside. Maybe that was where the bad hip came from. The damage made it difficult to see through. Too difficult. It would be easier to steal fresh wheels.

So he got dressed, turned off the engine and climbed out of the cabin with his holdall. Pity to leave the car. He'd enjoyed driving it almost as much as he'd enjoyed taking it. Still, it's only a car. He could take another. He threw the keys as far as he could down the bank towards the water. Just because.

One last job. He unscrewed the front and rear registration plates to take with him. They were fakes. Useful for keeping the coppers off the scent when the next car he took was reported stolen.

He zipped them into the holdall and stood. The hip was still bothering him but, apart from that, his movement was almost back to normal. Much more in control. He reached the road and wondered which way to turn. Left or right? There were no clues as far as he could see. Then he heard the distant sound of a lorry to his left. That must mean a main road. So he set off left, limping towards his revenge.

Chapter
Twenty-Two

I've had more comfortable nights, to be honest.

That was no great surprise. The suggestion that camping under the stars could somehow be a wonderful experience which puts you at one with nature always struck me as ludicrous nonsense. Give me a warm guest house or a room above a pub any time. I camped out for three nights at the Reading Festival in 1983, me and two mates in a one-man tent, and that was enough to put me off for life. And I was only seventeen then.

The notion of a night under canvas as a fifty-seven-year-old was even less appealing. With good reason, as it turned out. It wasn't even canvas. A night under carpet.

I did sleep for a while. A couple of hours, at best. That was when the soreness started to set in, but I didn't have the option of rolling onto my side to gain temporary relief because Gina was still asleep with her head on my chest. No amount of surreptitious bum-shuffling could make the aching go away under those circumstances. The discomfort wasn't made any easier to cope with by the fact that I badly needed to go for a pee from around half past two. I suppose

I could've awoken Gina or gently eased her off me but I didn't have the heart.

That wasn't just because she seemed so peaceful. I must admit I enjoyed our night-long cuddle. It had been a long time since I'd shared such physical closeness with someone. My relationship with Louise had not included any kind of intimacy for many years, not even at such an innocent level. I certainly wouldn't describe the pleasure I took from holding Gina that night as sexual, though. That wouldn't be right. But, for all the mad stuff she had put me through, she was a very beautiful woman and it felt good to cozy up to a very beautiful woman. That's not so wrong, surely? It reminded me how much I'd missed such a simple bliss. I think all of us need that in our lives. You can lose sight of just how much it means when it's been denied you for too long.

To soak in the warmth of her body against mine. To hear the soft sighs of her sleeping breath. To inhale the perfume of her silky honey-blonde hair. It was exhilarating! If it hadn't been for the growing paralysis in my arse cheeks and the cramping pain of a full bladder, I would have been utterly content.

But it was a relief when she finally stirred, shortly before sunrise.

She raised her head off my chest and stretched, rolling her neck to ease out cramping muscles that had been in the same position for hours.

'What time is it?' she yawned sleepily.

I lifted my left arm, which had been wrapped around Gina all night, to look at my watch and felt the prickle of pins and needles.

'Nearly quarter to six.'

'Nearly quarter to six? I don't feel like I got any sleep at all. Did you?'

'A little.' I didn't want to contradict her.

'When should we get moving?'

'Soon, I think. I've still not heard anything to suggest they've found the body yet but it can't be long until they do and it might be a good idea for us to be out of the way when that happens.'

Gina tensed her whole body into another stretch, cupping her hands above her head.

'What then?'

'We work out where we are, first off. Then we head towards the main road. There are a couple of pubs fairly close by. We should be able to pick up a signal there and I can order us an Uber to get us back to Sheffield. First things first, though.' I began to extricate myself from our carpet wrapping. 'I'm busting for a pee.'

It was only when I tried to get to my feet that I realised how badly my back had stiffened. I must've looked like an arthritic mantis as I creakily retreated a discreet distance into the woods to relieve myself against a tree.

When I returned, Gina was up and using her phone in selfie setting to attempt to fix her hair, insisting it was a 'complete mess'. It looked OK to me. While she also disappeared into the woods to do what she needed to do, I began to scrape out a trench, using the thickest fallen branch I could find, to bury the carpet. Carrying it back into Sheffield would not only be a complete bind, it would attract unwanted attention so, as much as I hated the thought of sullying nature by leaving it, I decided it was best to commit it to the earth.

I bade it a silent 'thank you' as we set off to find a way

out of the woods. It had served its purpose splendidly.

Within a few minutes, we had begun to pick up the sounds of traffic and carried on heading towards it. Soon, we emerged into an open field and could make out the start of the Snake Pass, with the west arm of the reservoir stretching out just beyond. We could see no sign of activity to suggest a police incident was in progress as we passed the entrance to the road we had driven along a few hours earlier to dump Thommo's body and thought that a good thing. We wanted to get away from there as invisibly as possible. Once we reached the Ladybower Inn and picked up a signal, I sorted out our ride and we were on our way back to Sheffield.

It was a quiet journey. Reflective would probably be the word. I couldn't tell you what was on Gina's mind. Maybe she was just thinking how glad she was I'd soon be out of her life. Perhaps she wasn't reflective at all. Maybe there was nothing more to say, as happens when people who don't really know each other run out of common-ground subjects to discuss.

But I was considering all the crazy stuff that had happened to us in the last couple of days. Believing it was all over made it feel like everything that had happened should belong in somebody else's life. Mine had been a strictly ordinary, borderline dull, existence before Gina sent it spinning into turmoil. Now it was wobbling to a stop again, the temptation was to question if it actually happened at all – or was it like that time on holiday when I got food poisoning from eating dodgy fish and had the weirdest nightmares ever?

I knew it was all real, of course. We were leaving behind a six-foot-four lump of flesh and gristle which, for all his unpleasant tendencies, had once been a living human being and that was not a responsibility which should be dismissed lightly. All I could do was impose the rational truth – that, for the sake of my family, I'd done what had to be done.

For the sake of my conscience, I hoped that would be enough.

We arrived at Gina's hotel. The end of the road. We got out of the cab and stood awkwardly facing each other, not really knowing how to wrap it up.

'Do you think you'll stay here for much longer?' I asked.

'One more day, I think. I have a few loose ends to tie up and some arrangements to make before I move on.'

'Another sting?'

She shot me a tolerant smile, noting the disapproval in my tone. 'No, I'm done with that. I reckon I should interpret the last couple of days as a sign that I shouldn't stretch my luck. I've made enough to set myself up very comfortably. Pushing for more would be greedy. Unnecessary. It's time to start a new life somewhere. Just a matter of figuring out where.'

I was glad she'd reached that conclusion, but realised there could still be implications for me.

'What if the police manage to track us down in connection with… you know? What should I tell them?'

She laughed. 'Tell them the truth. Tell them it was all my fault. I'll be long gone by then anyway and they haven't even got my real name to work with if they tried to start searching for me. You can leave out or add bits to the story as you choose, but you're not made for deception, Barry. You're an honest guy. If they come sniffing around, tell them what happened, but I can't see how any of this leads back to your door. You'll be fine.'

'You think so?'

'Sure so.'

I hoped so.

'I've still got all the documentation to do with the business I set up in your name and I'll put it in the post for you before I go. It has all the dates and reference numbers you need to sort everything with Companies House and the bank and such. I'd still recommend reporting it to the Fraud Squad to cover your backside. I'll take the website down as well.'

'When are you going to collect your car?' I suddenly remembered it was still outside my house. Going by the look on her face, she'd also forgotten.

'Keep it,' she announced. 'I don't need it. I'll sign it over to you and put the registration form in with the other stuff for posting. The keys are still in your spare bedroom.'

That left me a little taken aback. I could only mutter a confused 'thank you'.

'Let's call it compensation for all the shit I put you through.'

Gina glanced over her shoulder towards the hotel entrance, like I was now keeping her from an urgent task.

'Look, Barry,' she said. 'I'm sorry to have dragged you into all this. You probably think I'm a complete arsehole for what I've done but I meant you no harm. You're a sweet guy, Barry. I wish you all the best for the future.'

She held out her hand to shake. I took it and nodded.

'You, too.'

That was that. She turned to go. I watched her walk through the doors and then I turned to leave as well. No regrets, no recriminations. Move on.

I didn't actually think she was a complete arsehole

either.

Rather than head straight home, I decided to treat myself to breakfast. I was ravenous. I'd like to say it was just because it was the only café I knew that was close by, but I headed for the little place close to the cathedral where I'd first met Gina. A lifetime ago, it seemed. I chose to sit at the same table, even though others were available. Call it sentimental if you like. It just felt like the right thing to do. I already knew I'd never go to that café ever again. I was completing the circle.

They did a very good full English as well, by the way.

I was pouring a cup from my second pot of tea when my phone rang. The power bar was showing red, but the display said it was my daughter, Maisie, so I thought I'd better answer.

'Ey up, Maise.' My joviality surprised me. I hadn't realised I was that cheerful. It probably confused the hell out of my daughter.

'Dad?' she answered, uncertainly. 'Are you all right?'

Hearing her voice jolted me back to earth. It reminded me that matters could have worked out so differently if Thommo's threats had not been dealt with as we did. I shuddered.

'I'm good, love. How are you and how's my beautiful little granddaughter?'

'We're fine. We're at the leisure centre. Isla's been in soft play group while I've been in my class and we're going swimming after this. Dean's out golfing, as usual. Look, dad, we need to talk.'

Are there four more dreaded words for a man in the English language than when a woman tells him 'we need to talk'?

'It'll have to be quick, love. My battery's low.'

'It's about mum.'

So that was it. I prepared for a proper telling-off. If I'd had time to work it out, I probably would have figured that Louise would head for Maisie's next after being shunned by me.

'I can explain…'

'She was ever so upset,' Maisie pressed on, regardless. 'She said you've got a girlfriend. Why didn't you tell us you'd got a girlfriend?'

'It's not how it seems…'

'Mum said you were all over each other, like you'd just got out of bed. Honestly, dad. At your age! Mum said you made her feel really uncomfortable and then practically threw her out. She couldn't stop crying. She said she'd come to you because she was desperate for a friendly face after everything that happened to her in Mexico but you didn't want to know. How could you do that?'

'This isn't the time…'

'You need to come to see mum at ours and make it up to her. You owe her an apology.'

'Maisie, listen.' I needed to wrap the conversation up. 'My battery's almost gone. I will come round. Tonight, I promise. I'll tell you all about it then, but it's far too complicated to go into it over the phone.'

'Who is this girlfriend, anyway?'

'Tonight. I'll see you later. I've got to go. Bye, love.'

I hung up and rolled my eyes. Maisie was right. I did owe Louise an apology and an explanation, but I needed a few hours to develop a version of the story appropriate to the situation. Obviously, I couldn't tell them everything.

The exchange with Maisie had attracted a few flapping

ears at nearby tables, so I decided to leave without finishing my tea. I could start thinking through the task ahead on my way to catch the bus home.

The mental script was almost prepared as I turned on to Shinfield Drive. So absorbed in my rehearsals was I, though, that I didn't realise something was wrong until I was on my driveway.

The front door was open.

Not just open in an ordinary sense. Forced open. Smashed open. It was still on the hinges. Just. But a huge crack had been opened just below the line of the letter box, one of the panels had a hole in it the size of a football and the frame on the lock side was wrecked. It must have been hit with something very solid and with great force.

My heart practically stopped.

'He's not there anymore.'

I turned. It was Mrs Hemsley from next door. She remained her side of the low wooden fence which divided the front yards of our two halves of the semi-detached. She was a short, almost spherical, pinch-faced woman a few years older than me and her expression was fixed in deep disapproval, but she usually meant well. She was the street's unofficial guardian of tidiness and protector against any sort of anti-social behaviour. Not much got past Mrs Hemsley.

'Mrs Hemsley. Did you see what happened?'

'I heard the banging on the door and then I could hear a right kerfuffle from inside. I had a look. He's left it in an awful mess.'

Even from my position midway up the drive I could see an upturned armchair and several smaller items strewn across the floor in the room behind the shattered front door.

'Did you see them?' I asked. I was really hoping she was

about to tell me it was kids. But she'd said 'He'.

'Big bloke covered in tattoos with a cut on the side of his head. I shouted to him that I'd called the police. He swore at me and stormed off. I don't think he took anything. He drove off in a silver car. One of them USVs. Honestly, something like that going on first thing in the morning. It's a wonder you weren't in.'

No doubt I was meant to be. I felt sick to the pit of my stomach. This could only mean one thing. Thommo was alive.

'The police,' I blurted. 'You said you'd called them?' What was I going to tell them?

'I did. They asked if it was still all going on, but I told them he'd gone. They still haven't bothered to turn up. Typical. I should've said he was still here.'

I was struggling to get my head around it all. Thommo was alive. He'd clearly come to get me. He must have worked out what we did. Oh, Christ!

'Sorry, how long ago did you say this happened?'

'Half an hour, I'd say. Long enough for them to get a bobby here.'

Half an hour. If I'd come straight home instead of calling for breakfast, I'd have been here. It was a chilling realisation. Not as chilling as the next thought.

Where is he now?

'Jealous husband?'

Mrs Hemsley hung the suggestion out there like a net waiting for a passing butterfly.

'What?'

'Is that who he was? Hoping to catch you and your new girlfriend at it?'

I was too preoccupied to be either amused or offended.

'No. She's not…'

My phone rang. It startled me. I checked the display. Louise.

Christ! For the second time, her timing was dreadful. Would giving her the brush-off again make me more of a twat than ignoring her call completely? I answered it anyway.

'Love, I honestly can't do this now. Can I call you back?'

The laugh – dark, mean, menacing – curdled my blood. 'Sorry, lover boy. This won't wait.'

Chapter
Twenty-Three

How was he not dead?

Seriously. He'd been left to drown, unconscious, in freezing cold waters, and had then been knocked down by an accelerating chunky four-by-four monster car, all of which happened while he had enough drugs in his system to leave a rhino practically comatose. I was starting to wonder if the hardest man in Skelmersdale might be indestructible.

The thing is, he *was* dead. I truly believed that. I felt for a pulse, the way I'd been taught, and couldn't find one.

I Googled this some days later, by the way, just to make sure I hadn't done it wrong. Apparently, when exposed to extreme cold, the body cuts down the flow of blood to the limbs to stop the core from losing further heat and protect against hypothermia. It's called Peripheral Vasoconstriction and makes it difficult to detect a pulse from the radial artery which supplies the arms, but you can usually find a pulse if you push your fingers into the neck or groin. I think I know which of those two options I would have chosen if I'd been aware of this at the time.

So there you go. Every day's a school day.

But I hadn't been aware of any of that at the time, so when I heard Thommo's voice growling down the line at me, it was alarming, to say the least.

'You tried to bump me off,' he snarled.

There was no point in denying it. I could hardly claim there had been some sort of misunderstanding.

'You should've finished me while you had the chance because now you've made me very angry and that's not good. Not for you.'

'Thommo, listen. I'm so sorry. I panicked. I shouldn't have…'

'Oh, you will be sorry.' His words were almost dripping venom. 'I've got your wife.'

Louise! Maybe the initial shock of receiving the call was to blame, but I hadn't made the connection up to that moment. Of course, if he was ringing me from Louise's phone, there was only one way he could've got hold of it. She'd not been back in the country five minutes and already I'd humiliated her and exposed her to mortal danger.

'Don't hurt her. Please. Let me hear that she's OK.'

I could hear a squeal of fright in the background and then the sound of short, agitated breaths.

'Louise! Louise! Are you all right?'

'What's going on, Barry? Why is this…'

It was her, for sure. She screamed as the phone was snatched away from her.

'A wife *and* a pretty girlfriend. You have been busy.'

'Look.' I wasn't in the mood to go into details regarding relationships. 'Tell me what you want me to do. This is between us. Just don't hurt Louise.'

No reply.

'Hello?'

Silence. I looked at the phone screen. It was blank. The battery had gone.

I stared at it, disbelievingly. Not now! I was aghast.

I had to power up. Plugging it in at the wall in the house wasn't the best option. I had to get on the move so that when I could reconnect I could be quickly on the way to wherever Thommo told me to go. I kept a USB connection cable in the car for when I was out and about and let the battery run low. I needed the car keys. I dashed into the house.

On the other side of the battered door, the devastation was far worse than my first glance suggested. Thommo might only have had a short time to vent his anger on my living room but he'd made the most of his opportunity. Nothing was where it should've been. The car keys had been on the sideboard, but the sideboard was on its end against the far wall, close to the kitchen door, with everything that had once stood upon it scattered to the four winds. It looked a hopeless task to find the keys among all that mess, but I dropped to my hands and knees and began scrabbling through the debris.

In an increasingly frantic search, I thought I'd sifted through every smashed fragment and peered under every overturned piece of soft furnishing but still I couldn't find them. I rose up on my knees to catch my breath and a glint caught my eye. A silvery tag with the faded black enamel writing on it which had once more clearly spelt out the words 'Dad's Taxi'. I know it's corny but the kids bought it me for father's day years ago and I never found the heart to get rid. It was dangling from the middle of the TV screen, which was precariously balanced on top of the upturned sofa. The car key itself was half embedded in the screen. It must've been thrown with some feeling.

It meant I'd have to buy a new telly but I was so relieved to find the key I didn't care. I grabbed it and ran for the door.

'Where are you going?'

Mrs Hemsley was still stationed at her side of the fence.

'I have to leave,' I yelled as I pelted down the driveway to the road.

'But the police…'

There was no time for a discussion. I jumped in the car and connected the phone to the power, then started the engine and sped away.

Mrs Hemsley watched me go, a glare of deep disapproval on her face.

'Come on, come on, come on!' I yelled, willing the phone to come back to life. I didn't know where I was driving to. I only knew I needed to be mobile, ready for when the time came. For all I knew, I could be heading in totally the wrong direction.

The screen remained defiantly blank as I reached the junction at Sheffield Road and turned right, towards the city. I was half way up Normanton Hill before the phone flashed white and the little apple symbol showed. Seconds later, it prompted me to enter my passcode. I was in! I've never been so happy to see neat rows of app icons in my life.

There was a supermarket just around the corner, where the Rex Cinema used to be. I pulled in to make the call.

'I lost you. My battery ran out,' I blurted, as soon as the call was answered.

'You'd better not be trying to pull something.' He didn't sound happy, but then again he never did.

'I told you. The battery went. Tell me what you want.'

He paused. He was toying with me.

'Industrial park off a road called Hinkley Street. You know it?'

I didn't.

'I can find it.'

'There's a closed-down activity place for kids, last unit at the end past a car repair shop. Get there. Now.'

He hung up.

I did find the industrial park on the satnav. It wasn't far away. Quarter of an hour's drive. I reckoned I'd be able to work out which unit he meant when I got down there.

It was pretty obvious, once I was on the industrial park.

Krazy Kangaroo Kidz Kingdom

The multi-coloured lettering on a mint green background of the signage board was in stark contrast to the bare brick and cold grey corrugated metal of the building. It looked like one of those trampoline places that seemed to pop up everywhere a few years ago only to go out of business almost as quickly. Me and Charlie put down carpet tiles in the reception of one of them near Jordanthorpe. That one went bust as well.

It looked pretty sorry for itself now. The landlords had moved quickly to spoil the vandals' fun by boarding over the large panes of glass at the entrance to the unit but had played into the hands of the graffiti artists and fly poster stickers. There was no sign of anyone around, so I drove round the back. A silver SUV was parked there, out of sight. It matched the type of car Mrs Hemsley had seen Thommo drive away in from my house. I pulled up and got out to try to find him.

There was no sound of activity to lend a clue, no window to look through to see what was going on inside. But there was a green metal door with a sign on it saying 'Fire Exit. Please Keep Clear'. I gave it a push with the open palm of my hand. It wasn't secured. It moved stiffly, reluctantly, but it gave way enough for me to slip inside with a second, more purposeful, shove.

It opened directly into the large open space that had once, briefly, echoed to the yells of excited kids. It was empty now, except for two adults who were most definitely not in the mood for trampoline-orientated fun.

Louise was sitting on the exposed concrete floor against the wall, wearing jeans and a pale blue sweat top. She had drawn up her knees to her chest and had wrapped her arms around them to make herself into a comforting ball. Her eyes were fixed on the door as it creaked open and I stepped through. She was scared. Thommo was ten metres away, sitting on an abandoned office chair with his legs splayed unnecessarily wide.

His simmering presence could not be ignored but I didn't acknowledge it. I walked straight towards Louise. She rose to her feet and rushed to meet me, flinging her arms around my neck.

'Are you OK, love?' I asked.

She clearly wasn't. She was sobbing and shaking, but she appeared unharmed.

'I don't understand what's happening, Barry. Who is this man? He barged into our Maisie's house shouting "Where's the girl? Where's the girl?" He didn't mean little Isla, did he? Why would he want to hurt our little Isla? I said I was the only one at home and he wanted to know who I was, so I told him and he grabbed me and threw me in his car. I've never seen this man in my life. What does he want with us? What's this all about?'

The explanation would have to wait. All I wanted to do then was to attempt to reassure her.

'It's going to be all right. I'm going to sort it out.'

I turned my head to say something to Thommo but the words were slammed back into my throat as my head was jolted by a backhand slap from a large flailing fist. The blow was so heavy it sent both me and Louise tumbling to the floor. I instantly tasted blood from where my bottom lip had been ripped by his knuckles as I fell, dazed, on to my back. Louise rolled out of our broken embrace and I lay helpless, exposed to the hefty boot which sank into my left side just under the rib cage. I crumpled around it, every breath of air exiting my body with the violence of the blow. The second kick, into my ribs as I turned my back, seemed like it must have broken me in two.

Louise recovered her bearings and threw herself over me, shrieking 'Stop it! Stop it!' I don't know if I would've had to take further punishment otherwise, but I'm so grateful she didn't allow the opportunity to find out. Thommo pulled back. For now. He spat out some sort of vengeful bile but I was too deep into a world of pain to be able to make out what he was saying.

I reeled as if I was being tossed by waves; trying to refill my lungs, trying not to choke on the blood running into my mouth. Louise was attempting to restrain me, calm me, and eventually I gave in to her. The storm began to subside.

Thommo glowered down at us with bulging eyes, ready for more. I'm certain he could happily have launched into a further furious assault and would not have been satisfied until all life left my body, but he held back. I had the most horrible feeling he might be back for more before long but, right then, he needed me alive and able to function.

'Phone!' he yelled, pushing an outstretched hand almost into my face. 'The bitch's number! Now!'

My hand was trembling but I managed to unzip the front of my jacket and pulled out the phone from the inside pocket. Quite what the face recognition technology thought of my distorted features I can only guess, but it allowed access all the same and I scrolled through my contacts list to 'G'.

'Here.' I offered the phone and he snatched it away.

He circled, waiting for the call to connect. Impatient, incandescent. He screamed in rage. Voicemail message. I could hear it playing out faintly, tormenting Thommo with its cheerfulness.

'You know who this is, bitch!' he bellowed after the beep. 'You and me have business to finish. You'd better get your skinny arse down here now! Kids activity place on an industrial estate on Hinkley Street. Door around the back. You'd better make it soon cos I've got your boyfriend and his missus and, if you make me wait, I'm gonna start slicing them up. You hear me?'

He hung up and cast the phone aside, sending it skidding across the concrete. As he moved further away from us, I noticed Thommo was limping heavily. As much as I would have loved to claim the smallest consolation for pain inflicted by hoping he'd hurt himself kicking me, I knew I probably wasn't the cause. Not that way, anyway. Any damage was almost certainly all down to the impact of the car at the reservoir.

Louise knelt beside me and cradled my head on her thigh, stroking my face and attempting to soothe with gentle words. Like a poorly child, I succumbed totally. As she delicately pressed the cuff of her sweat top against my split lip to try to stem the flow of blood, a red blotch spread over the blue material of her sleeve.

'I'm sorry,' I gazed up into her dark eyes. Her soft, tanned face was framed by her long wavy hair as she leaned forward, smiling kindly down on me. For a moment, the years melted away. We were back in the cheap studio apartment in Corfu. Our first holiday together. After ten months of having to plan our sex life around times when our parents were out, snatching intimate moments together like thieves in the night, we had complete freedom to share and explore each other. We were so in love. We hardly saw anything of the island that week.

'It's OK,' she said.

'But it's not OK. Look what I've got you caught up in and that's my fault. You shouldn't be involved. You don't deserve to be dragged into this. It's my mess and I'm the one who should be dealing with it, but everything has been so out of control just lately and I don't…'

She held her forefinger to her lips to quieten me.

'Shhh! Don't worry about that now. We're together again and that's all that matters.'

Even in the state I was in, those words struck me. Louise could barely stand to look at me through the unhappy final years of our marriage. She'd divorced me and put distance between us as soon as the decree absolute was rubber stamped. How traumatic could her new-found freedom have been? She'd returned to me and I'd led her straight into the teeth of a savage beast, yet she was seemingly content to accept whatever gruesome fate awaited her.

All because we were together again.

Since the initial break-up and through our time apart, I'd been forced to face the regret of losing what I'd for too long taken for granted and found the weight of that realisation too much to bear. At times, I'd have given anything to wind back the clock and try to make things better. Maybe she'd also been confronted by regret. Was that what drove her back to me after escaping her shattered dream in Mexico? Had she also come to the conclusion that we should never have allowed what we once had to wither and fade?

I stared into her eyes and wanted, with all my heart, for that to be true. I also knew I wasn't prepared to lose her again.

'We're going to get out of this,' I promised. 'Somehow, we will get out of this.'

Chapter
Twenty-Four

Was she going to show?

Setting aside the high possibility she had decided she wanted no part of further confrontation with Thommo, I realised Gina might not have even picked up the voicemail message. No doubt the number I had for her was only ever intended to be active for as long as she was running this latest leg of her con job tour of the country. Finish the sting and then disappear under the cover of a new identity, leaving no trace pointing to what she was leaving behind. The phone number would become inactive. I'd already experienced how she operated when I'd tried and failed to get hold of her after Thommo first came visiting. At least this time the call had made it as far as voicemail, but it was far from a given that she would bother listening to it.

And what if she did? Why should she put herself in the face of danger again? To save two strangers? Why on earth should she want to do that?

Gina was a pragmatist. If she heard the message, she'd weigh up the risk and decide the possible losses far outweighed the potential gains. I couldn't imagine she'd be driven instead by an obligation to accept responsibility or by a sense of honour. She certainly didn't strike me as the sentimental type.

No. As the minutes ticked on and Thommo worked himself deeper and deeper into a state of fiery agitation, I honestly began to consider this might be the end for Louise and me. We'd just got back together and now we might die. Together.

But that didn't mean I was going to roll over and take it. I'd promised Louise we were going to find a way out of this situation and I was willing to do all I could to make that happen. I just didn't know how.

All I had to protect us was the retractable knife I used for trimming carpet, which was still in my jacket pocket from the previous night. Fully extended, the blade was only about an inch long, but, at the very least, I could use it to inflict some damage before we were taken down.

I strained to rise from where I lay with my head in Louise's lap, lifting myself into a seated position. We both shuffled back to rest against the wall.

'Is this position any more comfortable for you?' she asked.

It hurt to move. I was drawing in shallow breaths through an open mouth. I tried to breathe in deeper through my nose. That hurt as well.

'Not really.'

Louise took hold of my hand. 'Just try to keep still,' she said, adding after a pause: 'Do you think she's going to come?'

I wanted to put up a positive front but I couldn't lie. 'I doubt it.'

She accepted the sombre assessment with a nod. I'm

sure she'd already worked out for herself that we were in a pretty precarious situation.

'What is this all about then, Barry? What have you got yourself mixed up in?'

'All I did was sign up with one of those online dating sites.' Even to me, that sounded an utterly feeble explanation, considering our predicament.

'Gina responded to my profile and we met up. Everything was fine, at first. Then I found out she had no interest in me at all. Actually, she was running a financial fraud and was using my name as the front for a fake company to trick investors into putting money into a crypto currency scheme that would just swallow up all their cash. Thommo here…' I gestured with a nod towards the seething mass of a man who was limping furiously at the other side of the room, '… was one of the people who were conned. He came looking for Gina and because he got it into his head I had something to do with it as well, I was caught in the crossfire.'

'Good heavens!'

'Yeah, so you see…' I patted the back of her hand, '… you're not the only one who was taken in by a swindler. It turns out we've got more in common than we realised.'

'Mr and Mrs Gullible,' she said with an ironic snort.

'Quite.'

Louise absorbed this and then asked: 'Did she try to con you out of any of your money?'

'Ha!' I laughed. 'I haven't got any money to be conned out of. No. As I said, I knew nothing about it until a few days ago, when one of the blokes she'd set up in the past spotted us together in a bar and warned me. I had it out with Gina and I thought that was the end of it, but then Thommo came looking and I had to go searching for her.'

'Good heavens!' she said again.

I felt more in tune with Louise then than I had in years. Perhaps for as long as a decade and a half. We sat quietly, almost serenely, for a while, holding hands. Maybe that's how it is when you decide all hope is lost and abandon yourself to your fate. The impending threat of excruciating agony and possible death remained in the equation, but otherwise it was quite lovely.

'Online dating,' she said. She was clearly still churning over all the new information. 'I wouldn't have had you down as the type. All those decisions!'

'I know!' I smiled. 'I probably would've stayed single forever if it'd been down to me to make the first contact, but even when she messaged me, I didn't expect it would come to anything. I suppose I knew from the start she was probably too good to be true.'

'I bet you thought all your Christmases had come at once. She's very pretty, this…'

'Gina.'

'Gina. Even if she was using you as part of her scheme, it must've been nice to have a younger, good-looking woman in your bed.'

'As a matter of fact, there was never any of that.'

'Oh!' Louise appeared surprised and, dare I hope, a little bit pleased at this revelation. I could tell she was fishing for reassurance of some sort. 'So when I called in at the house yesterday…'

'It was all for show. We were expecting Thommo at any time and that was Gina's less than subtle method of getting you out of the way. She didn't want you there when he arrived and, in fairness, that was the right decision.'

'Oh!' She considered this for a moment. 'So you never slept with her?'

'Nope.' I reckoned a night in the woods wrapped in a carpet was not what Louise meant.

'Shame.'

'Yep.'

She paused. 'I suppose I should've known.'

'What do you mean?'

'I should've twigged when she said the sex was amazing.'

I was deciding whether I should be offended when I saw the smile spread across her face. In seconds, we were shaking with suppressed giggles like two naughty kids at the back of the class. The more we tried to stop, the more out of control we became.

Thommo made it stop. I didn't see him stomp over from the other side of the room but I felt his boot connect with my hip.

'Fucking shut up!'

I groaned. Louise gasped. It wasn't funny anymore.

We didn't speak again after that. It was an unwanted reality check. We sat still, holding hands, wondering what would happen next. Wondering if Gina would show. Unexpectedly, she did.

'Lewis Douglas Thomas.'

Three heads turned towards the fire exit door at the sound of a small female voice. She strolled into the room as if she owned the place. She had changed into a burgundy blazer with the sleeves turned up over a white scoop neck shirt and was carrying a white handbag. She looked sensational, to be honest. Out of place, but sensational. Like she was on her way to meet up with a few girlfriends for drinks but had been persuaded to stop off and deal with the boring inconvenience of a violent lunatic. If she was scared, she was making a real effort not to show it.

'A very interesting email had arrived for me this morning when I fired up my laptop. I thought at the time I might not need it because I believed we'd dealt with this particular problem, but I'm glad to have it now.' She stopped, around five metres from Thommo. Her eyes were fixed on his. 'You see, I like to make sure I know everything about the people who make it their business to interfere in my life, so while Barry was having his long lie-in at home yesterday morning, I decided to put out a few feelers for information about Lewis Douglas Thomas, aged thirty-six, of number two-one-six Epton Terrace in Skelmersdale. Those are the details you used on the application to invest in my crypto scheme, aren't they?'

Thommo was totally bemused. In truth, he was in good company.

'In and out of Secure Training Centres and Young Offender Institutions from the age of eleven, three spells in prison after that for a variety of loathsome offences such as assault causing actual bodily harm, burglary, the possession and supply of drugs and so on and so on. Nothing especially surprising there, but what did surprise me was to learn that you avoided a quite lengthy spell of detention at His Majesty's pleasure by providing the police with information which led to the arrest of three other undesirables. Were they former friends or enemies, Lewis? Do you mind if I call you Lewis? Do they know it was you who dropped them in it? I understand not very nice things can happen to people who cooperate with the authorities to stitch up other felons. Is that right?'

'Shut it! You're lying! Fucking shut it!'

Thommo's face practically matched the colour of her jacket. From the waistband at the back of his jeans, he whipped out a handgun and pointed it at Gina's head. Both Louise and I recoiled, grabbing tightly on to each other. Gina didn't even flinch.

'Put it down. You're not going to do anything to hurt me. You're not going to hurt anyone and I'll tell you why. After your call, I decided to put some insurance in place, so while I was waiting for the taxi, I wrote out a note saying that if any harm came to me, Barry or Louise, you were the one to blame. I said you were trying to extort money from us because you held us responsible for a failed investment.'

'You *stole* it!' roared Thommo, indignantly.

She ignored him. 'To help prove it was you, I've collected an interesting couple of bits of audio. The first I made at Barry's house, when I very generously offered to split the loss incurred in the said failed investment only for you to reject the offer, demand repayment in full with an extra ten grand a month and, if I remember rightly, threaten to kill everybody, including Barry's three-year-old granddaughter in an arson attack. The second is your voice message from this morning, when you again made some very crude threats. I'm sure the police will have no trouble finding DNA evidence all over Barry's house and in this place. The taxi driver will corroborate that he brought me here. I tipped him well enough. I've downloaded the two clips onto a flash drive and left it, with the note, in an envelope for the manager at my hotel, with the instruction that if he doesn't hear from me in twenty-four hours, he's to pass it on to the police.'

'You don't scare me. If they don't find bodies, they've

got nothing.'

Gina nodded. 'You could be right, but I do have a back-up plan. I've also sent an email to a trusted associate which details how information you gave to the police led directly to the conviction of three members of a notorious Manchester gang for armed robbery and the murder of a security guard. Similar kind of arrangement. If he doesn't hear from me in twenty-four hours, he's to pass on the information to connections in Manchester who, I'm sure, will be very interested in learning the name of the informant. I doubt they're quite as diligent as the police in their need for evidence before exacting their brand of justice.'

The gun was still aimed at Gina's head but Thommo's hand was now trembling. She had him and he knew it.

'So that's why, Lewis, you're not going to hurt anybody. You're going to let these two good people go, you're going to get into your car and you're going to drive back to your little shithole town where you can carry on pretending to be the main man. If you don't, the best you can hope for is that the police pick you up first, but I doubt even your friends on the force can keep you safe for very long once word about your deal with the cops reaches the right ears. Either way, Lewis, you harm us and you're dead.'

She leaned defiantly closer to the barrel of the gun.

'So dead.'

Thommo did not move, almost as if he couldn't move. The wise option would have been to listen to the advice, accept the loss and leave, but he didn't strike me as the type who took advice. From his point of view, to go would have been to lose too much face. He was floundering to try to find a better alternative, a way of wrestling back the upper hand.

'You're lying!'

'Try me.'

He snorted down his nose like a wild bull straining at its tether. 'You think you're so smart, don't you?'

'Huh!' Gina contemptuously looked him up and down. 'Believe me, it doesn't take much to outsmart you.'

'Somebody should've taught you to watch that mouth of yours.' The tremor in his voice betrayed the strain he was under. 'It's gonna get you in big trouble.'

'Nobody gets to tell me what I should do and what I shouldn't say.' I saw the flames ignite in her eyes. I reckon the days when she had allowed herself to be controlled were too recent, still too painful, and she was never going to let that happen again. She should still have let it go this time, but I guess she'd had enough of biting her lip.

'You think you can teach me how, big man? Put me in my place? Keep me in order? Men like you think you can bludgeon your way to whatever you want, just because you fancy yourself to be a hard case, but you're pathetic. You'll never rise above the streets because to succeed in this world you've got to be smart. You're not smart. You're a small-time thug and the only way you'll ever be useful is as muscle to enforce the will of others. On your own, you'll bully and exploit the weak and the desperate but only for as long as you're allowed to exist. When those who hold the real power decide it suits them to move in and take over, they'll wipe you off the face of the earth like you're shit on their shoe. You strut around like you're everything, but you're nothing. You're a petty crook, a hooligan. You're a blunt instrument.'

I winced as I listened to Gina tearing into Thommo. Not because I was sorry for him. Christ, no. Not even remotely. It was too much. She'd got the win. She'd saved the day and for that I would be eternally grateful, but having trapped the tiger there was no need to pelt it with stones. She was brave beyond belief but was pushing it too far.

Thommo cracked. He lunged at Gina with a swinging right arm and the butt of the pistol grip caught her on the left temple. She didn't have time to react. She buckled and twisted, out cold before she hit the floor.

He towered over her limp, unmoving body.

'That blunt enough for you, bitch?'

Chapter
Twenty-Five

Louise shot quickly to her feet and scurried to where Gina had fallen. As might be expected from someone who had spent just about all their working life tending patients in hospitals, she stepped straight into nurse mode. It took me longer to rise and cover the short distance because I wasn't moving too easily after wearing a few kicks, but I was just as concerned as Louise plainly was. Gina had taken a fearsome blow.

'She seems to be breathing OK,' said Louise, her head tilted close to Gina's mouth, listening. 'No obstructions, as far as I can tell. Can you hear me, Gina? Can you open your eyes?'

Nothing. She was out cold. I was just so relieved she was still breathing. I feared the worst when I saw her crumple to the concrete floor and hit it so heavily. Gina was on her right side, her right arm reaching out awkwardly behind her and her left foot seemingly stuck under her right leg. Of all the things, I was worried she might be uncomfortable lying in such a posture.

'Do you need me to help you move her or anything?'

You feel so useless in situations like that. Thank goodness Louise knew what she was doing.

'We have to keep her still in case she's got a serious neck or head injury. We need to keep her warm as well.'

Louise started to peel off her sweat top but she only had a bra on underneath. That didn't seem right. I stopped her pulling it over her head by holding out my hand.

'Here,' I said. 'Use my jacket instead.'

She pulled her top back down and I took off my jacket. Before handing it over, I remembered the retractable knife and transferred it stealthily into my jeans pocket. It wasn't exactly the deadliest of weapons, but having it with me provided a tiny bit of reassurance.

'We have to call for an ambulance,' she shouted across the empty room. Thommo was on the other side of it, hobbling and cursing to himself. I'm not certain he was the type to ever regret allowing his temper to get the better of him, but maybe this was as close as he could come to that. I'm sure he realised, the second the pistol grip butt connected with Gina's temple, that it wasn't the smartest move. She had threatened to unleash the forces of the law and the lawless on his head unless we three were all able to walk away safe and sound from that building and now the only person who could call off the hounds was lying flat out, unconscious, on the floor. That was a problem for him.

'No ambulance! No ambulance!' he roared.

'She could have a fractured skull. She could be bleeding on her brain.' Louise was desperately trying to make him realise the gravity of the situation but she wasn't getting through.

'She shouldn't have talked to me like that. She should've watched her mouth. No ambulance!'

'Think about it, man!' I was angry. If Louise said Gina needed urgent care, she needed urgent care and I had to try all I could to get it for her. I saw my phone where it had been flung aside, only twelve metres or so away on the floor, but to try to reach it would have been too much of a risk. Thommo was the one still calling the shots. And holding the gun to shoot them with.

'She might die unless we get her to a hospital and if she dies, where does that leave you? The letter to the police and the message to the gangs will be sent out unless Gina says otherwise in less than twenty-four hours. You'll be a marked man. There'll be nowhere for you to hide. You need Gina if you want to stay alive.'

'Shut up!' he yelled, pointing the gun shakily in my direction. I backed off and raised my hands in submission. 'I need time to think. She shouldn't have talked to me like that.'

I could come up with nothing more to do or say without antagonising him further. Louise crouched next to Gina, watching closely for any change, lightly holding her hand.

'This is bad, Barry. I can't do anything more for her. We need to get her to a hospital as soon as possible.'

Much as I appreciated the urgency, I was powerless. 'I don't fancy our chances of trying to rush him, even two against one – and even if he didn't have a gun. If only I could get to my phone, but it's too far away to try it without him noticing. I'm guessing you've not got your phone either.'

She shook her head. 'He took it when he first brought me here.'

All three of us were at the mercy of a maniac with a weapon. A maniac who had totally lost his grip and didn't have the nous to figure out what to do next. Our outlook –

and particularly Gina's – was dire.

'Thommo, please! Just let us go so we can get Gina the medical attention she needs. I promise if you do we'll not mention any of this to the police.'

I wasn't sure how I might deliver on that promise, but I was willing to say anything. He was a man desperately in need of a way out of a predicament that would destroy him. Any lifeline offered might be grasped.

'No, no, no, no!' he said, shaking his head frantically. 'I don't trust nobody. You'll blab and then… No, no, no!'

He started tapping the butt of the gun handle against his own skull, as if that might help jolt a solution to the surface. It kind of did. But it wasn't an ideal one from our perspective.

'You two! Get away from her. Go over there.'

He pointed the gun towards us and flicked his head towards a far corner of the room. We were reluctant to comply, of course, but he sort of insisted.

'Move!' he yelled.

Louise started with fright. I held out a hand to help her to her feet and then pulled her close as we shuffled towards where we were being sent. Thommo kept us in his sights all the way.

'She's coming with me.' He gestured towards Gina's still body. 'When she wakes up, I'll make her call off her people and then…'

'But she might not wake up unless…' pleaded Louise.

'Shut up!' The gun was jabbed in our direction again. I squeezed Louise gently, hoping to convey in it that any attempt to reason with him at this stage might not go down too well. I'm sure she'd probably worked that out for herself as well.

'I'll make her call off her people. Tell them not to send out the stuff. I'll make her do it. If she doesn't, I'll, I'll…'

He had to think some more before figuring out the next bit.

'I'll make her watch while I chop pieces off her boyfriend. You're coming with me as well.'

Louise let out a stifled yelp of horror. I'm sure every drop of blood must have drained from my face. Obviously, no part of this intended plan appealed to me in the slightest, but the fact that it only involved me and Gina was something.

'Only if you let Louise go. I'll only go with you if she can walk away.'

'Fuck off!' he snarled.

Louise grabbed my arm. 'Barry, no!'

I touched her hand, hoping to assure her I knew what I was doing. I wasn't certain I did, to be honest.

'This has had nothing to do with her all along. You'll have me and Gina. We're the ones you have a grievance with. Louise hasn't done anything to you. Let her go.'

For the smallest of fragments of moments, I thought he might be seriously considering the suggestion. Then again, it might just have been because he took longer to process than most.

'Nah!' he said. 'She's seen too much. She can't be trusted. She has to be silenced.'

He slowly raised the gun and wheeled his aim directly at Louise. She screamed and recoiled. I froze. It was like being trapped behind a window while a heavy object was about to topple onto an unknowing victim's head but, this time, I was able to smash through the barrier in time.

I stepped into the line of fire. 'I won't let you do that.'

A sneer spread across his face.

'Out of the way, lover boy. Don't think I won't waste you as well.'

I stepped slowly closer to the muzzle of the gun.

'You don't want to do that. Shoot me and you've lost your power to make Gina do what you want her to. The only way this ends with you not being hunted down and killed is if you let Louise go.'

Oddly, a strange calm had enveloped me. I should've been absolutely shitting myself and just about every time I've thought back to that incident since I have come close to needing a change of underwear but, in the moment, I was utterly at peace. I even had the cool presence of mind to slip my hand into my jeans pocket and subtly, silently, slide the blade of the retractable knife out to its full extent.

I was ready for a fight.

With every small step I drew closer and closer to the small black hole at the end of the hand-held weapon, knowing my life could so easily have ended there and then with a gentle increase in pressure on the trigger and the flash of a small explosion as the firing pin struck the percussion cap and ignited the propellant. That easily. Yet I wasn't afraid. I edged to little more than a couple of feet away and stopped. The gun was angled straight at the middle of my forehead. Neither of us moved.

A groan.

Gina. It was the first sound she had made since being hit. Though it was such a small noise, it was amplified by the tension of the stand-off. My eyes darted towards the source of it. Thommo jerked his head around to see.

An opportunity. I whipped out my hand from my pocket, gripping the knife, and jabbed the blade with all the power I could muster into the muscle of Thommo's extended gun-holding arm. It sliced as deep as it could go into the flesh of his forearm, midway between the wrist and elbow.

He screamed with pain and surprise. In reflex, he pulled the trigger but the bullet, as his arm was diverted down and away by the force of my stabbing motion, pinged off the concrete floor and ricocheted harmlessly into the high roof. I lost my hold on the knife but so, too, did he relinquish his grip on the gun. It dropped to the floor as he grabbed his injured right arm with his left hand. Quickly, I kicked the weapon away from us, as far as I could, sending it spinning towards the far wall.

'Run!' I shouted, turning to Louise.

She was jolted into action, sprinting towards me and the door. I barged with everything I had into Thommo who, disorientated by the sudden agony and caught off-balance, tumbled over. It was our chance to get away.

Louise, unhampered by the after-effects of Thommo's boot, was soon up with and past me in the race for the door. Out of the corner of my eye I saw Gina, who was motionless and silent again, and I wanted to try to scoop her up and try to get her to safety as well, but I glanced back to see Thommo, on his feet and scrambling over to retrieve the gun. There was no time. If I'd stopped to try to rescue Gina, we'd both have been easy targets. I carried on, as fast as I could, towards the exit.

The first bullet thumped into the wall far too close to my right ear, though in reality it probably missed by quite a margin. It didn't seem that way at the time and I almost stumbled as I ducked instinctively. The next bullet was no better directed – thankfully, from my point of view – and then I was outside. I heard the crack of two more shots, one of which fizzed through the open doorway, a second or so after I made it through. It ripped into the dense hedges bordering that end of the industrial park.

Louise was holding back, waiting for me. She had run left out of the door and was almost at the corner of the building.

'Come on!' she called in panic. The adrenaline rush of being shot at had done wonders for easing the pain in my aching ribs and I set off at full pelt to catch up, all the time dreading the sound of more bullets being fired my way. I reached the corner without having to dodge any and carried on running, past the stark coloured signage of the boarded-up entrance and towards where Louise had dipped behind the temporary shelter of a metal skip.

We crouched, wide-eyed and gasping for breath, leaning against its side. I, for one, wasn't in any kind of shape to handle any burst of physical exertion, but it's amazing what you can rise to when the incentive is there. I dared to poke my head above the top of the skip. I could see both sides of the building. There was no sign of Thommo coming after us, which was obviously a good thing.

'Jesus!' I rasped, bending with my hands on my knees.

'We need to get help,' said Louise between gulps of air. 'Gina's still in there.'

I nodded and looked around us, beyond our little corner of the industrial park. I hadn't noticed activity at any of the other units as I drove in and could see none now. Doesn't anybody else work on Saturdays these days?

'You're right. There's a main road not far from here. You head there and find somebody who can call the police. I'll try to stop him driving away with her.'

Louise didn't appear to have full confidence in the strategy. 'How are you going to do that?'

'I don't know.' I wished I'd held on to the knife after I stuck it in Thommo's arm. I could've used it to slash his tyres. I thought there might be some broken glass or whatever down there to do the job instead. 'I'll figure it out.'

'OK.' She still didn't sound certain, but we both knew allowing him to get away would probably mean curtains for Gina. Louise suddenly grabbed me and planted the biggest smacker on my lips. It took me by surprise, to be honest. It was a nice surprise, though.

I grinned at her in what I hoped was a non-dopey, grateful, steeled-for-action way.

'Let's go,' I said.

'Be careful,' she replied.

'You, too.'

I left the comforting shelter of the skip and crept back towards the Krazy Kangaroo Kidz Kingdom.

Chapter
Twenty-Six

Remember those slasher horror films of the seventies and eighties? The ones where a homicidal axe-wielding maniac or a flesh-eating monster from another dimension would wreak mayhem on a small, sleepy community?

Inevitably, there would be one scene where a minor character, often an attractive young woman, would be alone in the house and would hear mysterious noises coming from the long-abandoned attic or the dingy, creepy basement. Naturally, they would think it was a good idea to investigate and this would make you want to shout at the screen: 'Don't do it! Haven't you heard there's a homicidal axe-wielding maniac or a flesh-eating monster from another dimension on the loose and it's already massacred half of the neighbourhood? Just get out of the house and run as fast and as far away as you can!'

But no. They decide to take a look anyway, armed only with something hopelessly inadequate, like a small kitchen knife or a rolled-up newspaper. Guess what? They soon come to a very messy end and you think: 'Do you know what, pal, if you're going to do something that daft you deserve everything you get. You're your own worst enemy.'

If somebody had been looking down on me as I stalked tentatively, like an aging commando, back towards the Krazy Kangaroo Kidz Kingdom, they might have been saying similar things.

'What are you doing, going back there? You only just escaped by the skin of your teeth and now you're going to give him another chance to get you? You want your head examining.'

Well, they would probably have had a point, but I knew I couldn't just walk away without at least *trying* to save Gina from whatever nastiness Thommo had in mind for her. I might not have owed her a thing, because it was true that if she hadn't scammed her way into my life, exploiting my good name and trusting nature, then none of the bad stuff would have happened. I'd have carried on with my ordinary, hazard-free existence and Thommo the oversized nutcase would still have been conducting his personal mini-crimewave in Skelmersdale.

But we'd been through stuff together, Gina and I, and that sort of shared experience creates a bond. That was it. We'd been bound together, unwillingly, by being made to deal with a crisis neither of us expected to face and you can't just ignore that kind of connection. After all, Gina didn't have to go to the Krazy Kangaroo to try to get Louise and myself off the hook, but she did — and that was because she knew we shared that bond, too. I had to do the same for her.

She wasn't a bad woman. She had her faults, but she wasn't evil. She didn't deserve to be left to the mercy of that psycho.

It wasn't as if I intended taking him on, anyway. All I wanted to do was stop him driving her away. Find a way of delaying him long enough for Louise to alert the police and for them to descend on the industrial park to save the day. It wasn't in my thoughts to play the hero – and neither was I going to allow myself to become the hapless victim who stumbled towards a bloody oblivion.

It was something I had to do, that's all.

I made it back to the far corner of the building without encountering Thommo coming at me from the opposite direction and that was a bonus. I peeked warily around the edge of the wall towards the fire exit door I had darted through only a few minutes before. Both cars were still there – my battered little red Mazda2 and, closer to me, his stolen silver SUV. There was no sign of him. Or her.

I had a look around to see if there was anything useful as a tyre-puncturing aid. Nothing obvious came into view. It occurred to me only then that if I'd taken a second to have a rummage through the contents of the skip I'd hidden behind there might have been something I could use, but it was a bit late to realise that then and I wasn't turning back.

A noise. The heavy fire escape door was creaking wider open. I leaned sideways as far as I dared to be able to check out what was going on and saw, through one eye, Thommo emerging from the doorway. In his arms was Gina, limp and compliant like a very well-dressed rag doll. He carried her towards the back of the SUV and, balancing his load to free a hand, opened the tailgate. He tossed her inside like she was a bag of rubbish and slammed down the door. Clearly, even if he appreciated how badly Gina might be hurt, he didn't care. That made me cross again. He hobbled back across the asphalted parking area and into the building.

Maybe he'd decided that, rather than chase after Louise and me, it was better for him to get Gina in the car and get away from Sheffield as soon as possible, before the police could arrive. My window of opportunity was closing. I didn't have anything to hand to burst a tyre or two and there was no time to let them down by sticking a twig in the valve, like we used to do sometimes when we were kids. I had to quickly come up with an alternative plan.

As I saw it then, I had one chance. I could make a mad dash across the car park, hope the tailgate door didn't lock automatically when it was shut, open it, grab Gina, close it and run. Hopefully, I could be out of view by the time Thommo stepped back out, climbed into the driver's seat believing Gina was still safely stored away in the back, and then drove off. If I could make a mental note of the registration number as he went, the police would be able to pick him up soon enough and, most importantly, we could get Gina to a hospital for the treatment she needed.

Without much opportunity for my usual dithering, it was as good a strategy as I could come up with. I set off. My side and hip had stiffened up again after the earlier bullet-induced burst of adrenaline, but I was still moving fairly freely.

I reached the back of the SUV and pressed the door catch. It rose open with a hiss of pneumatic air. Gina appeared so peaceful that you might have thought she'd just fallen asleep, but, for whatever reason, she was bound around the ankles and wrists with thick grey tape. A strip of it had also been stuck over her mouth. Perhaps he reckoned she might regain consciousness at any time and he didn't want to risk her screaming blue murder when they pulled up next to a police car at traffic lights, or something like that. It seemed excessive to me. She looked so tiny and defenceless. I reached out to pick her up.

Just then, I was alerted by the noise of something metallic being dropped on a hard floor, followed by the sound of an irritated man cursing 'bollocks'. It seemed to me to have come from just the other side of the fire escape door. He was heading back!

I was caught in no-man's-land. If I made a bolt for it, carrying Gina, I would almost certainly not be out of sight by the time Thommo stepped back into the daylight and either he'd catch us easily or shoot us. Presumably, the gun was the something metallic I'd heard him drop. If I stood there, like a cat on the kitchen worktop about to take a nibble out of the Sunday roast joint, he would either shoot me right there, or he would catch me, beat me up, chop bits off me and then shoot me. I didn't fancy any of those potential scenarios.

I panicked. I jumped into the back of the SUV and pulled the tailgate door shut.

It's all right saying now that wasn't the wisest move. It was the only thing I could think to do.

The first possible new danger I'd left myself open to came to mind almost as soon as the door clicked shut behind me. What if Thommo was bringing something else out of the building that he wanted to put in the back?

I held my breath. I could hear his heavy footsteps approaching but they passed in front of the car, not behind it. They stopped at the driver's side front door. A rush of air and background noise entered the cabin of the vehicle as the door was opened and he settled, with a grunt, into the seat.

Relief! I exhaled long and slow through my mouth. But then he started the engine and I realised I was far from out of peril. I was trapped in the back of a car and Christ knows where we would be heading. I tried to open the door. Maybe it wasn't too late to jump out before we started moving and run for all I was worth before he could react.

So much for that idea. Is it even possible to open those doors from the inside? If it is, I'm buggered if I could work out how. I don't suppose the need crops up all that often, but you'd think the manufacturers would build in a release button, just in case, wouldn't you?

The car began to pull away. I could hear no police sirens racing to cut off his escape route. I could only settle down for the ride and see where it led.

At least I had company. Sort of. It was very cramped in the back for two people, but Gina was only petite and, unfortunately, she was in no state to complain.

I turned on to my side to face her and, in the almost total darkness of our confines, tried to assess how she was doing. She lay on her back. I shuffled to place my left ear close to her nose, as I had seen Louise do earlier, and could hear her breathing; feel the lightness of it on my cheek. Number one on the priority list had been ticked.

Maybe I could make it easier for her to breathe if I took the grey tape from her mouth. I wanted to do that anyway because I didn't like seeing her trussed up like an Easter turkey, so I began to peel it off. Carefully, carefully, in case a sudden jerking tear provoked a reflex yelp of pain and gave Thommo cause to pull up to see what the cause of it had been. She didn't stir at all as I eased away the final strands of the adhesive tape and screwed it into a ball. I started to pick at the edges of the tape securing her wrists together and then, with greater difficulty because of lack of room to move, from her ankles. It was all I could do for her at that time. A shred of dignity restored. But I was so conscious that, with every minute that ticked by, potentially irreparable damage was being suffered inside her head and there was nothing I could do about that.

Above us, only a thin fibreglass parcel shelf divided our hiding place from the car cabin. I pushed at it lightly, to see if it moved. It was held in place by two plastic pins which slotted into housings fixed to the inside of the boot. I reckoned I'd be able to push the pins out of the housings easily enough. That struck me as a possible route to freedom. Perhaps if Thommo stopped on the way to wherever we were heading – to get a coffee from the services or have a wee or something – I could wait until he was far enough away from the car, then burst through the parcel shelf, clamber over the back seat, out of the rear door, back to the tailgate to rescue Gina and run off to raise the alarm. The thought restored my hopes of getting out of there without detection and lifted my spirits. It's surprising how quickly you start to see the world through the eyes of an escaping prisoner of war.

Until then, the thin divide meant I could hear everything that was going on in the cabin. Thommo was quiet, at first. I imagine he was still aware that the police could soon arrive to thwart his getaway. No such luck. After ten minutes or so, his increasing confidence manifested in his swearing at fellow road-users. I distinctly made out an instruction to 'get out of my fucking way' followed by a 'yeah, fuck you as well, dickhead'. By then, we appeared to be travelling faster, as if we'd hit a dual carriageway. All the time moving further and further from the relative security of familiar ground.

I didn't mind the swearing. I much preferred it to the rap metal he decided to have blaring through the sound system speakers at top volume. I've never been a fan of rap metal. I'm even less of one now, and as the miles and the minutes ticked over with no sign of him slowing to take a comfort break, the journey became less and less comfortable with every bump in the road for me laying in the back.

Attempting to restore circulation to parts of me that were being starved of blood flow, I stretched my legs and felt my foot sink into something soft. I managed, with some effort, to twist and reach whatever it was, apologising to Gina for accidently pressing my knee into the side of her thigh. It was a rolled up exercise mat. The type people use when they do yoga and stuff. It probably belonged to whoever Thommo stole the car from. I dragged it back with me and used it as a cushion, to try to make Gina more comfortable.

What if there was something else in the back I could make use of? A tyre iron or a heavy-duty tool of some other sort that could be employed as a weapon, if needed? I hadn't thought to find out what was on the other side of where Gina lay. Perhaps her white handbag, the one I'd seen on her arm at the empty activity place, had also been tossed into the back. It might have her phone in it.

I manoeuvred myself over her body, trying as much as I could not to press down on her. It was hard work in an increasingly breathless space and I was starting to sweat. Thankfully, any noise I made was easily drowned out by the rap metal. Down by her left knee, I touched a bag. It wasn't hard, like a handbag, but made of softer material. Like a holdall. I pulled it to my side of Gina and fumbled for the zip to open it.

Inside, I could feel clothing, silky to the touch like exercise gear. It was exercise gear. It was an exercise bag. Made sense, in view of the earlier discovery of the exercise mat. Not much use to me, though.

But then I delved deeper. I found stuff that I figured out could well come in useful.

Chapter
Twenty-Seven

Nearly two and a half hours I was in the back of that car. Nearly two and a half hours!

Until you, too, have spent that long – and I wouldn't recommend you try – sharing a space which is a little over a metre wide by less than a metre deep with another human being, a space which has practically no ventilation on a warm day and no padding beneath to absorb the many bumps and potholes of the road, where you are constantly buffeted from end to end with every turn of the steering wheel and from side to side by every harsh braking followed by rapid acceleration, all accompanied by top-volume heavy metal and hip-hop fusion music which is made even more intolerable (if such a thing is possible) by the driver's hopelessly tuneless attempt at singing, then you have no idea how uncomfortable an experience that can be.

Very, let me tell you.

Thommo showed no inclination to stop for a break, so there was no chance of attempting an escape through the parcel shelf. I could only grit my teeth and try to roll with every movement of the car as best I could, as if I was the passenger on one of those high-speed sidecar racing bikes.

All the while I was also trying to protect Gina from being jolted around and I suppose, in that respect, it's a good job I was in there with her. The last thing she needed was for her unconscious body to take more blows, especially to the head.

She was out of it for practically the whole long journey. Once or twice I saw her eyes flutter briefly as if she was coming awake and I heard her mutter something at one stage. It sounded a bit like 'frayed nipples' but I might have got that wrong. I was very concerned for her. I'm no doctor, but I knew being unconscious for all that time was not good and that the boot of a speeding car was not an ideal place for her to be.

For both our sakes – but especially for Gina's – we had to get out of there. The big problem was that the only person likely to release us from our captivity was the person who intended to inflict far worse pain and suffering on us.

The odds of us escaping unharmed were slim to negligible – but we might have one chance. I had a plan.

After a long stretch of straight and mercifully smooth motoring at a higher speed, which I assumed meant we were on the motorway, the car slowed to a crawl before a longer, sustained right turn. A queue of traffic before a roundabout, maybe. I guessed we might be nearing the end of our journey.

As to our final destination, I wasn't even thinking about that. I'd assumed all along it would be Skelmersdale. Thommo was, I reckoned, heading back to home ground to execute (an unfortunate choice of word, I know) the next phase of his plan, starting with trying to coax Gina out of her shut-down state. He needed her to send word to the two people who were on stand-by, preventing them from releasing information to the police and to a Manchester gang that, if it got out, would put Thommo in the firing line from both sides of the law. I shuddered to think what lengths he would go to in order to make Gina comply.

But I wasn't going to let him hurt her any more. Not if I could help it.

We slowed right down; short bursts of straights followed by a series of right and left turns. Two more rights in quick succession and I heard him pull on the handbrake then turn off the engine. Wherever it was, we had arrived.

Thommo opened the driver's door and slammed it behind him. The sudden relief from car noise and loud music was welcome, but I was in too much of a high state of nervous excitement to appreciate it. The blood pounded in my temples. I crouched, ready.

He didn't come to lift the tailgate door straight away, adding another level to my spiralling anxiety. I still couldn't see a thing outside my claustrophobic prison for two, but I didn't think we were now in an indoor space, like a garage or whatever. I certainly hoped we weren't.

Footsteps were approaching. The steps moved closer and closer. This was it. A click released the door from its catch and it began to rise, steadily, gradually revealing the form of a large man, from thigh to midriff to chest. But before it reached his eyeline, I sprang from my cramped confines. Surprise was on my side.

In my left hand was the can of deodorant spray I'd found in the exercise bag in the boot. Before he could react or fully comprehend what was going on, I leapt at Thommo and pressed hard on the nozzle, spraying straight into his eyes from very close range.

Thank goodness it wasn't one of those aerosols that releases its contents in a gentle mist. That might have made him smell nicer but wouldn't have given me what I needed, which was to temporarily blind and disorientate him. This one dispensed with all the force I hoped for. He yelped and recoiled, raising his right forearm to his face to protect himself. Not quickly enough. The spray was already burning his eyeballs.

In my right hand I had the half-kilogramme hand weights I'd also found in the bag. One was clutched in my palm for ballast. The other was strapped around my knuckles, for impact. I swung my arm for all I was worth and hit, with a satisfying loud crack of bone, the exposed left side of his jaw.

It silenced his reaction to the stinging pain in his eyes. His knees collapsed. His once imposing frame buckled and crumpled to the ground. I didn't dare to think I'd done enough to disable him for very long. All I wanted was to buy precious seconds to scoop Gina out of the back of the car and get as far away from there as possible.

I gripped her tight to my chest, one arm around her back and the other under her thighs, and willed my legs to find the power to propel me quickly away, which was not easy when your mobility is limited by the stiffness of two-and-a-half hours in an enclosed space.

As I attempted to run, I tried to assess our surroundings. We were on a long narrow driveway separating the back yards of two rows of two-storey terraced houses. The loose ground was pitted and uneven, making progress more difficult, but I was heading for the opening into a road, around fifty metres ahead. The distance hardly seemed to be closing, no matter how fast I tried to make myself move. It was like being stuck in a panic dream.

Gina was by no means a heavy woman but weighed enough to make it decidedly trickier for a desperately out-of-shape fifty-seven-year-old to make his getaway. Already, I was gasping for breath – a combination of my lack of fitness and the extra burden – but I could not stop.

Bang!

The bullet pinged into the concrete fence to my left and caused my heart to leap into my mouth. I was no more than a stride or two from the end of the driveway.

Bang! Bang!

Both were aimed too high this time. I heard them whoosh harmlessly into the emptiness above another long driveway which mirrored the one I'd just run down, between two more rows of terraces on the other side of the road.

Surely, someone in one of these houses heard the shots and was just about to alert the police. I couldn't imagine there was any place this side of Los Angeles where the sound of gunfire was so commonplace that it didn't raise an alarm.

I couldn't stop, though. I certainly wasn't about to turn to see how far Thommo was behind me either.

I turned on to the road, fighting the burning tightness of rapid fatigue in my leg muscles and my swirling light-headedness. Up ahead was another road. Options were right, left or straight ahead. I chose left and waddled along until, thirty metres on, I could run no more. On top of everything else, I had stabbing pains in my back from where I had been kicked in the ribs, making it agony to draw the deep breaths I needed. I dipped behind the back of a parked blue car and set Gina down as carefully as I could on the ground. I needed the relief of a break, but it was a risk. Thommo was after us.

Through the windows of the car I could see the four-way junction we'd just come from. No sign of him, at first, but then… He stopped, head darting in each direction searching for us, holding the pistol at shoulder height. I tried all I could to suppress the wheezing sound of my panting breaths, just in case he could pick up the sound, though he would have needed ears like a bat's to hear me from that far away.

He didn't know which way to go. With every fibre of my soul I was desperately imploring him to go right, go straight on – but please don't go left! If he did, we were surely done for. The inward debate raged within him for torturous seconds before he made his choice.

Right.

I wanted to shout with joy. I settled instead for watching him moving awkwardly away, precious small distances further from us with every step. Thank goodness for his bad selection and thank goodness for the damage to his hip he suffered when we knocked him over with the car at the reservoir. If he hadn't still been seriously hampered, he might have been quick enough off the mark to see which way we went.

I watched him hobble further along, twitching his head from side to side to check out every potential glimpse of his escaping prey, until there were seventy, eighty metres between us. I had to move. He could double back on himself at any time, once he realised he had chosen the wrong direction. The advantage I already had could've been the best I would get. My recovery had been brief but just enough to replenish energy levels. Enough to pick Gina up and get ready to go again. I had to find a haven. Settling in a hiding place might not be safe enough. I had to get someplace where there were lots of people. He wouldn't dare pursue us then.

Further down the road, not far, was a turning on the left. I decided my best option was to head down there. With luck, I could be around the corner and out of sight before Thommo saw us break cover.

Clutching Gina tightly, I made my bid. The junction was only a few steps away when she suddenly gasped, her eyes springing wide open. The surprise caused me to stumble. I almost fell forward and by the time I'd regained my balance, I was perilously close to toppling off the kerb, onto the side road.

A car was making a turn on to it, going much too fast. There was a young guy behind the wheel, hunched intensely like he was on a speed lap at Silverstone. He blasted his horn and howled at me through the open window.

'Watch where you're fucking going!'

No concern for the clearly stricken woman I was struggling to carry or acknowledgement of my obvious state of emotional distress. No 'Are you all right, mate? Can I help?' He just revved his tatty Vauxhall Corsa to within an inch of its life and sped off. What's wrong with people these days?

Anyway, I had more pressing concerns then than declining standards of common courtesy. I turned to see a large figure lumbering towards us. We'd been rumbled.

Gina, after her momentary awakening, was out of it again. I carried her across the road, aiming for the junction with another road which met the one I was now on. I figured the more diversions I could take, the more we could stay out of view and the more chance we had of losing our stalker. My fear was the next turn might prove to be a dead end – a term which could take on a whole new meaning if we were trapped down one.

It wasn't. It was much better than that. My hopes soared.

At the end of that narrow street of neat red brick terraced houses, beckoning to us like a shining beacon offering comfort and salvation, was the entrance to a supermarket. A really big supermarket. Cars were driving in and out from the car park. Pedestrians were hauling away heavy bags or were on their way to fill empty ones with their weekly provisions. It was the most commonplace scene, yet the most glorious sight.

A fair stretch of street still separated us from liberty but I tore towards it with every scrap of speed I could muster. I was renewed, a surge of second wind pouring strength into weakened limbs with every pounding step. I've never been into doing marathons and stuff like that, but it was how I imagine it feels when the 26-mile marker and the finish line looms into view.

The yellow circle set in a blue square of the shop sign above the main doors of the store drew me ever closer, encouraging one final spurt of finishing power to set the seal on a medal-winning performance. Who knew how close my nearest challenger now was? I only had eyes on glory. Fifty metres, forty-five, forty metres to go.

There was one last obstacle. A busy main road ran between me and the car park entrance. Of course I wasn't even going to break stride. A white van screeched to a halt just in time as I vaulted the kerb and a distracted green hatchback almost ploughed into the back of a bemused red family saloon as I crossed the other side of the carriageway, but I made it. I was almost there.

I shouted breathlessly, as loud as I could, as soon as I was close enough for people to hear.

'Call – police – please – man – gun – coming – after us – please.'

There were so many folks about, as you might expect at a big supermarket on a Saturday afternoon. Most of them just stopped and gawped, but then I suppose we must've been quite a sight. One or two drew their children closer, as if we were the dangerous ones. I didn't wait around to see who might be the first to actually take action and do as I was pleading for them to do. The doors were so close. Once I was inside, I believed we would truly be safe.

A bloke in a white shirt and black tie stood cross-armed beside the main doors, watching the lumbering progress towards him of a sweaty old guy carrying a floppy woman. I was guessing he must've been security.

'Police – call – gun – hurry!'

For a moment, I thought he was going to try to tackle us, to stop us entering his store, but then I saw his eyes widen as he stared over my shoulder and he called out.

'Down! Everybody! Get down!'

Nobody did. Well, you wouldn't, would you? You'd think 'what the hell is he going on about?' and carry on doing what you were doing.

But when they heard the gunshot, followed instantly by the crash of the huge pane of glass next to the main doors as it shattered into a million fragments, then they reacted.

They screamed, they ran, they dived behind cars, they ducked behind trollies.

The security man dropped to his haunches with his hands on his head but, fair play to him, was straight back up and barking instructions into his walkie-talkie to alert everyone to the emergency situation now unfolding.

I carried on running into the store. Fleetingly, I'd allowed myself to hope Thommo might give up trying to get us when he saw so many people around, but I should've known better. I felt like that bloke in Terminator. No matter what you did to him, he never seemed to stop coming after you.

I dashed past the display of ready-made sandwiches and skipped around the end of the fresh fruit and veg aisle. I cut past the stacked cans of baked beans, chopped tomatoes and mushy peas, pushing on deeper within the store. There had to be a staff-only door towards the far end that I could take us through and lock from the other side.

From the echoing screams and cries now within the store, I gathered Thommo had made it past the security man. I couldn't blame him. If a tattooed nutter wielding a firearm bore down on me I'd get out of the way as well. I'm sure he doesn't get paid well enough to warrant taking a bullet.

But by then there had to be armed police hurtling their way towards the supermarket in response to the emergency calls. I had to get to a part of the building where I could shut us in – and him out.

Past the crisps and snacks, with panicked shoppers pressing their bodies against the shelves to keep out of our way, I nipped left and then up between biscuits and chocolate on one side and a weird variety of miscellaneous random goods on the other, pushing for the far corner of the building, behind the frozen goods compartments, where I was hoping the store offices were to be found.

My progress had slowed to a plod by then. I was so tired. But I had to keep believing I could find a sanctuary. I had to keep going.

Bang!

The bullet whizzed so close to the side of my skull that I could've sworn it had shaved a new parting through my hair. It spat into the shelves of health and beauty products, sending a shower of shampoo and body lotion into the air from punctured bottles.

I fell forward, just managing to twist in time to prevent me from tumbling with all my weight on to Gina, or risk her head hitting against the hard floor. We were close enough to the end of the display cabinet on my left for me to scramble behind it for cover, pushing Gina's body ahead of me.

But we were in big trouble. I knew we were not going to make it to the shelter of a secured door then. He was too close.

I raised myself to my knees to peek over the arrangement of anti-allergy mattress protectors and see just how close he was.

Close enough to see the hatred in his eyes reddened by the deodorant spray. Close enough to see the half-sneer of triumph on his lips as his mouth drooped open because the left side of his jaw was broken. Close enough to see the still-gaping gash on the side of his head caused by its impact on the car windscreen when he was run over. Close enough to see the wrapping of grey tape acting as a makeshift bandage around his right arm where I'd stabbed him with the retractable carpet knife.

Yet still he limped on, towards us. He was unrelenting. Indestructible. How could any man stop that?

In desperation, I grasped at anything, everything that was close at hand. I threw a squirrel-proof bird feeder at him. A set of a half-dozen various sized spanners. A paddling pool designed especially for dogs. They all missed or fell short. He trudged inexorably closer.

I threw a stainless steel insulated flask, a one hundred piece jigsaw of two puppies playing with a ball, a toy car stunt track that did loop-the-loops. Finally, a hit. A cordless multi-sander struck him on his left upper arm but, still in its box, it bounced off him without inflicting any damage. It only seemed to annoy him.

I was on my feet by now and he was no more than a handful of metres away, on the other side of the display cabinet. I stared straight at him and I gave up. I couldn't beat this beast. I could only stand and accept what was coming to me.

Thommo raised his right arm, deliberately slowly. He was relishing the moment of his glorious victory. Hard-earned and not without its cuts and bumps along the way, but victory.

I, the defeated, faced him and gulped, then drew a long, final breath.

He squeezed the trigger and – nothing.

Click!

He pulled it again. And again.

Click! Click!

Out of ammo.

He ejected the magazine to make sure. He was off guard. I had one last chance to do something to save myself. I frantically scanned the racks of bizarre goods for one more object to cast. A loose bundle of solar lights. Each one was only about a foot long. A lamp fitting on top of a silvery metal spike for driving into the ground. I picked one up and threw it, like a spear.

As it glided through the air, Thommo looked up from

his spent gun, aware too late of the item of garden decoration hurtling his way.

The last thing he will have seen was it heading directly for his right eye. It pierced the soft shell of his cornea, passed through his lens, and cut through the retina. Though it hadn't been thrown with great force, it was with sufficient power and was freakishly accurate enough to burrow all the way through his eye and skewer into his brain.

He toppled straight backwards, his head crushing packets of plain digestives and rich tea on the shelves behind him as he flopped to the floor.

And this time he didn't get back up.

Chapter
Twenty-Eight

Do you know those long road tunnels you sometimes come across on car journeys, the ones that cut through mountains or go deep under rivers? Driving through them can be a real assault on the senses. The artificial light strains your eyes, the tight walls around you seem to squeeze the width of the lanes, the ordinary noise of engines echo and reverberate to fill your ears and the harsh concrete panels of the road surface judder under the tyres so you feel each bump through your hands on the steering wheel.

Then you see a small shaft of daylight drawing you on and the aperture of the tunnel end opens wider and wider until whoosh! You're out in the open air. Suddenly, you can see far ahead in every direction again. The road is somehow smoother and wider. You feel able to breathe easily. Your stress levels are reduced. You become a calmer driver.

That's a bit what it was like in the immediate aftermath at the supermarket. We'd emerged from the chaos and all around was peace again.

Thommo was dead. He wasn't going to terrorise us – or anybody else for that matter – ever again.

That didn't make me happy. I wasn't even especially relieved – though that feeling did wash over me later in a flood of tears. At that moment, straight after his lifeless body collapsed into the shelves of own brand biscuits, an enormous aura of serenity enveloped me, enclosing me in its warm, comfortable, protective bubble.

The shop had been crowded with customers when we got there, but they quickly – wisely – headed for the exits as soon as the shooting started and now it was just me and Gina, among the rows of abandoned, half-filled trollies. I lowered myself to sit beside her and pulled her to me so that her head rested against my chest. I supported her with my left arm and gently stroked her soft honey-blonde hair with my right hand, talking to her in low, soothing whispers.

'It's OK now, Gina. Everything's going to be all right. Everything's going to be all right.'

I caressed her not like you would a lover, but more like a daughter. All thoughts of romance between us, which had only existed on my side anyway, had long since vanished, but we were closer then than we ever could've been on any other level of a relationship. We were the only two people in the world, wrapped in harmonious, perfect silence.

No doubt I was a little bit in shock. I can see that now, weeks after it happened, but I'd always associated shock with deep anxiety and there was none of that. However, I realise my state of mind was far from normal. One clue.

As I held Gina close, I could swear I heard her draw a deep, long contented breath and I looked down to see her beautiful hazel eyes wide open and sparkling up at me. She smiled and spoke.

'Thank you, Barry. I knew you wouldn't let me down.'

Did that really happen, or did my trauma-addled brain

imagine it? I know which of those options I think is the most likely because the noise of approaching boots made me look up and when I glanced back down again, Gina was as she had been. Unconscious. Unresponsive.

'They're here.'

Two figures were closing in, dressed head to foot in heavy, black protective gear, the word 'POLICE' emblazoned on their military-style helmets and their eyes shielded by black-rimmed goggles. They shuffled cautiously ahead behind the handguns in their outstretched arms, sweeping side to side for signs of danger. The cavalry had arrived.

'Shooter is down and neutralised,' came the call from the other side of the aisle. They'd found Thommo.

At that news, the two advancing on Gina and me holstered their weapons. They'd plainly been briefed by witnesses outside – the security guard, maybe – that the only armed threat was from the big guy with the tattoos and we were his intended victims.

'Sir, are you injured?' asked the first of the police officers.

'Not injured, no,' I said. 'But she needs urgent attention. She's unconscious.'

'Get the paramedics in here,' he ordered and his colleague scuttled away to relay the message.

The policeman peered over the display aisle of random items to where the dead body of Thommo lay among spilled packets of crunchy sweetmeal treats.

'Bloody hell!' he said. 'Is that a solar light?'

'Looks like it,' answered one of the other officers, clearly not leaping to assumptions until the CSI people arrived to provide confirmation.

'Christ! My sister's got some like that in her flower beds.'

Two paramedics, a man and a woman, ran towards us in their bottle-green uniforms. Both had bulky green bags over their shoulders and the man was carrying an orange basket stretcher. The armed officer stepped back to allow them to get on with their jobs and walked around to the other side of the aisle to join his colleagues, no doubt curious for a closer look at the big guy with a solar light stuck in his head.

They encouraged me to give up my hold on Gina and asked questions about what her name was and how she came to be unconscious. They talked to her all the time as they checked her breathing, blood pressure and heart rate and prepared to put her in a neck brace. I'd never seen paramedics in action up close before. It's very impressive.

Then the female paramedic, who had bright orange hair tied back in a ponytail and didn't seem that much younger than I am, turned to me and asked: 'And how are you, my love?'

I wasn't expecting to be asked that, for whatever reason. I guess I was still numbed. I was watching everything going on around me like it was happening to somebody else.

'Fine,' I replied, in what could go down as a classic example of British stoicism. 'A few bumps and bruises, but fine.'

She saw straight through me.

'I think we'll take you in to have you looked at, all the same. That lip might need a stitch, for a start.'

I'd forgotten about the split lip.

She gave me a bottle of water. I hadn't realised how thirsty I was either. Several other police officers, other than the ones in combat gear, had joined us by that time and one of them, a fresh-faced guy with a very precisely-shaped beard, crouched beside me and introduced himself.

'Are you up to answering a few questions before they take you away?'

I told him my details and as much as I knew about Gina and Thommo's. I gave him the outline version of everything that had happened that day. Just the basics so they could start to make sense of the scene of supermarket bedlam.

'We'll need you to give us a full statement as soon as you feel up to it,' he said, folding away his notebook. 'We'll be asking the same of Miss McKenzie. Do you two know each other well?'

'Not really. We only met for the first time a couple of weeks ago.' Then I felt the need to add, for whatever reason: 'She's not my girlfriend.'

He gave me a look that suggested he was struggling to see the relevance of this piece of extra information, but left it at that.

'Well, if you want a lift to hospital, I'd better let you go. We'll be in touch.'

He helped me to my feet.

'Where exactly are we, by the way? I mean, what's the name of this town?' I thought I should ask.

'Skelmersdale,' he replied, a bit puzzled. But then, I had just told him I'd spent much of the last few hours in the boot of a car.

'Thought so.' I started to walk away, following the paramedics carrying Gina on the stretcher between them. 'Just one more thing. Could I ask a favour?'

'Sure,' said the officer, walking beside me.

'Could you phone someone to let them know I'm OK. I haven't got my phone.'

I gave him Louise's number. It was the only one I knew off by heart. That includes my own, which I'm always forgetting. I hoped she'd got her phone back from the Krazy Kangaroo by then.

***

Three hours later, I was in a waiting room close to the ward where they'd taken Gina, sipping a cup of tea that one of the pink-tunicked Health Care Assistants very kindly brought for me, when Louise and my eldest, Maisie, bustled through the door.

It was late in the afternoon by then and I'd well and truly come down from all the earlier excitement. I was dog tired and starting to feel in the way. Like a spare part. I was thrilled to see them. They looked as if they'd just remembered they'd left a pan boiling on the hob.

Maisie, being younger and nimbler, reached me first and threw her arms around my neck.

'Dad, we've been so worried. Are you all right?'

I nodded. I was a bit choked, to be truthful.

Daughter ceded to mother and backed away discreetly. I'm not sure kids ever grow out of the unease they feel at the sight of their parents showing affection to each other.

Louise squeezed me tightly around my chest. A bit too tightly.

'Oh, I'm sorry!' she remembered. 'How are they?'

'A couple of cracked ribs,' I said. 'I'll live.'

'And how's she?'

I wasn't sure if Louise had trouble remembering Gina's name or if she still didn't really want to acknowledge a potential rival.

'Not in danger, thankfully. She started to come to in the ambulance and was responding to the paramedics before they whisked her off into A&E. I'm told they've done a CT scan and X-rays and didn't find anything to worry them, so she's on the ward where they'll keep an eye on her for a couple of days, just to be safe.'

I screwed up my eyes and rubbed them with the tips of my fingers.

'Long day,' said Louise. 'Let's get you home.'

'Yeah.' There was nothing I wanted more, but then I recalled the disarray of the last time I stepped into the front room. I didn't want to face all that alone. 'Will you come and stay with me? I'm afraid the house was in a bit of a state after he went rampaging through it this morning.'

'I will,' she replied, then, uncertainly, 'but are you sure?'

'What do you mean?' I honestly didn't catch on.

'About staying. I've no right to expect you to let me back in, after everything I did to you, so just tell me if you only want me to help clear up and then go. I'd understand.'

'No, no!' I saw again in her eyes the desolation I noticed when she turned up on my doorstep the previous afternoon. So vanquished. Since then, we'd reconnected at the kids activity centre, when I was sure we both recognised what we once had was still alive. I didn't need any further proof that we belonged back together again, but perhaps her battered self-confidence had left unresolved nagging doubts in her mind. She needed it spelled out.

'Of course I'm sure. I love you, you daft sod. Always have, always will.'

The shadows lifted and she kissed me, carefully avoiding the cut side of my mouth.

'I love you, too.' She hugged me, gently this time. 'I

should never have walked out on you.'

'Well,' I shrugged. 'That's in the past. We don't have to get into that now.'

'No, I need to explain this to you. I need you to understand.' I could tell by her expression that it couldn't wait. It had been simmering too long.

'I felt my life was slipping away. One minute I was twenty-two and carefree and the next I was fifty-two with a grandkid. I love Isla to bits, you know that, but I didn't feel old enough to be a grandma. It kind of compounded what I already feared. It was as if we were crawling towards old age and it annoyed me that you seemed so content to do that. I allowed all my insecurities to turn into resentment and instead of staying to try to fix it, I ran away. It was selfish of me, but I was convinced I needed to leave to feel alive again.'

She sighed. 'It's funny, though. I flew off to Mexico seeking excitement and adventure and all I discovered was that I missed the boring old security of my life back home.'

'With boring old Barry,' I added.

'That's not what I was going to say, but yes.'

I was glad she had been so honest with me. I can't say I did completely understand her perspective, but I accepted her view and her words did stir my conscience. At the time, she'd sent enough signals for me to know how unhappy she had become and I chose to ignore them. Why didn't I act on them instead?

'I'm sorry I made you feel that way. For my own part, I've realised since how much I'd taken you for granted and what a stick-in-the-mud old bugger I'd turned into. I promise not to be as boring ever again.' I kissed her on the forehead.

'I think a bit of boredom would be nice after what we've

been through,' she suggested.

'Fair point.'

We stood for a while, absorbing the significance of the new commitment we were about to take. The one we both wanted. It felt right.

'Let's go,' I said.

I looked over to Maisie, who opened her bag to retrieve her car keys.

'Give me a minute, though. I'd better let the nurses on the ward know I'm leaving and look in to see if Gina's awake.'

She wasn't. She lay in bed, not flat out but propped and cushioned by a multitude of soft, white pillows, and looked so peaceful. She was out of the protective collar, though still connected to monitors beside the bed which quite contentedly performed their function with no suggestion of sign for alarm.

I smiled at the nurse who'd kept me so well informed earlier and mouthed 'I'm going home.' She waved back, cheerily.

I took one last look at Gina and knew I would never see her again.

Chapter
Twenty-Nine

An officer from West Lancashire Police phoned me four days later. Gina, against the advice of medical staff, had checked herself out of hospital within forty-eight hours of her admission and had disappeared. Did I know where she was?

I didn't. I told them which hotel she'd been staying at in Sheffield but I knew she'd have already checked out and be long gone. She was probably on the other side of the world by then. Good luck trying to track her down when you don't know which name she's using on her passport.

I'd already given them my full statement. I say full. I didn't include the doping with illegally obtained drugs, the attempted drowning or what was, effectively, a hit and run driving incident. I figured the police had enough on their plate already without getting bogged down in unnecessary detail.

That day, not long after the police called to say she had vanished, I did receive a package through the post from Gina. It had a Sheffield postmark and contained the Companies House and bank documentation she'd promised, plus the V5C logbook, officially signing the black VW Golf over to my name. I was grateful for that.

No note or anything, though, which I thought a bit odd, bearing in mind I sort of saved her life. Then again, I suppose she sort of saved mine. She certainly shook it up and, let's face it, it needed shaking.

My near-death experience (as Louise so melodramatically likes to call it) and the whole episode of Gina has lifted the scales from my eyes. I see what I had become.

Though her intentions were dishonourable, Gina reawakened me. I don't think I did properly fall in love with her, but first she rescued me from drifting deeper into self-pity and then she made me live again. Through chasing the beautiful, unattainable fantasy that was Gina, I rediscovered all those important little factors that go into keeping a relationship fresh and recognised the timidity, the complacency, that suffocated my marriage. Louise was right. We did get stale and I accept the largest share of the blame for that. Louise got bored because I got boring.

But I promised her she'd see a new me and I've set about proving it. I decided I should sell the VW and use the money to take Louise on a trip she'll never forget. Not the Isle of Man this time. We're going to hire a camper van and drive all the way down the Australian coast, from Brisbane to Melbourne, arriving in Melbourne in late January in time to take in a few big matches at the Rod Laver Arena in the climactic final days of the Australian Open Tennis Championships. It's been her dream for years, but the old Barry always managed to find a reason why such a grand venture was out of our reach.

No more. I suggested we go for it, she said yes, and I

planned it all. How's that for new me?

Maybe we'll even remarry while we're in Aus. Get Roger Federer and Pat Cash to act as the witnesses.

I might be lapsing into the realms of fantasy now, but I'll tell you one strange fact.

It came to light while I was giving my statement to the police. We were putting dates to the sequence of events and, what do you know, the pandemonium in Skelmersdale, the day Louise and I properly got back together, fell one year to the day since she first told me she wanted a divorce. September the ninth.

That's not all.

I calculated the number of days I'd known Gina, from the day she sent me the first message on clickforlove.com to the day I saw her for the last time in hospital, and you'll never guess how many it was. You probably already have, actually.

Twenty-three.

I know it's all a coincidence. Gina told me herself she never planned with such precision how long she stayed with one of her lonely heart victims before vanishing into the night to pull the same stunt on the next hapless chump. It was all down to how long it took for her fraudulent business to start roping in gullible people with too much spare money and not enough good sense.

I know all that.

Still. Weird, isn't it?

ACKNOWLEDGEMENTS

Every day's a school day, as my narrator Barry reflects in the midst of all I subjected him to through this novel.

The statement is certainly true for the writer as well.

None of us know it all. The key is finding people who can fill the gaps in your knowledge and I am grateful again to those who helped this time.

In particular, I leant on Jack, Cho, Ruth and Ann. I'm so lucky to have so many medical advisors at hand. It means my partner, Sue, doesn't have to deal with all my daft questions. I rely on her for plenty of other guidance through the writing process as it is.

On non-medical issues, I've drawn regularly on the knowledge of Andy Wilson, a fine bloke and fellow long-suffering Blade. He helped again this time. I forgot to acknowledge his contribution to the last novel, which was a bit rubbish on my part. Sorry.

A word, too, for Sumaira and Nikki at SpellBound Books, for showing faith in me in the first place and for their continuing work and support.

Andrew Rainnie has again provided a great cover image and thanks also to everybody who have not only read my books over the years but have taken the time to say and write kind words about them. You make so much difference.

ABOUT THE AUTHOR

Mark Eklid's background is as a newspaper journalist, starting out with the South Yorkshire Times in 1984 and then on to the Derby Telegraph, from 1987 until he left full-time work in March 2022.

Most of his time at the Telegraph was as their cricket writer, a role that brought national recognition in the 2012 and 2013 England and Wales Cricket Board awards. He contributed for twelve years to the famed Wisden Cricketers' Almanack and had many articles published in national magazines, annuals and newspapers.

Writing as a profession meant writing for pleasure had to be put on the back burner but when his work role changed, Mark returned to one of the many half-formed novels in his computer files and, this time, saw it through to publication.

The Murder of Miss Perfect (July 2022) was his first novel for independent publisher SpellBound Books and was followed by *Blood on Shakespeare's Typewriter* (September 2023), but Mark had previously self-published *Sunbeam* (November 2019), *Family Business* (June 2020) and *Catalyst* (February 2021).

All five are fast-moving, plot-twisting thrillers set in the city of his birth, Sheffield.

ALSO BY MARK EKLID

BLOOD ON SHAKESPEARE'S TYPEWRITER

When Dan Khan buys a unique piece of cultural history for £50 from a man in the pub, he thinks his troubles are over.

He is told it's the actual typewriter William Shakespeare used when he wrote all his plays. Dan and his girlfriend Shannon reckon it must be worth millions!

But they don't realise the vintage machine was stolen from the city's most notorious crime boss. And he will stop at nothing to get back the sinister secret it contains.

THE MURDER OF MISS PERFECT

Detective Chief Inspector Jim Pendlebury almost died at the end of his last big case.

Three years later, he is struggling to cope with forced retirement and the frustration of failing to convict the teacher accused of killing an 18-year-old student after seducing her.

Now, he must try one more time to search for the vital piece of missing evidence the police failed to find during the initial investigation and make sure justice is served for the cruel murder of the beautiful young woman the media dubbed Miss Perfect.

CATALYST

Sheffield is being steered towards an ecological disaster which will put thousands of lives at risk by an unscrupulous city council leader who is chasing one last big backhander before he gives up power.

With time running out to avert a potential catastrophe, fate takes a hand.

An old lady is injured by a falling branch from a tree during a storm. It is the unlikely spark for a chain of coincidental events which sets one man on the path to save the city.

FAMILY BUSINESS

Family historian Graham Hasselhoff thought there were no skeletons in his cupboard. That is, until the day he met the son he never knew he had.

Getting to know Andreas, who is now the boss of a road haulage firm, soon leads him to a trail of arson, beatings, mysterious warnings – and murder.

Can his son really be behind this deadly business?

Graham has to quickly work out if Andreas is an impetuous eccentric – or a dangerously ruthless criminal.

SUNBEAM

John Baldwin has been on a downward spiral to self-destruction since the day he witnessed the murder of his best friend, Stef. It has cost him his marriage, his business and his dignity.

One year on from the day that turned his world upside down, he sees Stef again. John fears he has finally lost his mind but Stef is there to pull his friend back from the brink, not tip him over it.

He offers John a fresh start, a new destiny.

John rebuilds his life. He has everything again but there is a price to pay. The killer is still on the loose and Stef wants revenge.

Visit his website, markeklid.com, for further details.

Printed in Great Britain
by Amazon